The man intrigued her

She had no fantasies of anything more than that. It was better to be a realist where romance was concerned. She enjoyed Rico's company—but there couldn't be a future for them.

They were polar opposites. Worlds apart philosophically.

She headed to the bedroom to change her clothes and took the envelope with her. Sitting on the edge of the bed, she kicked off her shoes, then ripped the package open.

Her heart stalled. In ragged cutout letters pasted on a sheet of paper the message read, "Stay away or you'll regret it!"

Dear Reader,

Have you ever found something so interesting you couldn't get enough of it? That's the way I felt when I finished my book about a Los Angeles police detective working on a cold case. I became fascinated with the methods and discovery process used to solve old crimes. Thus my new series was born—welcome to the first book of COLD CASES: L.A.

The series opens with handsome Detective Rico Santini, who first appeared in *The Man in the Photograph*. *His Case, Her Child* is first and foremost a love story between Rico and Macy Capshaw, two people who couldn't be more opposite and who might never have crossed paths had it not been for Billy, a lost little boy under Macy's care as his court-appointed child advocate.

As an attorney and the daughter of an attorney, Macy grew up with the proverbial silver spoon in her mouth. But money can't replace a childhood without love. She's chosen to make her own way in the world, working mostly with battered women. Her life is devoted to keeping her clients safe—even if it means bending the rules a little. Rico is a by-the-book detective, born and raised in New Jersey. When Rico's cold case uncovers something in Macy's past that's unfathomable, the two are forced to work together. It's then they find out just how different their philosophies are. And yet how similar.

I'd love to hear what you think of *His Case, Her Child*, or any of my books. You can reach me at P.O. Box 2292, Mesa, AZ 85214 or LindaStyle@cox.net. To read about my upcoming books and other fun stuff, visit www.LindaStyle.com and www.superauthors.com.

May all your dreams come true.

Linda Style

His Case, Her Child
Linda Style

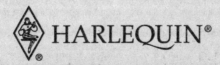

HARLEQUIN®

TORONTO • NEW YORK • LONDON
AMSTERDAM • PARIS • SYDNEY • HAMBURG
STOCKHOLM • ATHENS • TOKYO • MILAN • MADRID
PRAGUE • WARSAW • BUDAPEST • AUCKLAND

ISBN 0-373-71281-2

HIS CASE, HER CHILD

This edition published by arrangement with Harlequin Books S.A.

® and TM are trademarks of the publisher. Trademarks indicated with ® are registered in the United States Patent and Trademark Office, the Canadian Trade Marks Office and in other countries.

www.eHarlequin.com

Printed in U.S.A.

For my family, who are always there for me. And for my writer friends who keep the creative juices flowing: The Phoenix Desert Rose Chapter of RWA and the Golden Heart 99ers, the most loving, supportive group of people ever.

My deep appreciation to those who contributed to the research for this book: the Los Angeles Police Department and the City of Los Angeles. Since this is a work of fiction, I've taken some liberties. Any errors are mine.

Books by Linda Style

HARLEQUIN SUPERROMANCE

Don't miss any of our special offers. Write to us at the following address for information on our newest releases.

Harlequin Reader Service
U.S.: 3010 Walden Ave., P.O. Box 1325, Buffalo, NY 14269
Canadian: P.O. Box 609, Fort Erie, Ont. L2A 5X3

CHAPTER ONE

"THEY FOUND THE BOY scavenging through trash cans at the bus station." Detective Enrico Santini shifted his cell phone from one ear to the other and scanned the reception area of Macy Capshaw's upscale law office. "He doesn't know his name or where he's from."

"And you think it could be Chelsey's kid?" his partner asked.

"He's the right age."

"Him and how many others out of the 800,000 kids who go missing every year. You still feeling responsible?"

Rico didn't answer. He'd been the one who suggested his niece stay at Haven's Gate to have her baby, and less than twenty-four hours after the birth, the infant had been abducted.

"We did everything we could," Jordan said.

Yeah, so why did he feel he could have done more? "I need to check it out."

The receptionist nodded at Rico, indicating the lawyer was ready to see him.

"Gotta go. I'll get back to you later." He stood, pocketed the phone and followed the young woman into the attorney's spacious office.

"Detective Santini," the receptionist announced to the woman behind an oversize mahogany desk. Her blond hair gleamed like the patina on the champagne-colored Benz he'd seen in the parking garage with the vanity plate MC2LAW, her tailored suit screamed Gucci or some other designer name and the subtle lift of her chin warned that a cop, the son of Italian immigrants from Hoboken, New Jersey, wasn't in her league. Not even close.

She stood to shake his hand, a quick, firm move that was all business.

As the receptionist left, Rico noted that Macy Capshaw, with her hair pulled back into a sleek, long ponytail, looked as if she'd just graduated high school. Except the Harvard Law certificate on the wall said otherwise.

How someone her age could afford digs in the L.A. Citicorp Building without any partners was a mystery.

The lawyer motioned for him to sit in the chair across from her. "What can I do for you, Detective?"

"I understand you're the court-appointed advocate for the boy found at the bus station."

"I'm the court-appointed *attorney*...not quite the same." Her cool blue gaze flicked over him, lingering on his faded jeans and JC Penny button-down shirt.

"I'm working a cold case in which an infant was abducted five years ago. The boy would now be about the same age as the child in your charge. I'd like to find out if they might be one and the same, and I understand that I need your okay to see him."

She relaxed against the back of a tanned leather chair, arms at ease.

"LAPD?"

He nodded.

"But you're not from California, are you?"

"New Jersey, born and bred." He gave her his best smile. "Did the accent give me away?"

The corners of her mouth moved, but didn't make it into a smile. "The child is in protective custody and under a physician's care. Being questioned by more police is not in his best interests right now."

"Isn't it in his best interests to find his parents?"

"We want to find his parents as much as anyone…but as I said, he's under a physician's care." Her firm words belied her relaxed body language.

Rico leaned forward, elbows on his knees. "Was he abused?"

"Possibly. He has several physical problems, and he doesn't remember anything about himself or his family. We don't know if he wandered away from his parents or if he was abandoned. But since it's been well publicized and no one has come forward, the likelihood is the latter." Her ice-blue eyes locked with his. "We may not know anything for quite a while."

"Are you refusing to let me talk to him?"

She frowned. "Whatever he's been through was obviously traumatic and more people questioning him might send him over the edge. If your case is five years old, Detective, it can't hurt to wait a little longer, can it?"

Rico's blood rushed. He was too close to this case and he knew it. He took a calming breath. "The case might be old…but the child's mother has been grieving for five years over the loss. The boy in your charge could be her son."

Her eyes seemed to crinkle around the edges, and he saw an almost imperceptible wince. Maybe he'd touched her nurturing side. He hoped.

As if she knew what he was thinking, she pulled herself up and squared her shoulders. "I can sympathize, Detective. But that's all I can do. Right now numerous authorities are involved. Child Protective Services, the court that appointed me, the hospital and a number of physicians and the police who took him into custody. I've had three other detectives call me because each had an old case with a missing child and they want the same thing you do. As the child's advocate, my responsibility is to the boy, and if we found his parents right this minute, we wouldn't spring them on him immediately. Not until we have some answers."

Her voice had softened and maybe she really did sympathize. Whether she did or not, he had to admire her conviction. Her concern for the boy. He drew a breath. It was obvious he wasn't going to get anywhere by pushing the issue. If he'd learned anything in his ten-plus years in law enforcement, it was that making nice on someone won him more points than bullying ever did.

"And exactly what *is* your responsibility?" he asked. "I've never worked with a child advocate before."

She moistened her lips with the tip of her tongue, which oddly had him wondering what it might be like to unravel that cool, you-can't-touch-me attitude of hers.

"It's my job to represent the child's best interests—

to ensure that any abuse suffered at home…or else-where, doesn't continue as abuse and neglect at the hands of the system."

Back to the canned legalese.

"And *you* are the system, Detective Santini."

Maintaining eye contact, he stretched his legs and forced himself to appear at ease, the posture at odds with the tension building in him. "I'd like to see him, not in-terrogate him."

She picked up a folder on her desk and thumbed through it. Finally she said, "All in due time. Right now it's more important to determine his physical and men-tal state. Surely you can understand that."

His nerves tensed even more at her condescending tone. "I can. And surely you can understand that, like you, I'm doing my job—and I'd hoped you'd be able to help me."

"As much as I'd like to, Detective Santini, I can't. Not today."

Right. She'd like to help him about as much as she'd like to spend an afternoon at a baseball game swilling beer and chowing hot dogs. "Well, if you won't let me talk to him, perhaps you could come to the station and take a look at the case file. Maybe you'd see something that would allow us to rule out the possibility?"

Her lips formed a thin line and he knew she was going to refuse his request. "I can't tell you how devas-tated this mother has been, searching the faces of every child she sees. Five years is a long time to be doing that. Can you at least think about taking a look at the file?"

After a moment, she gave a reluctant nod. "My schedule is full. But I'll see what I can do."

At that, Rico stood, stuck out a hand and, pasting on his most charming smile, said, "Thanks. I appreciate it."

She reached to shake his hand. This time he was surprised at the warmth. Apparently ice *didn't* run through her veins. He turned and on his way out, he gave a two-finger salute. "I'll be in touch."

AN HOUR LATER, Cheryl, Macy's receptionist, beeped her. Macy hit the intercom.

"It's that detective again. The cute one."

The cute one. Yes. He had it going on all right. But she wouldn't describe him as *cute.* He commanded attention. And like most cops she'd worked with, he wanted to call the shots. He hadn't been in her office for two minutes before she knew he was a man who had to be in control.

Hell, he'd barely left and was already calling back for a decision. "Put him through, Cheryl."

Annoyed, she let the phone ring twice, then picked up the receiver. "What can I do for you, Detective?"

"How about meeting me at the coffee shop downstairs?"

His voice, a deep resonant baritone, was low and seductive, his East Coast accent noticeable when he said *cauwfee.* She knew the drill. He wanted something from her and she'd bet he usually got what he wanted. Most women would find a man like Rico Santini irresistible. Tall and dark, with a big white smile and those soft brown "I'm available" eyes, he was hard to resist. Well, unfortunately for him, she'd had her fill of tall, dark and irresistible.

"I want to show you something," he added. "Can you spare a few minutes this afternoon?"

She had a deposition to do, a brief to write and she had to file a restraining order on Ginny Mathews' estranged husband. *And* she had to be in court at one o'clock. She didn't have time to have coffee with anyone, especially someone with an agenda. She needed a paralegal. Desperately.

This mother's been grieving for five years over the loss of her child.

She closed her eyes. Remembering things she didn't want to remember. "I'll have a few minutes around 3:00 p.m. if that works for you."

"I'll be there."

Macy let the handset slip into the cradle, a dull ache of loss heavy in her chest as painful memories played in her head. The darkened room, the contractions that never went anywhere, the scent of alcohol and somewhere in the drug-induced fogginess of her brain, hushed, disjointed voices, words like Cesarean and breech. All she'd wanted was to have her baby and take him home. Instead she'd been given drugs to ease the pain, and then it was all over.

And her baby was gone.

Twelve years ago and the memory was as vivid as if it were yesterday.

The jangle of the phone brought her to attention. She punched the intercom. "Yes?"

"Miss Creighton is here to see you."

"Good. Send her in." Macy opened her file drawer, pulled out *Billy's* case and waited for the social worker to enter.

Karen Creighton was on a mission. Get Billy out of the hospital and into foster care ASAP. The hearing to make Billy a temporary ward of the state was on Monday, and the financial considerations when a child was a ward of the state were always a prime concern for the social workers.

Karen Creighton came in, nodded at Macy and then headed for the chair in front of Macy's desk. From her first introduction, the woman eschewed the formality of a handshake.

"Karen, what can I do for you?"

Gaunt, with pale skin and lifeless brown hair, the social worker looked as if she could use a good nutritionist herself. "I'm working on foster care placement for Billy. It isn't easy. The lists are full and his special needs make it more difficult."

"He's not ready for that anyway, so there's no rush."

"From what I understand, he's physically able to be discharged, and I have to make a decision."

"A financial decision. Only Billy's physician hasn't said he's ready for discharge. In fact, the doctor told me that while proper nutrition may have him back to normal in no time, his mental state isn't that easy to evaluate."

"He's been interviewed by several psychiatrists and psychologists—"

"And none have been able to determine if his inability to answer questions about his past has an organic cause or if it's psychologically induced. And there's also the possibility that the memory loss is deliberate on Billy's part. More tests have to be done."

"Whether he remembers or not, we have to find placement for him."

"Yes, but nothing can happen until after the hearing Monday morning. And I'll need to interview the prospective caregivers before any decision is made."

The woman's lips formed a straight thin line. "I have two interviews set for Monday afternoon."

Macy's muscles tensed. Karen knew her afternoons were usually booked.

"The first is at one o'clock and the second at three."

"Fine. Give me the addresses and I'll be there."

The social worker shoved a piece of paper at Macy. "I'll see you at the hearing, then."

Watching her leave, Macy's irritation spiked. She shouldn't be annoyed. Karen had a job to do. But then, so did she, and she was going to do it, regardless of what other people wanted.

As she picked up Billy's file, the card Detective Santini had left on her desk fluttered to the floor. She stared at the small piece of paper, wondering why he was so invested in the cold case. And what did he want to show her that was so important he had to meet with her today?

RICO DROPPED the Ray file on his desk in the LAPD's Robbery-Homicide Division and fell into his chair. Even though smoking was banned in the House and had been for years, the stale scent of tobacco still hung in the air, imbedded in the fabric on the chairs and other old furniture in the room. Between the stale smoke and a lot of sweaty guys, he hated being cooped up on such a great spring day.

But he had to find something to convince Macy Capshaw that his taking a look at the boy wasn't going to damage the kid's psyche any more than it already was.

"How's it going?" his partner asked.

"It's not."

"You mean you didn't charm the socks off her?" Jordan St. James set his midmorning cup of coffee on the desk and smiled. "You losing your touch, Romeo?"

"You can't charm a rock." Rico liked women, and not much kept him from pursuing one he wanted to get to know. But he never got involved with someone on a case. "She's not my type. Besides, you know the rules."

"She's not involved in your case."

True. Not directly. But he wasn't looking for anything else. Not even a date.

"I thought you liked smart women."

Yeah, that was a plus. He also liked women who were fun and accessible, and who didn't want something permanent within the first week of dating. Someone who could go with the flow. Macy Capshaw might be smart, but she didn't seem to have a fun bone in her body, and she was about as accessible as Mount Everest. "She's a control freak."

Jordan laughed. "Nothing like you," he said, perching on the corner of Rico's desk. "I think she's okay. Besides, I thought you liked a challenge?"

"Some challenges are more interesting than others, my friend. You know her?" Rico and Jordan had covered a lot of cases in the five years they'd worked together, and Jordan's knowledge of L.A.'s movers and shakers never ceased to amaze Rico. Growing up with the crème de la crème of L.A. society had its advantages.

Jordan nodded. "My father was on the board at Pennington and so was her father while she went to school there. We've attended some of the same charity functions."

Only families with fortunes out the wazoo sent their kids to Pennington. "I guess that means she doesn't have to worry about where her next rent money is coming from."

"I'd say so. Her father is Wesley Capshaw and her grandfather is Ira Delacourt III. I heard she inherited a lot of money from the old guy. A trust."

Wesley Capshaw, the famous Hollywood palimony attorney. It explained a lot. "Oh, that makes me feel a whole lot better," Rico said facetiously. He'd worked too many cases where people with money felt entitled to different treatment, that they didn't have to live by the same rules as the rest of society.

Excluding Jordan, who came from a wealthy background, but never acted as if he was anything other than Joe Average. But then Jordan had been adopted and had known from the time he was a kid that he wasn't really a blue blood.

"You know her well enough to convince her to help me?"

Jordan shook his head, gulped down more coffee, went to his own desk and pulled out one of the files. "Not really. We don't hang in the same circles. The last time I saw her was when I testified in a case she defended for her father's firm, and I have to say she made my testimony a hell of a lot more stimulating. She knows her way around a courtroom."

"Well, she has her own offices now in the Citicorp Building."

Jordan's phone rang and he picked up.

Rico was thumbing through the case when Luke Coltrane entered the room and drifted toward Rico's desk. Damn. He knew what Luke wanted.

Luke, the oldest, and the most cynical detective in the unit, had been with the LAPD for fifteen years and mostly worked Homicide's high-profile cases. He had the highest percentage of solved cases of any officer in the district, and his reputation was legend.

But three weeks ago Chief MacGuire decided to run for mayor in the next election and had told their captain to reduce the number of cold cases in the basement by half. They all knew MacGuire wanted the numbers to look good *before* he made his public announcement that he was going to run. The cold cases had been culled and the most likely to be solved had been assigned. The Ray case wasn't one of them.

Luke stopped at Rico's desk and picked up the glass paperweight that one of his nieces or nephews had given him.

"Got a minute?" Luke studied the glass ball, shook the snow around and set it back down.

"Sure. What's up?"

"I heard you're working one of the missing kid cases again." Luke's dark eyes were shuttered so you couldn't tell what he was thinking. But Rico knew.

"It's not on the list." Rico's mouth was dry. He never knew what to say to his friend when the subject of missing kids came up.

"Well, you have my help if you need it," Coltrane said.

"Thanks. I appreciate it." Luke always offered to pitch in when a child was involved, but Captain Carlyle knew Luke's objectivity was tainted because of his own son and never put him on a missing kid case. Carlyle wouldn't have allowed Rico on his niece's case five years ago, either—if he'd known she was his niece. The one time he went against procedure, he'd paid the price. Guilt dogged him, hung like a chain around his neck.

When Coltrane left, Rico went back to his research, scouring the old file. He wished to hell he knew what pushed the attorney's buttons.

His phone rang. "Santini."

"It's Suz. I have the information you wanted on Macy Capshaw."

He liked Suzy's easy manner. Why had he stopped dating her? He couldn't remember. Thanks to her numerous jobs as a legal assistant, she knew practically every attorney in the city and could find out anything about anyone. Then he realized that *was* the reason. As sweet as she was, she couldn't keep her mouth shut.

"Your lady does family law. Mostly cases that involve kids and battered women. I'd say she has some screws loose, leaving her father's firm to represent low-income families. No money in that."

And what act of God had made Macy Capshaw leave her father's firm?

"She does a lot of child advocacy."

"Anything else?"

"That's it."

He said his thanks and hung up, still thinking about what Suz had said. He'd thought he had the attorney figured out, but maybe not.

Maybe she had strong feelings about the inequities in the justice system? A system where the rich hired top attorneys and were acquitted, and the poor were stuck with public defenders and got squat. Yeah, right. And if he believed that, he'd be a good candidate to buy a bridge.

But it seemed Ms. Capshaw had a soft spot for kids, which, instead of being in his favor, might make her even more protective of the boy in her charge. Convincing her to let him talk to the child might be harder than he'd thought.

Still…she had agreed to meet him. Though he didn't know why. Curiosity? Sympathy for the baby's mother? It sure as hell wasn't because she wanted to help him.

THE COFFEE SHOP on the mezzanine level of the building was a hangout for legal types and was usually jammed to the rafters. Except on Fridays when all work seemed to end at noon. Today was no exception.

Reaching the restaurant, Macy smoothed the front of her "court suit," a business navy, meant to impress judge and jurors with her lawyerly appearance, but with a bright red power blouse to accent her blond hair. The skirt was long enough for decorum, but short enough to show off her legs. She brushed a wisp of hair from her eyes, opened the door and went inside where the rich scent of coffee and baked pastries permeated the air.

She saw him immediately. She couldn't have missed him if she wanted to. Rico Santini wasn't the only guy in the place, but standing at the counter in his jeans and black leather jacket schmoozing with the waitress whose white sweater was so tight, her black bra showed through the threads, he couldn't be missed.

The girl laughed and then nodded toward the door.

Rico turned, acknowledging Macy with a lift of his head. He said something to the waitress and then started toward Macy. "This okay with you?" she asked, indicating the first booth.

He smiled. Big and white. "Perfect." He gestured to one side of the booth and waited for her to be seated.

Old-fashioned manners. Unusual, at least among the men she worked with. Most of them treated her as if she was one of the guys. Macy slid into the booth. Rico shrugged off his jacket and sat across from her facing the door. Within seconds the love-struck waitress sashayed over.

"What would you like?" The girl's eyes were glued on the handsome man in front of her.

"I'll have coffee," Rico said, then motioned to Macy.

She shrugged. "Why not. I'll be awake all night anyway."

The waitress kept her focus on Rico until Macy cleared her throat and said, "I'll have the same."

"Okay. Two coffees it is."

As the waitress walked away, Macy couldn't help saying, "Looks like jailbait to me."

As soon as the words left her lips, she wanted to snatch them back. Who was she to monitor this man's flirting? But Rico didn't seem to mind and instead of being angry, he let go with a burst of laughter.

"She is that for sure. In fact she's the same age as one of my nieces." One eyebrow arched sardonically. "They went to school together back East."

Macy felt heat creep up her neck—something that hadn't happened since, Lord, she didn't know when. Thanks to her father she'd learned early to hold her own in just about any encounter. She never got embarrassed. Not even in situations where she should be. So what was different today?

"Sorry. I made an assumption—and you know what they say about people who make assumptions."

Rico laughed again, his dark gaze catching hers. "No big deal. I get that all the time."

"Get what all the time?"

By his expression, she saw he was mildly amused. "Nothing. It's not important."

"Okay… So, why don't we get to what is important. I have work to do."

"Right to the point. I like that." He fumbled with his

jacket on the seat next to him, pulled out a small brown envelope and handed it to her. "I wanted you to see this."

Macy pulled the tabs on the envelope to open it. But before she looked inside, she said, "You know this isn't going to change anything, don't you? I meant what I said earlier. I can't let you talk to Billy. Not right now."

He leaned back. "I understand. That's why I thought if you saw these photos you could tell me if you thought there was any resemblance."

"A picture? I thought the child was only hours old when he was abducted."

"He was. The shelter where the child's mother was staying takes photos of all the babies born there. There's also one of the baby's mother and father, which are probably more significant."

Macy reached in and pulled out a picture of an infant with a full head of dark hair. She gave a quick glance. "Sorry. All babies look alike to me." She flipped the photo over and saw the baby's measurements on the back. And a stamp that said, #051500 Haven's Gate.

She caught her breath. *Haven's Gate.* The same shelter where she'd had her child twelve years ago. Of all the shelters in Los Angeles, what were the odds that this child would've been born at the same place as her son?

She studied the picture of the baby's mother, a sweet-looking girl with brown hair and haunting green eyes, then the photo of the father, a very young man with dark hair and dark eyes. Her heart raced as she fought back the memories. She stuffed the photos in the envelope and handed it back to him. "Sorry, I can't help."

He sighed. "Yeah. I'm sorry, too."

The disappointment in his voice revealed how much he cared about this case. Surely he didn't feel this way about all his cases. He was a cop and, as in her profession, a certain amount of dissociation was necessary. But hearing his emotion touched her. "Once the physicians determine the state of Billy's health, and if his parents don't show up, the court will order DNA tests with parents of missing children who would be of the same approximate age. I'll see what I can do to have your case come up first."

Rico tapped his fingers on the envelope, a dull hollow sound. Like the thud her heart was making in her chest. Had Haven's Gate taken a photo of her child, too? Did they do that with stillborn babies? "It might help if the police could do a computer-aged photo of the baby…"

He shook his head. "They'd need a photo of him at an older age."

She nodded.

"Will you let me know if anything changes?"

"Of course." Macy suddenly wished she could do more.

Somewhere in the middle of their exchange, the waitress had brought coffee. Macy reached for her cup and holding it with both hands, took a sip.

"Not quite like Starbucks, is it?" Rico winked at Macy.

Her pulse quickened at the intimacy. "No, it's definitely not Starbucks. And I should know. I live on the stuff."

He leaned forward, elbows on the table. "Because you need to stay awake to work all night. Right?"

"Something like that."

"You don't take time off to have fun?"

"Not when I have work to do."

"Ah, I see."

Macy frowned. "You see what?"

"Work is a good excuse."

"Excuse for what?"

"For not having anything better to do."

She opened her mouth to give him a sharp retort, but nothing came out. Maybe because what he said held a kernel of truth. Actually more than a kernel. She didn't have anything better to do. But that was her choice, and what she did with her time wasn't any of his business.

"I could help out in that area if you were interested," he said.

A teasing glint shone in his eyes and she knew he wasn't talking about helping her prepare briefs. Normally she'd be put off by such swagger, but Santini's charm drew her in and she couldn't help but smile.

While the idea held more than a little appeal, especially after a two-year relationship drought, she already knew enough about him to know he was the kind of man who'd take over your life if you let him. And she wasn't about to go down that road again.

"Thank you for the generous offer, Detective. As much as I'd like to take you up on it, I'm going to be extremely busy."

She paused, flicked a strand of hair away from her face and gave him a saccharine smile. "Doing my laundry."

CHAPTER TWO

HAVEN'S GATE. Macy hadn't known about the photos, and she couldn't stop wondering if someone had taken a photo of her baby. She'd been so sedated, she'd never even seen her child.

She should've questioned Rico, but at the time, all she could think about was getting out of the café. Rico hadn't told her the specifics of his case, so maybe she should take a look at the file. If nothing else, to satisfy her curiosity.

The man had unnerved her. She never let people unnerve her. He'd taken her by surprise with his comment about helping her out, yet she handled remarks like that all the time. So what was different about Rico Santini that got her all flustered?

He'd let her remark about doing laundry bounce off him like a soccer ball and insisted on walking her to her car. A gentleman. A quality that only added to his appeal. But…she wasn't going to let temporary insanity get the better of her.

She glanced away from the work on her lap and checked the clock. Eight o'clock on a Friday night and she was a lump on the couch—in her pajamas—and alone. Working on a brief that wasn't due for weeks.

Santini was so right. Work was an excuse for having no life.

Well, what if it was. She'd had her fill of empty dating and relationships that were so-so—relationships that never had any spark. It had been years since she met a man who flipped that switch for her.

Not since Jesse. She leaned her head against the soft pillowed cushions and closed her eyes, imagining the face of the boy who'd captured her teenage heart. Jesse had set her soul afire. He'd been everything to her. And everything her father despised. If he hadn't been killed in a car accident the night they were going to elope...

Curling a pillow into her chest, Macy still felt the loss, dulled over time, but not forgotten. Realistically, they'd probably have screwed up their lives and the life of their child by marrying so young with no resources, no skills and no family to help. Her parents had threatened to disown her if she kept the baby.

None of the boys she dated ever fit Wesley Capshaw's standards, and she'd loved Jesse for all the reasons her father hated him. Unlike her father, Jesse had loved her—no strings attached.

And...sometimes she still wondered what might have happened if Jesse hadn't died. Would they be a happy family today? Would they still be in love?

She'd never told anyone about her stay at Haven's Gate because her father said it would be a stain on his political aspirations. But over the years his law practice became so lucrative, he'd never gone into politics.

And to this day, no one knew about her so-called indiscretion. Not her grandparents, not her friends, though she had few of those these days, and especially not her business associates.

Now with her law firm just getting off the ground and working with children as she did, it seemed prudent to keep the past in the past. But if Santini decided to reinvestigate Haven's Gate who knew what might come out?

She nipped at the soft skin on her bottom lip. What could it hurt to go to the station and look at the detective's file? If there was any way to tell if Billy was the abducted child Santini hoped he was, she'd want to make sure they did all the right things in reuniting him with his parents. Right now, the poor child was disoriented, confused and undernourished. Even if Billy turned out to be the missing child in Santini's case, telling the boy that he had parents he didn't know and probably wouldn't recognize could be traumatic.

But if by simply looking at Santini's case she might be able to get him to back off, it would be worth the visit.

SATURDAY MORNING, an hour after Macy Capshaw said she'd be at the station and she still hadn't arrived. Well, what made him think she'd have any respect for *his* time.

Jordan wasn't in, but Will Houston, another detective on the team sauntered by. "That woman sure has you tied in knots." As his name indicated, Will hailed from Texas and he had the drawl to prove it.

"I guess when you've been raised with the proverbial silver spoon, you get used to doing whatever you please." Rico opened the Ray file. "Even if it inconveniences someone else."

"That's bad manners in my book, but maybe she has a good reason."

"Yeah? It would have to be better than good since she didn't bother to let me know."

"So, blow her off."

"I would in a New York minute if I didn't need something from her."

Will raised his eyebrows, his craggy face a testament to life in the fast lane. "First time I ever heard those words comin' out of your mouth."

"It's a job. That's my only interest."

Walking back to his own desk, Will said, "If you say so, buddy. If you say so."

Annoyed at his coworker, and annoyed at himself for getting more upset than he should, Rico tore open the file to see if some new evidence might miraculously appear. It didn't.

Just as he was about to chuck the file, he saw her at the door. Tall and blond, she was a striking woman. Not movie star beautiful, but she commanded attention. Wearing a pink jogging outfit and with her hair hanging loose around her shoulders, she sure had his.

"Sorry I'm late."

That was it? No reason, just *sorry?* "No big deal." He motioned to the chair at his side. "Have a seat."

As she sat next to him, she flipped her hair behind

her shoulders and leaned forward, elbows on his desk, her face much too close to his. He didn't know what fragrance she wore, but it made him think of dimly lit bedrooms and satin sheets.

"I was surprised to find you in the Robbery-Homicide Division."

"Otherwise known as the we-do-it-all unit," Rico quipped. "Murders, bank robberies, extortion, sex crimes and kidnappings."

"I'm impressed. I've studied some of the more famous cases that your department has investigated. Manson, the Robert Kennedy assassination and O. J., to name a few."

"All before my time," Rico said, leaning back in his chair, hands clasped behind his head. "I guess that's a good thing. In at least one of those cases, the division got a lot of flack that I hear wasn't warranted."

She looked skeptical.

He shrugged. "That's what I heard."

Picking up a photo, one of the many of his nieces and nephews that cluttered his desktop, she asked, "Yours?"

He laughed. "Nope. That's my nephew. All nieces and nephews."

"So far," Will, now sitting at another desk interjected.

Rico stared at him. "How about I get a little privacy here?"

Grinning, Will got up. "Okay. I'm gone."

Rico turned back to Macy.

She put down the photo and checked her watch, as

if she had only so much time to give him. "What would you like me to do, Detective?"

He slid the busting-from-its-seams case file toward her. "Look at this."

"You want me to look at the whole thing? What possible good would that be?"

"I want you to see if anything in the file strikes a chord with anything you've uncovered about Billy. There are more photos. Maybe you can see if there's a resemblance between the parents in this case and the boy in your case." He'd tried to get Chelsey Ray to come down, but couldn't reach her. Mostly, he wanted the attorney to find an ounce of sympathy and let him meet with the boy in her charge.

But he kept silent, watching as she flipped through the pages, her face expressionless. She stopped only when she landed on another of Chelsey's photos. "Did she plan to give up her child for adoption? That's why most girls go to Haven's Gate, isn't it?"

He nodded. "Yes, she did. She was a teenager, unmarried, had no money and no way of caring for the child."

"And the baby was kidnapped from the nursery?"

"Yeah. We covered all angles. The most likely scenario was that the baby's father had abducted the infant since he hadn't wanted the mother to give the child away. But later we discovered that she'd changed her mind about the adoption and told the father, so there was no reason for him to take the boy. When that lead fizzled, we had few others. We interviewed the staff, checked lists of anyone who was allowed in the nursery during that time, and still came up with nothing. Our leads went cold and the baby has never been found."

Macy picked up a copy of the boy's birth certificate, then looked at Rico. "The baby disappeared *after* the mother told Haven's Gate she didn't want to go through with the adoption—or before she had a chance to tell them?"

"What does the entry in the file say?" He caught her gaze, her blue eyes making it hard to stay focused on the case. He went to the file again and flipped a couple pages.

"I didn't see anything about it… But it's a big file."

Rico's muscles tensed. It was a good question. Only he didn't know the answer. How many times had he gone through the case—and yet he didn't know the answer to something that could implicate Haven's Gate in the kidnapping?

She shrugged. "It was just a question. It probably doesn't matter."

Maybe not to her, but it did to him. This was his niece's baby they were talking about. Besides, he prided himself on doing a thorough investigation, everything by the book. He should've *known* the answer. "I'll check the file later."

Later when she was gone…because right now sitting next to her had him thinking of things that had nothing to do with the case.

High maintenance, Santini. Not your type. Now he just needed to convince his body of the same.

Frowning as she looked at the file, Macy said, "I—I

have another appointment, so unless you have anything else…" Her voice trailed off and she pushed away from the desk. "I don't see how this is doing any good."

Rico sensed that something she'd seen in the file disturbed her. But within seconds, she'd collected herself. She leaned forward. "I hope you didn't think my coming down here to look at the case was going to make me change my mind about letting you see the boy."

He almost laughed. Was he that transparent? "No, I didn't think that at all," he lied.

She raised one of her fine blond eyebrows in question, her expression dubious.

Now he *had* to laugh. "Okay, maybe I did…a little."

Her full mouth turned up in a smile, but there was no smugness in her voice when she said, "An honest man. I like that."

At which she stood, turned and walked toward the door, pink velour clinging in all the right places.

He sprang to his feet and followed. Before she reached the exit, he touched her shoulder. "Thanks for coming down. If you have a change of heart, please let me know."

She turned. "It isn't going to happen. I can tell you, though, after looking at the photo of both parents in the file, I don't think there's a resemblance."

Disappointment, sharp and quick, shot through him. "Kids don't always look like their parents."

She nodded. "True. As I said, if someone doesn't show to claim him, there will be DNA testing, and I'll do what I can to ensure your case is one of the first tested."

It wasn't the answer he'd wanted...but it was something.

"Thanks. I guess it pays to know the right people."

MACY HADN'T INTENDED on going to her office on a Saturday afternoon, but she didn't have any other plans and she had to do something to get her mind off what she'd learned at Santini's office. She unlocked the big double doors, went in, pulled out one of her other client files and sat at her desk, forcing herself to focus on the papers in front of her. The Joffrey case. A welfare mother was bringing suit against one of the largest health maintenance organizations in the country for not giving her daughter the same quality of care that other clients received.

Even though Macy wanted more than anything to see Marilyn Joffrey receive monetary compensation for her loss, she knew all the money in the world could never replace the woman's child.

And the Joffrey case couldn't keep her mind from going back to one thing. Chelsey Ray had agreed to give up her child for adoption, but had changed her mind.

A chill crawled up Macy's spine.

No matter how many times Macy's parents had impressed upon her that she was unable to care for a child, she'd finally realized she couldn't do what they'd wanted her to do. Her baby was a part of her—and a part of Jesse. She couldn't just give their child away like an old pair of shoes. At the last minute she'd changed her mind about the adoption—just as Chelsey had.

But young girls changed their minds all the time,

some even after taking their babies home. Because that's when reality set in.

It also bothered her that the same physician that delivered her baby delivered Chelsey's child. She'd had no idea Dr. Dixon worked at the shelter. Her father had told Macy the physician was a personal friend and that he would come to the shelter, deliver Macy's baby and keep everything confidential.

Back then, naive and barely seventeen, she hadn't known medical records were always confidential—that any physician who delivered the baby would have to abide by the laws of confidentiality.

So what was the big deal? Twelve years had passed. What difference did it make whether Dr. Dixon was on staff at Haven's Gate or not? Still, the question niggled at her. Why would her father lead her to believe Dr. Dixon wasn't on staff?

The easiest thing would be to talk with her father and see if what she remembered was correct. If her father would even talk to her.

They'd had little communication since Macy left his firm. But her mother kept calling Macy, urging her to come for dinner and make up with her father. She hadn't taken her mother up on the invitations, but maybe it was time she did.

The decision made, she picked up the phone and punched in the number, hoping her mother wouldn't be engaged in her usual activity—shopping.

"Hello," a woman's voice trilled.

"Mother. How are you?"

"Macy? Is that you?"

"Ye-e-es," Macy drew out the word. "Who else would call you mother?" Granted she hadn't called the house much since the fallout with her father.

"I'm surprised to hear your voice, that's all. Is something wrong?"

"No, of course not. I called to…to find out how you are."

Macy heard a sigh of relief on the other end of the phone. "Oh, sweetheart, I can't tell you how good that makes me feel. Let me get your father so you can talk to him."

"No, don't do that. I want to talk with you, Mom."

"Sure, sweetheart." Ever the peacemaker, Sarah Delacourt Capshaw wanted everything to be fine with everyone, no matter that she was married to a tyrant who directed all aspects of her socialite life. Okay, that wasn't fair. Her mother's life was just different. It wasn't how Macy wanted to live hers, but so what. Passing judgment was exactly what her father did.

If her mother found her importance in life through keeping ahead of the pack in just about everything, then who was Macy to say it wasn't right for her.

"What do you want to talk about, dear?"

"I…uh…was wondering when I might come for dinner?"

Her mother's excited squeal nearly perforated Macy's eardrum.

"Tonight? I'm having your grandparents for dinner and they'd be oh so happy to see you."

"Okay. What time?"

"Is seven all right? I can change it if it's not convenient for you."

"No, Mom. Seven is perfect."

When she hung up, Macy felt warmed by her mother's reaction. She'd made her happy. Such a little thing, and the woman was ecstatic. Knowing her grandparents would be there had made the idea of dinner with her father less stressful for Macy.

Wesley Capshaw wasn't going to steamroller anyone with Ira Delacourt in company. It was her grandfather's name and money that put her father where he was, and Ira Delacourt doted on his only grandchild. Her father wouldn't win any points being rude to her in front of Ira.

Comfortable with her decision, Macy spent the rest of the afternoon on other cases, four of which involved women who'd fled from abusive husbands. She could never understand how one person could physically hurt another, but it happened all the time.

Even as she worked the other cases, her mind drifted to Santini's cold case—and to Detective Santini himself. How warm his hand had felt when he'd placed it on her shoulder. How gentle, yet firm. Strong. She liked strong men, both physically and mentally.

A muscle tightened low in her belly. Damn. You'd think she was a teenager with a crush on the captain of the football team. Okay. She had to admit that Rico Santini was a mighty appealing man—even if he was a cop. Cops and attorneys were like fire and water. Always on opposite sides in the courtroom. A combustible combination that rarely worked.

Looking for something to take her mind off the sexy detective who was only being nice because he wanted something from her, she began to write down things she remembered from when she'd stayed at Haven's Gate.

She remembered Carla…what was her last name? Carla was one of the girls Macy had made friends with while they were at the shelter…and Macy had promised to keep in touch. Somehow that promise had been lost along the way, what with college, law school, a trip to Europe and then starting work at her father's firm.

Carla…Carla Monroe, that was her name. She and Carla had commiserated over what they were about to do, wondering if there was any other way. But there wasn't. The father of Macy's baby was dead, and Carla was only fifteen, living with her single mother and seven siblings on welfare.

Acting the big sister, Macy had impressed on Carla the importance of finishing school, and she wondered now if Carla had taken it to heart. She noted the girl's last name.

Macy also wrote out tidbits she remembered from Rico's case file. Before she knew it, she had a pad full of notes and it was time to go home and change for dinner. Her mother and grandmother would die if she came in her sweats.

On the drive home, Macy decided on a pair of black dress pants and a lightweight black cowl-neck sweater. Just right for a crisp spring evening. And to top it off, her best Manolos. No matter what she wore, she always felt more confident in great shoes.

At her condo, Macy heard the phone as she was pulling the key from the door, but by the time she got to it, the message had clicked off. She glanced around for Hercules, forgetting he was at the vets overnight. She missed the dog. It was the first time they'd been apart overnight since she'd brought him home three years ago.

Setting her briefcase on the couch, she kicked off her shoes, retrieved a soft drink from the fridge and then went back to the phone and punched the message button. She dropped onto the couch to listen.

"Hi, Macy. It's Rico. Detective Santini. When you get a minute, please give me a call at 555-2531. I'm going out now and it'll be late when I return. So call tomorrow if you can. Thanks."

She played the message again, enjoying the sensual quality of his voice. *Call me,* he'd said. But not tonight.

Of course not. What guy who looked like Rico would be sitting home on a Saturday night?

A tiny pinprick of envy needled her. She wondered what kind of women he dated. Wondered why she was even thinking of him, and why she couldn't stop.

But she knew why.

In a way, Rico Santini reminded her a little of her first love. Dark hair, soft brown eyes and long, black eyelashes that most women would kill for. Both men owned any room they entered. Jesse because he looked very much the rebel, and Rico because he possessed a charm and self-confidence that made heads turn.

An hour later, she was knocking at the front door of her parents' home in Bel Air, her palms sweaty and her nerves tingling on the surface of her skin. She knocked one more time and then opened the oversize carved wood door, as was her custom. Never barge in, she'd been taught. Not even in the home where she'd grown up. Manners, manners, manners. Her mother ran a close race with Emily Post in all things related to etiquette.

"Sweetheart," her mother sang out as she floated toward Macy.

They hugged. Sarah gave Macy an air kiss on each cheek, then smoothed the front of her lavender silk shirt, which perfectly matched lavender silk pants. Svelte at sixty-two, with golden hair, perfectly coiffed, her mother wore little jewelry. Just the three-carat rock she wore on her left hand and matching stud earrings. Sarah didn't need to wear much makeup.

"Come in, dear. Your grandparents are in the library with your father."

"Am I late?"

"Just a little. But don't worry about it. We're simply happy you're here."

They walked into the library together and immediately, her grandmother was at her side. Her father and grandfather stood near the window talking. When they saw her, her grandfather started toward her. Her father didn't budge.

She gave the older man a loving hug, then went over to her father and hugged him, too, a perfunctory gesture.

"You look beautiful, young lady," her grandfather said.

"Thanks, Gramps. You look pretty spiffy yourself."

Her father looked good, too. He always did. At sixty-one, he was still a handsome man with silver hair and a golden tan that said he had time to spare for many vacations in the tropics. Tall and elegant, Wesley Capshaw was a Renaissance man. When he entered a courtroom, he put everyone on notice.

Before Macy knew it, dinner was over and they were having coffee and dessert and she hadn't had a single opportunity to talk with her father.

"Dad, do you remember Doctor Dixon?" she asked around a mouthful of tiramisu.

Her father's head snapped up, his lips thin, and it took a second for him to respond. "Yes, of course." He looked to Sarah and then Macy's grandparents, and without further acknowledgment of her question, he said, "I think you should all know that Sarah and I plan to go to Paris for our wedding anniversary next week." He smiled with satisfaction and patted her mother's hand.

"How wonderful," Macy's grandmother sang out. "And how romantic." Marion Delacourt played the addled old lady far too often, but Macy knew her gran was as sharp as a fillet knife. "How many years is that, dear?" Marion asked her daughter.

"Thirty—" Sarah hesitated "—thirty-one."

"That's good since I'm already thirty," Macy joked.

"Mind your manners, young lady," Sarah reprimanded with a tight smile, as if nobody at the table knew that Macy's parents had married because Sarah was pregnant. Which, she guessed, was part of the reason they hadn't wanted Macy to keep her baby. They'd regretted their mistake and didn't want their daughter to do the same. To make sure, they'd refused to help her if she kept the child.

At the reminder, Macy pushed to her feet. "Dad, can I talk to you in private for a minute?"

Wesley looked surprised, but he wasn't going to refuse her request in front of guests. *What's in the family, stays in the family. The immediate family.* If she'd heard it once, she'd heard it a thousand times.

Macy followed her father into the library and closed the door behind her, dreading any discussion with her father because the outcome was always the same. Bad. But this was something she needed to do—for her own peace of mind. "Do you remember telling me that Dr. Dixon delivered my baby as a favor to you?"

Wesley shrugged. "That was a long time ago. I've put it out of my mind."

Sure. So had she until something came up to remind her, and it seemed something always came up. "I had no idea he delivered more babies at Haven's Gate. I thought he was there just that once."

Her father's eyes narrowed and a frown creased his tanned forehead. "I really don't want to discuss any of this. For God's sake, Macy, that's all in the past."

He was shutting her down. It was what he did when he didn't think a subject worthy of discussion. "Well, maybe for you, but it isn't for me." As the words came out, she felt her hands start to shake. "There isn't a day that goes by when I don't think of the child I lost."

Wesley let out a sharp breath. "Keep it down or your grandparents will hear you."

"You know what? I don't give a damn if they know. I never did. In fact it might be better for all of us to acknowledge my so-called indiscretion than to pretend it never happened. I kept the secret for you, not for me, and now I want you to listen," she said, talking fast so he couldn't shut her down again. "I was working with a detective today on a case in which an infant was abducted five years ago—from Haven's Gate." She stopped, caught a quick breath, then went on. "Dr. Dixon delivered that baby, too."

He gave her a blank stare. "So what?"

"I thought it a little strange since you told me he was delivering my baby as a favor to you. A one-time thing. That way we could be assured it would be kept confidential."

He shrugged. "I don't see the point. Apparently Dixon decided to continue working at the shelter after that. What does that have to do with anything?"

Before she had a chance to respond, he yanked open the door. "I don't want to hear anything more about this. I'm not going to let you spoil your mother's happiness tonight."

Guilt. He was good at that, too. "You're still ashamed of…of me. Aren't you?"

"And you're not?" He turned on his heel to leave, but on the way out he reiterated, "Leave well enough alone, Macy. Don't bring this up again."

Macy's stomach sank. The room closed in on her.

She tried to draw a full breath but felt as if her lungs had collapsed. She held on to the door, and when she'd managed to regain her composure, she forced herself to walk back into the dining room.

She should have known nothing would come of talking to her father. Which made her all the more determined to get some answers.

He'd lied to her twelve years ago, and she was going to find out why.

CHAPTER THREE

CARLA MONROE. CARLA MONROE. Macy thumbed through the phone book, scanning for her former roommate's name. If she talked with Carla or even one of the other girls who'd stayed at Haven's Gate back then, she might learn something.

Her friend would likely be married and the chances of finding her in the white pages weren't good. Finished with the phone book, she turned to the computer in her home office and did an Internet search. Nothing there, either.

She could call Charlie. She used the private investigator when she needed someone to do background on a case that she couldn't get through normal channels. She was about to punch in his number when she remembered Carla's mother's name and went back to the phone book. Mary Monroe... There it was—along with four others of the same name and a dozen more with the initial *M*. She started at the top.

After six futile calls, she was ready to give up and call Charlie when, after Macy explained who she was and who she was trying to find, the woman who'd answered said, "Yes, I have a daughter named Carla."

"Oh, thank heaven," Macy said. "Carla and I were friends several years ago and I've wanted to get in touch with her, but I lost her phone number." It was true. If she'd had Carla's number before, she didn't know what she'd done with it.

"Oh, I remember you, Miss Capshaw. Carla talked about you all the time. Said you helped her a lot."

Macy felt even worse for letting time and circumstance keep her from maintaining the friendship, but she couldn't change that now. "I'd like to get in touch with her. Do you have her number?"

"Yes, of course."

Mrs. Monroe rattled on about how Carla was married now and had three children and couldn't be happier. Then she gave Macy Carla's number and said goodbye. Though glad to hear her friend was doing well, Macy felt a twinge of envy. There was a time when she wanted more than anything to have a family of her own, but four years ago, that door had been closed forever.

After talking to Mrs. Monroe, Macy called Carla. No answer, so she left a brief message and her number. She hoped Carla would call, but couldn't blame her if she didn't.

Macy went into the kitchen, prepared some tea and went back to her office. Work would take her mind off what was quickly becoming an obsession. She pulled up her e-mail and found several messages from her admin assistant and plowed through them, making notes in her Day-Timer of court dates, due dates for briefs, and then she read some case law that she'd asked Cheryl to find.

A half hour later, the phone rang. Macy snatched it up. "Hello."

A woman's small voice said, "Hi, Macy. This is Carla."

As reluctant as Macy had been to call Carla, she was more than happy that she had. In seconds, the years slipped away and they were as comfortable with each other as if they'd never been apart. "Your mom says you're doing fantastic," Macy said. "Instead of talking on the phone, why don't we get together? It would be so much fun and a lot easier to catch up on each other's lives.

There was hesitation on Carla's end, but Macy persisted. "Any time you want. Anywhere you want. I can pick you up, take you to lunch or—"

"It's…it's hard for me to get a sitter," Carla said. "But I take the kids to the park sometimes in the morning and maybe you could meet us there one day. We can talk while the rug rats play."

"Sure. I'd like that. Whenever you want."

Carla suggested the next week, but Macy didn't want to wait that long. "I'd love for it to be sooner if we could."

Again, Carla hesitated, then said, "I have some time this afternoon when the kids are napping. Could you come here?"

"Of course I will. I can't wait to see you."

"Me, too," Carla said, but Macy didn't hear conviction in her voice. And after giving Macy her address, Carla added, "It's not the best neighborhood, but we're planning to move soon."

"I'm coming to see *you,* Carla. Not your house."

"Okay," Carla's voice rose as if pleased at the response.

Macy asked for the address and they agreed on a time. Now all she had to do was decide what she was going to ask Carla and yet not bring up unhappy memories. Her friend had wanted desperately to keep her child. They'd both wanted that.

Two hours later, Macy was cruising the streets in one of the older L.A. neighborhoods. While some older parts of the city had been designated historic, the area she was looking for hadn't made the grade.

She located the address, an apartment, and then parked in the back as Carla suggested. The rundown building reminded Macy of the projects where she had visited one of her pro bono clients. Uncomfortable with the guys hanging out a few cars down, nonetheless, she went inside, only to be greeted by dingy walls and the sweet, telltale odor of marijuana filling the hallways. No elevator, either.

She walked up the two flights, found apartment 234 and knocked softly so she didn't wake her friend's children.

The door parted a crack and a pair of brown eyes peered out. The door shut again. She heard a chain slide, a click, and then Carla—as pretty as ever—was standing there and Macy felt as if she'd been flung back in time.

The women reached out to hug each other. "It's so good to see you," Carla said, her dimples making dents in cheeks that were still girlishly plump.

"You, too," Macy said.

Carla motioned for Macy to come in and then locked and bolted the door. "Can't be too careful around here."

After a few awkward moments, they launched into conversation, their rapport as easy as if the years hadn't come between them. They looked at several photo books of Carla's family, laughed at some of the silly things children do, and then caught up on where they were in their personal lives.

"My mom told me you're a lawyer now, and I know your life must be really busy," Carla said, looking lovingly at the photographs of her children. "But having children is one of God's greatest gifts. I hope you're blessed with that happiness someday."

Macy swallowed. She'd hoped for that, too. Once. But her fate was sealed when her gynecologist confirmed that it would be impossible to conceive again. The disappointment had cut deep. But like other things she couldn't change, she'd grieved and then made a personal decision to devote her life to helping children.

"I have a…female problems. So, it looks like I'll just have to enjoy other people's children," she said, trying to make light of it.

But she couldn't forget the loss. The disappointment.

Carla glanced away, obviously embarrassed. "I'm so sorry. I shouldn't have assumed—"

"It's okay. I've adjusted."

A long pause ensued and then Carla asked, "Do you ever think about your baby? Where he is and what he's doing? If he's happy?"

The question surprised Macy, but then it shouldn't have. Carla had left the day before Macy had delivered, so she couldn't have known Macy's child had been stillborn. But Macy didn't want to get into all that. What she really wanted to know was if Dr. Dixon delivered Carla's baby, as well. She nodded. "Of course. All the time. Do you?"

Carla hesitated. "I think about it sometimes, but then I think what happened might have been for the best."

Macy nodded her understanding. "Giving up a child for adoption is one of the biggest sacrifices a mother can make. But when it's what's best for the baby…"

Carla's eyes went wide. "Oh, I didn't give him up."

Macy stared at Carla. "I…I don't understand. Do you mean you changed your mind and took your baby home?" Her gaze darted around the room searching for photos of an older child. She hadn't seen any in the photo albums.

Furrows formed on Carla's brow. "You didn't hear?"

"Hear what?"

"My baby was dead. He was stillborn. When that happened, everything changed."

But…Macy had been told that everything had gone fine for Carla…that the adoption had been completed and Carla was happy her child would have a good home.

When Macy finally found her voice, it was only a whisper. "No, I didn't know."

"They said it was for the best. He wouldn't have been normal and would have had severe medical problems all his life. Something about the heart. And I know now, I was way too young to take care of him properly. I blame myself sometimes."

"But it wasn't your fault."

"I know. That's what the doctor said."

"Do you remember the doctor's name?"

Carla shook her head. "Why?"

"No reason," Macy said absently.

Ten minutes later, Macy left Carla's and drove back to her office, her mind reeling as she tried to make some sense of what she'd just learned. Why would anyone lie to her about Carla's baby? And it wasn't just one person who'd lied, it was the doctor and the rest of the staff. *Her father.* Did they think she couldn't handle the news after hearing her own baby had been stillborn?

Two stillborn babies within hours of each other? What were the odds? Immediately the lawyer in her rose to the fore. Had the doctor or the staff botched something in one of the births—or both?

She parked and went inside the tall, contemporary Citicorp building, rode the elevator up to her office on the seventh floor. The only conclusion Macy could draw was that there was culpability on the part of either the physician or the staff when her child died, and they didn't want the facility to get slapped with a lawsuit. If they lied to Macy about Carla's baby, there'd be no reason for Macy and her family to think there was any problem with the standard of care when her child was stillborn. If her family knew about two dead infants within twenty-four hours of each other, someone might have had a few questions.

Preoccupied, she crossed the reception area, barely acknowledging Cheryl, went into her office and sat at her desk. Even if she'd heard about Carla's baby back then, she'd been so naive, she might not have thought anything of it. But her father would have. Then again, since he wanted the whole thing to disappear, and Dr. Dixon was his friend, he might not have done anything. Wesley Capshaw looked out for himself.

Her head hurt. She didn't work well on possibilities or assumptions. She had to find out exactly what had happened that night. But how? She couldn't waltz into the shelter and start poring over confidential records. Requesting her own records would take time and wouldn't necessarily show anything. She needed Carla's records, too.

Rico Santini. The Ray case was connected to Haven's Gate. He could get a search warrant to look at the records. Take her with him.

Anyone who knew the circumstance would think it suspicious. All she had to do was tell him why he needed to check the records.

Only if she did that, she would have to tell him about her involvement.

BERNIE'S SPORTS BAR AND GRILL was the nearest watering hole to the *House,* aka the station, and while Rico didn't frequent the place as often as the rest of his unit, he managed to make every Yankees game he could. As a kid, Rico, his dad and his brothers watched them all. His dad worked hard at his small restaurant in Hoboken and the family had barely scraped by, but attending ball games was part of Mario Santini's life.

Initially, his dad had had to force Rico to go along,

because Rico was more interested in his computer. Now, even though he was three thousand miles away, he still participated in the ritual from afar whenever he could.

Three televisions blared with the most important game of the season. Yankees versus their archrivals, the Boston Red Sox, and Rico had convinced his buddies that they better root for his team.

"My round." Luke slid first one pitcher of beer across the table and then another.

Deep voices reverberated with each out, hit or run. Jordan, Luke and Rico hooted along with everyone else and gave high fives when their team came home. They sat at a table directly in front of the big screen and were on their fourth round of beer, the Yankees were down by two runs and the bases were loaded when the room came to a sudden hush.

Rico did a 180. A blond woman stood just inside the doorway, looking to the left. When she turned his way his mouth fell open. Macy.

What the…

"Come to Papa," one of the guys at the next table said and whistled loudly. A few other drunks joined in.

Rico's first instinct was to get up and punch the guy with the biggest mouth, but he restrained himself. He didn't have a clue what she was doing there. And the fact that she was there at all annoyed the hell out of him.

Tilting back on two legs of his chair, Jordan clapped Rico on the shoulder. "I think she's here for you, Romeo."

"You want us to leave?" Luke asked.

"No. Stay here. I need protection," Rico joked.

"Yeah? If you want protection from that woman, you've got a major problem."

"I'm not into high maintenance."

"I'd have no problem with that," Jordan injected.

"Yeah, I know." That was because Jordan's family had nearly as much money as Bill Gates and he was used to dating women of the same ilk.

As Macy Capshaw walked toward them, all eyes were upon her. His, too. He couldn't take his eyes off her creamy smooth skin exposed by the open collar of her shirt. Her suede pants looked as if they were hand tailored for every curve. She was fine, all right. Too fine for him.

And she knew it better than anyone. It wasn't likely she was there to seduce him, so he had to wonder. Had she reconsidered letting him talk to her client? Did she have new information on the boy's identity?

Luke placed a hand over his chest and thumped it a couple of times. "Be still my heart."

As she reached their table, Rico, Luke and Jordan clanked chairs in an effort to stand, but she gestured for them to stay seated.

"Excuse me, gentlemen." She looked at Rico. "Can I talk with you for a minute?"

He felt drawn to her and was annoyed at himself because of it. "Now?"

Just then she looked away from him and her eyes lit up. "Jordan? Jordan St. James?"

Jordan stood and held out a hand. "How are you, Macy?"

"I'm fine, thank you. You guys work together?"

Jordan nodded. "Yep. We're partners. I was promoted right after the trial."

"The trial. Oh, yes. Don't remind me."

"Why? You won the case."

"But it wasn't a good win."

Rico had enough experience with attorneys to know what that meant. She'd won the case, but she didn't like how she did it. It was either that or she thought her client was guilty.

"Well, it's nice seeing you again, Jordan."

"Thanks. I'm hoping you can help out my partner so he won't be so cranky."

Macy glanced at Rico.

He kept his expression somber.

"Do you have a minute?" she repeated.

"If you want to tell me you're going to let me see the kid, sure, I've got a minute. If not, I'm busy." He'd said it jokingly, but he was sure the message was clear. He didn't play games with rich girls.

Her gaze flashed to Luke, then to Jordan and back to Rico again. "That's not why I'm here."

"Okay… So, why are you here?"

A loud roar went up from the guys at the bar, and because she was blocking his view, Rico missed the play. "Dammit." He launched to his feet, and his chair scraped backward, falling over with a crash.

Macy's blue eyes rounded like dinner plates. Seeing her expression, Rico bit back his frustration, took a breath and picked up his chair. He said, very quietly, very gently, "This is my day off, Macy, and I'm trying to watch a game. In fact, we're at a critical point for my team. So, if you're not here about Billy, can it please wait until this is over?"

Her eyes narrowed. She pulled out a chair and said, "Okay. I'll wait."

Rico ran a hand through his hair. How the hell could he focus on the game with her at the same table? Her scent alone was enough to raise his testosterone level a couple notches. His body obviously didn't recognize high maintenance as a flaw.

"Have it your way," he said, then moved to face the television.

And dammit if she didn't pull her chair right up beside his. He inched his a little to the side, though out of the corner of his eye, he could still see her. As irritated as he was, he admired her chutzpah. She wasn't a quitter. But then she was probably used to getting whatever she wanted.

"Thank you," he heard her say to someone behind him. And a few seconds later, she said, "Cheers."

Somehow he managed to watch the rest of the game, but it wasn't easy listening to her laugh and joke with the other guys. Apparently a sexy woman with a great smile was all it took to capture their interest. Hell, who was he kidding? That was usually the case with him, too.

When the game was over, and his team had lost, he felt even more irascible. And with her sitting there, he couldn't voice his frustration.

"Sorry your team lost," she said.

"No big deal. They've lost before and they always come back."

"Sounds like you're one of those die-hard fans."

He snatched the pitcher and poured himself another beer, then he filled her nearly empty glass. "Depends on who you talk to."

She looked at Luke and Jordan. "What do you guys say? Die-hard or not?"

Both men nodded and gave a thumbs-up. "Die-hard," they said in unison.

"Stop talking about me as if I'm not here." He leveled his gaze at Macy. "What is it that you wanted to talk to me about?"

She leaned toward him and said under her breath, "Is there somewhere that's private?"

Rico considered. He gestured toward the back of the bar where there was an empty booth. "There."

She didn't look particularly enamored with his choice, but said, "Fine."

Rico picked up both glasses and followed her to the back booth. What could be so important that she had to track him down on his day off? Her day off, too, wasn't it?

They edged into the booth, one on each side, and he slid a glass toward her, the condensation leaving a beaded trail on the table. "So, why are you here? I'm sure trolling the local sports bars isn't your idea of a good time."

Defiance flashed in her eyes. "I called the station and the officer in charge said it was your day off. He said I might find you here."

He let his gaze travel over her. "And you dressed for the occasion?"

She looked down, as if embarrassed. "After I looked at your file, I was curious about some things and did some research myself."

"Curious about what things?"

Macy curled her hands around her glass. She didn't want to lie, but she didn't want to tell him the real reason for her curiosity, either. "Nothing anyone else would notice, but it relates to a case I once worked on." She lifted her glass and took a gulp of beer.

He nodded. "Go on."

"I can't tell you the details of that case, but it was similar to yours in that both girls had babies at Haven's Gate."

He frowned. "Not unusual. It's a home for pregnant girls."

"Yes, that's true. Lots of women have had babies there. But something about these two cases came together for me. Call it intuition or whatever. It also struck me that the Ray baby investigation wasn't all that thorough."

He sat up, squared his shoulders. "The investigation was very thorough," he said tersely. "I know because I was part of it."

"Sorry, that came out wrong. I meant that after looking at the file, I had some questions." Damn. She didn't want to put him on the defensive, but she seemed to have a preternatural gift for it.

If she wanted him to help, she was going to have to be more cautious.

"My former client had been told her baby, the child she'd given birth to at the shelter, had been stillborn."

"So?"

"The staff at Haven's Gate told me my client's child had been adopted. There was no reason to question it because it had nothing to do with the case at the time."

Liar. She hated liars and here she was doing exactly what she hated in others.

His frown deepened. "And this is important to me because…?" He lifted his hands, palms up.

"Because they, the staff at Haven's Gate, lied to me. And because another baby had been stillborn not twenty-four hours before that."

"How do you know that?"

Macy waffled, searching for a quick answer. "My client told me."

"Why do you think they lied to you?"

She shrugged. She had an idea, but she wanted to find out for sure. That's why she needed his help.

"Maybe the staff at Haven's Gate thought it wasn't any of your business because their records are confidential," Rico said.

"I could accept that. But they out and out lied."

His forehead furrowed. "So how does this relate to the Ray case?"

"Same place, same physician, same staff. Two babies dead, one they lied about. If they lied once, they may not have given your people the correct information on the Ray case, either. Maybe there's culpability on the part of the staff or the physician. Maybe the delivery was botched and the people at the facility said the baby was abducted to cover up what really happened."

Leaning against the back of the booth, he didn't say anything at first. Then he smiled, one of those lopsided, half-grin smiles. "I think you're watching too many police shows."

She clamped her mouth shut. His glib remark made her feel as if her opinion wasn't worth anything. One of her father's favorite tactics.

"So what did you think I could do with this information?" He leaned back against the padded booth.

"Take a look at the shelter's records."

"You're joking, of course."

She shook her head. "No."

"Well, first of all, we looked at all the records that were available to us five years ago. And as an attorney, you should know I can't just go in and rifle through records. I'd have to get a warrant."

"So get a warrant."

"And to get a warrant, I'd have to have probable cause. I'd need new evidence. Believe me, if there was new evidence in the Ray case, I'd be on it like white on rice. But as it stands, no judge in his right mind would sign off on a warrant for the reasons you just gave me."

"I know a judge who might."

Rico looked surprised. Or maybe shocked.

"He owes me a favor."

At that, Rico's whole body seemed to tense up. "That might be how things work in your world, Macy. But I don't take liberties with the constitutional rights of others."

His words were sharp. Succinct. And she didn't like his accusatory tone. "I'm not asking you to trample anyone's constitutional rights. I'm asking you to get more information on an old case. People do it all the time."

"I don't need a warrant to get public information."

"No. But without a warrant, all you'll get is what they tell you."

"Sorry."

Macy was at a loss. He was a stubborn man. Rigid. Her nerves felt stretched like rubber bands. He reminded her of another inflexible man she knew.

"Laws are laws. I've taken an oath to uphold them."

"And you always play by the rules?"

He looked her straight in the eyes. "Always."

"You don't bend them even just a little?"

"Nope."

"No matter what?"

"No matter what."

She leaned forward and stared back at him. "Well, you know what I think? I think you just haven't found anything important enough for you to bend the rules."

"You're right. And I doubt I ever will."

CHAPTER FOUR

MACY CAPSHAW CONFUSED the hell out of Rico. She was adamant about adhering to the letter of the law in her job as an advocate for Billy, but she was willing to bend it to get information she needed on something else. He shouldn't be surprised.

While spouting all their legal platitudes, most attorneys were only concerned with one thing—getting their client off, guilty or not. Twisting truth to serve their purpose. He spent all his time trying to put criminals behind bars and the lawyers did all they could to get the perps back on the streets.

Rico swung around in his chair and pulled another file. He was just getting to like her and then she threw that at him.

While he wasn't as altruistic about police work as he'd once been, he wasn't as cynical as many longtime cops, either. The job had a way of changing people, but he hoped he never reached the point where he'd disregard his values and beliefs. Not even a little, because once you crossed that line, it was easier and easier to go just a little bit further. He'd seen it happen too many times.

"I say we go through every old missing-child case within the past ten years and see if there are any similarities." Jordan's cultured voice cut through Rico's musings.

Rico looked up. "We did that before."

"Yeah, but time changes things. We have new ways to look at evidence now. And we might come at it with a new perspective."

Jordan may have been away from the case, but Rico hadn't. Although he wasn't thumbing through the file every day, he wondered all too often if he'd missed something. If he could've done more.

"Good idea. Let's go back an even dozen." Rico stood, instantly ready to go to the morgue, the warehouselike room in the basement where the cold cases were stored. "But this is my gig. I don't want to drag you into it. You've got other cases to take care of."

Jordan bobbed his blond head and said, "I'll get some coffee and meet you there."

Three hours later, Rico punched in one last note on his PDA. The most important note he'd taken so far. Jordan had left an hour ago. But he had a gut feeling there was something he wasn't seeing, something they'd all glossed over—and he'd been right. He didn't know if it meant anything or not, but it certainly was an interesting bit of information—and one more lead to follow.

MACY PACED OUTSIDE Billy's hospital room waiting for the doctor to finish. She wanted all the information she could get before going to the hearing.

Billy's room had changed and he was now on the children's floor, which was surprisingly quiet. She heard laughter coming from one room and whimpering from another. Her heart melted knowing how hard it must be for a child to be away from his family. How hard for the parents. Yet Billy hadn't shown any sign that he missed his family and she guessed it was because he didn't remember them.

Dr. Stanley came out of the room. "Billy's waiting for you."

"How is he?"

"He's remarkably well. His spirits are good, and physically he's improved a great deal. With proper nutrition he'll keep improving. Healthwise, he can go home at any time. There appears to be no organic cause for his amnesia, so we have to believe it's psychologically induced."

Which meant they couldn't find a natural cause, no head trauma or other physical problems such as a brain tumor. "So he does have amnesia then?"

"He has a block that won't allow him to remember. He could remember everything an hour from now—or never. Either way, it'll be a big adjustment."

"The social worker is pushing for foster care immediately. Do you think he's ready?"

"We can't do anything more for him here that couldn't be done in the home. Wherever he goes, I recommend therapy."

"I can make sure that happens."

"I'll sign off on the discharge papers tomorrow at the latest. I can't justify keeping him any longer."

She thanked the physician and went into the room. Billy was dressed in the hospital pajamas that had been provided for him and was sitting at a small table with some puzzles on top. But he wasn't playing with anything.

His eyes lit up when he saw her.

"Hi, pal. How are you today?" She ruffled his tousled brown hair and then sat in the small seat next to him, careful not to crush the chair. "I brought you some clothes." She placed the bag on the table and pulled out a red T-shirt, jeans and white Nike tennis shoes, some underwear and socks.

"Did you find my mommy or my daddy?"

"No, I'm sorry to say we didn't. But we're going to keep looking. And in the meantime, we're going to find a nice place for you to stay."

The wary look on his face said he'd had a bad experience with places to stay.

"It'll be with some really nice people who're looking forward to meeting you."

"Can I come with you?"

Her heart wrenched. "I wish you could, Billy. But I work with many other children. My job is to help find a good place for you to live."

His bottom lip protruded.

"I'm not at home very much," she added, hoping he'd understand.

His eyes glazed over, as if he was used to hearing bad news.

"I promise I'll come to see you and we'll go have some ice cream. How does that sound?"

He nodded, but the brightness had left his brown eyes.

Macy's heart ached for Billy, and she left the room feeling more than a little animosity toward whoever had so callously abandoned him. How could anyone abandon a child? She vowed to make sure whoever took him in wouldn't be doing it just for the money. In her job, she'd had experience with all kinds of foster parents—good and bad.

She went directly from the hospital to the hearing, which lasted less than fifteen minutes. On the way out of the chambers, Karen Creighton caught up with her. "I'll be moving Billy into a foster home as soon as a decision is made on a caregiver. Will you be there this afternoon?"

"I'll be there."

The social worker went to leave. "Oh, I had a call from a detective who wanted to see Billy. I told him that wasn't my decision and suggested he speak with either you or the doctor."

"When was that?"

"This morning."

Macy clenched her hands at her sides. She'd bet her law license the detective was Rico Santini. Apparently he wasn't going to give up—no matter what she said.

RICO ROSE FROM HIS CHAIR in the waiting room of Macy's office when the attorney suddenly barreled in. Seeing him, she rolled her eyes and kept going through the doors and into her private office. Rico followed.

"What is it now, Detective?" she asked without turning. "I've had a really busy afternoon and my patience is as thin as rice paper."

"I need to talk to you for a few minutes."

She turned abruptly to face him. "I don't have a few minutes. And most people make an appointment to see me."

He checked his watch. "Isn't it quitting time? Your receptionist has gone."

"It's my business. I have to work until the job is done."

He sighed. "It's a real pity if that's all you do."

She shot him a narrowed gaze. "Excuse me?"

"A person's got to take time to have fun."

She raised her head, a little defensively in his mind. But then her shoulders seemed to relax. "Well," she said, her voice softer. "I'm sure your idea of fun and mine aren't the same."

Nodding, he said, "Probably true."

"What is it you came to see me about? I really hope it isn't about seeing Billy again."

Macy was still standing behind her desk, but Rico sat in one of the chairs anyway. "Billy's doctor says he's ready for discharge."

Her back stiffened and he knew he'd said the wrong thing. He could almost see the steam rising.

"So it was you. You disregarded my request and went to the hospital anyway."

"I didn't disturb Billy. I'm not as insensitive as you apparently think I am." Besides, he hadn't actually talked to the doctor. One of the nurses at the desk had given him the information.

Finally Macy sat, but she didn't say a word. Just stared at him, not giving an inch. He didn't give an inch, either. After a few moments of hard eye contact, she said, "I don't think you're insensitive. Just persistent. And while I admire the quality, it isn't going to help in this instance. Billy is going to be discharged tomorrow and placed in foster care. He'll need some time to get oriented to new people and new surroundings."

He was ready to protest when she added, "When he's settled and I'm sure he's not suffering any trauma from the move, I'll make arrangements for you to see him. Hopefully, it won't be too long."

It took a moment for him to absorb what she'd said. His spirits lifted. "That's great."

"So now you can go home, or to your sports bar, or wherever it is you go to have all that fun you've been talking about."

"Thanks, but Billy wasn't actually the reason I came to see you. I came about Haven's Gate."

Her eyes flashed with apprehension. "What about it?"

"I was researching missing kids and I noticed that four mothers had some connection with Haven's Gate, or the same doctor."

"Dr. Dixon?"

He nodded.

She sat forward in her chair, elbows on the desk. "What do you think it means?"

"I think it deserves further research. I contacted a couple of the mothers, but I didn't find anything to hang a warrant on."

"And you came here to tell me this because you've changed your mind about getting help with that warrant?"

He couldn't tell if she was serious or joking. But it was serious to him. "I'm telling you because I wanted to apologize for discounting your theory when we were at the bar."

She sat up, suddenly attentive. "Really? Does that mean you think my theory has some basis?"

"I think it's worth checking out, and since you had a client who'd been at Haven's Gate maybe—"

"You know that's protected information. Client confidentiality."

He grinned. "Hey, it was worth a try."

She returned the grin. "So, how will you pursue it if you can't get the records?"

"We have a list of those who stayed at the facility when the Ray baby was kidnapped. It might be helpful to reinterview those women and also some of the previous residents."

Macy's face paled. "I guess you'd have to have a warrant to get that information, too."

"For the earlier stuff, yeah, we would. But without probable cause, it's not going to happen."

Just then, the office door flew open and a woman who appeared to be in her fifties or sixties breezed into the room. It was hard for Rico to tell how old any woman was anymore since natural aging seemed to be a thing of the past in California.

"Mother." Macy's voice rose when she said the words. "What are you doing here? Is something wrong?"

"Oh, no." Then the woman saw Rico. "I—I'm sorry. I was out shopping and thought I'd…well, I didn't know you had a client. It's after hours and no one was out in front and—"

"He's not a client," Macy quickly clarified.

"Oh. A friend then?" The woman looked from Macy to Rico, and she was smiling. Pleasant.

Macy seemed a little rattled. Maybe she wasn't impervious after all. "Yes," Rico said. "We're good friends."

Macy's mother gave her daughter a look he easily recognized. The bad manners look. His mother was good at that, too.

"I'm sorry," Macy said. "This is Rico Santini." She gestured toward him. "And this is my mother, Sarah Capshaw."

Rico stood and extended a hand. "Pleased to meet you, Mrs. Capshaw. Although I'm surprised. You two look more like sisters than mother and daughter. But then you've probably heard that more than once."

Macy's mother beamed. "Please, call me Sarah."

"And please, call me Rico."

Macy glared at him.

"Well, dear," said Sarah, clutching her bag. "I won't keep you. Why don't you come to dinner tonight? We'd love to have you join us, too, young man."

"I don't think—" Macy began, searching for the right words.

Standing next to Macy's mother, Rico saw the woman's hurt. Apparently Macy saw it, too. "Well, let me check my schedule," she said, hitting a few keys on her computer. "Okay. It looks like I'm free."

Sarah's face lit up like Yankee Stadium during a night game. It made him wonder when Macy had last brought a friend to dinner.

"And how about you, Rico?"

Watching Macy's expression, he said, "I'm always up for great company. Sure, I'd love to have dinner with your family."

"It's settled then," Sarah chirped, already on her way out. "Your father will be delighted. Seven okay?"

Macy nodded, her lips pressed into a thin line, as if it was all she could do to hold her tongue.

"Ta, then." And with that, Sarah glided out the door.

Macy eyed Rico. "You want to explain?"

"About?"

"That *good friend* thing."

He shrugged. "I was being polite. Maybe *you* should explain why you didn't tell her we weren't good friends."

"I didn't want to hurt her feelings."

"And the dinner? You could've told me not to come but you didn't."

She straightened, raising her chin. "Maybe I thought dinner with my parents would be the perfect punishment for lying about our relationship."

"Our relationship. I like that. But for me, food is never punishment." He grinned.

She cleared her throat. "With my parents it is. Anyway, you don't have to go. I'll make an excuse for you."

"No need for that. I'd like to go. In fact, I'd like it very much."

Macy's expression shifted from uncertainty to resignation. Maybe she'd just realized he wasn't a quitter, either.

"Shall I pick you up or would you like to drive separately?"

"Pick me up?" He scoffed. "I think it would be more appropriate if I picked you up. Just tell me where and when."

She puzzled on that for a few seconds. "Yes…I guess that would look better, wouldn't it."

Look better? He didn't care what other people thought. He shifted uneasily from one foot to the other. Why did he feel as if Macy had manipulated him?

RICO LEFT MACY'S OFFICE on a mission to get more information about Haven's Gate. When he was finished at the station, first on his to-do list was the Board of Health and the office that regulated licensed health-care facilities.

"I went through the Ray case again," he told Jordan, who was sitting at the desk diagonally across from Rico's. "There wasn't much information on the actual facility."

Jordan frowned. "Is that significant?"

"I don't know. Right now anything could be important."

"Right now—" Jordan looked at his watch. "—a cold beer seems pretty important. How about it? The others are already at the bar."

Rico closed the file. "Can't. I have other plans."

Jordan didn't look surprised. "Hot date?"

"Business. Dinner with Macy Capshaw at her parents' home."

His partner, who had been pulling files together, getting ready to go, stopped what he was doing. "That's an unusual way to conduct business, my friend."

"Strictly business," Rico said. "Information gathering. After you left the morgue, I went through another box from the Ray case and discovered that Wesley Capshaw used to be on the board of directors for Haven's Gate. He may have been their legal consultant, too, but that wasn't clear. I don't know if he's still on the board, but he was at the time of the kidnapping."

"You think the two are linked?" Jordan frowned.

"I have reason to believe the doctor or the facility might be covering up some quality-of-care issues."

"And that relates to the kidnapping how?"

Rico expelled a long breath. Right now, all he had was Macy's theory that there could be negligence since two babies were stillborn within twenty-four hours and someone had lied about one of them. "That's what I'm trying to determine."

He told Jordan everything Macy had told him and when Rico finished, Jordan said, "Now it makes sense. If someone lied about that, they could've been lying about the kidnapping. That if Chelsey recanted her decision to give up her child, someone might've taken the infant so he could be adopted anyway."

"That's one scenario."

"One that doesn't make sense. There'd be other ways to do it that wouldn't involve the police."

"The police were brought in because Chelsey Ray called them in. The management of Haven's Gate had balked, saying they'd conduct their own investigation. I guess that's understandable if they didn't want anyone nosing around."

"Didn't we check with the Board of Medical Examiners back then to see if the doctor had received any complaints?"

Rico nodded. "Yes, but I'm going to do it again. See if he was licensed in any other states and check there, too."

"What makes you think Wesley Capshaw's going to spill anything? And if he's on the board, or was in the past, wouldn't Macy know? Wouldn't she have a problem with your questioning him?"

"Maybe. But I don't think she knows. I only discovered it myself when I was scouring the old file. It wasn't something that had any significance in the earlier investigation, but it does now, and while I can't question him at dinner, I might get some insights. You never know where a nugget of new information might come from."

"Uh-huh. And dinner with a sexy heiress isn't too hard to take, either."

"Not even a thought."

Jordan clapped Rico on the back. "Right. And I'm Donald Duck."

"That's right. And you're quacking up the wrong tree." But he had to admit, having dinner with Macy was not an unpleasant thought.

"Okay. Since you're not up for the bar, I'm outta here. But the guys are gonna be pissed that you're not there."

"They'll get over it."

"Right. Well, good luck with the dinner date." Jordan looked back at Rico over his shoulder. "I think you're going to need it."

Rico knew what Jordan meant. He probably wouldn't get a thing from Capshaw. But Macy would be there, and he felt drawn to the attorney and her cause to get to the bottom of Haven's Gate. And if it helped him, too, all the better.

"So, get outta here then, and leave me to my misery."

WHY? WHY HAD SHE AGREED TO that whole friend thing and dinner? Part of it was the disappointed look on her mother's face when she thought Macy was going to say no. And maybe it was also because she was tired of Rico needling her about not having any fun. And she was tired of her parents thinking she didn't have a social life.

But the instant Rico had started grinning like a fat, satisfied cat, she'd felt her blood burn in her veins. *"I'd love to have dinner with your family."* He was so stinking sure of himself. She was going to regret opening that door. She just knew it.

On the other hand, her mother was ecstatic.

Of course Sarah would be excited. She wanted her only child married. She wanted grandchildren. Desperately. The last man Macy had brought to dinner—three years ago—was an attorney at her father's firm who she discovered only wanted to be a partner, one way or another. When she'd explained she was going to open her own practice and have nothing to do with corporate law, he'd disappeared faster than the speed of light.

So, okay. She was going to have dinner with Rico. Nothing she couldn't handle. She just hoped the event didn't give her mother false hope. But if it did, her father would soon squelch it. Rico, a cop, wasn't her father's idea of prime son-in-law material.

The thought gave her pause. Had she accepted the invite to spite her father? The man always used to say she'd dated boys he didn't approve of because she wanted to get back at him. It was probably true at the time. But she wasn't a teenager anymore. She didn't give a fig what her father thought.

And this wasn't a date. Yes, she liked Rico. She was drawn to him because he was a nice guy. He was an honest man and he was charming. But it wasn't a date and they weren't even friends.

Even though his touch made her stomach flutter.

Macy stepped into the walk-in closet and flipped on the light. What to wear to dinner? She shifted the hangers to see what appealed to her. What would Santini wear? She'd only ever seen him in jeans and a shirt, or T-shirt with a blazer. If he wore that, her mother would probably faint. She almost hoped he'd come as is.

CHAPTER FIVE

THE SECURITY GATES at the Wilshire Boulevard high-rise condominiums where Macy lived swung wide to let him in. The Golden Mile—the high-rent district. Everything in the Hollywood Hills area was the high-rent district. Beverly Hills, Bel Air, Sunset Boulevard. He smiled as he envisioned bringing Macy to his little place in Anaheim. Yeah.

He parked in one of the guest spaces and noted the lush greenery, bright flowers, palm trees and shrubbery he didn't recognize. He'd never had much interest in scenery, preferring instead to experience the outdoors in a more physical way. But he had to admit it was a pretty nice place—if you liked living in high-rise stacks.

He nodded to the uniformed man standing at the doors, pulled the numbers for the security lock from his pocket and punched them in. The front door opened into a large marble-floored foyer. A giant bouquet of flowers on a round mahogany table in the middle of the entry announced this was where rich people lived.

If he'd had any interest in Macy Capshaw at all, this place told him what a fantasy that was.

He punched the elevator button and the doors silently slid open. Reaching her unit on the top floor, he rang the bell and almost before he took his hand away, she appeared.

"Hi."

He could barely get out a response. She was a knockout in an off-the-shoulder sweater and a short skirt that revealed her great legs. And sexy, strappy high heels. "You look great."

"Thanks," she said as her gaze swept over him. "You look nice, too. Different."

"Gave up the jeans and T-shirt just for you."

"My mother will be most appreciative. Come in. I'm on the phone, but I'll be done in a minute."

He stepped inside.

"Make yourself comfortable," she said before walking into an adjoining room—an office with a large desk and matching bookshelves lining the walls. Law books, he guessed. She apparently worked at her office downtown *and* at home.

He went into the living room and did a quick inventory, noting the exits. In addition to the front door, there were three sets of Arcadia doors on a wall of glass opening onto a large balcony. She had a pretty good view of the city from there.

The rest of the place was designer perfect, but if felt as if something was missing. No photographs of family, no sentimental things.

Just as he was about to sit in one of the plush easy chairs on the other side of a gargantuan marble-topped coffee table, something rustled behind him. He swung around to find a ball of fluff nudging his pant leg.

"Hey, little guy. What's up?" He'd never seen a dog so small. "Go ahead and sniff. I'm no threat." He reached down and picked up the pooch.

"Okay," Macy's soft voice came from behind. "Sorry about that."

"No problem. This little guy's been keeping me company."

A wide smile crossed Macy's face when she saw him holding the dog. "That's Hercules."

She took the dog from him and cradled it in her arms before placing the fluff ball on a large plush pillow next to one of the chairs.

"Big name for a little guy."

"Yes, I thought it would boost his self-esteem. And when I have to listen to him bark, I'm inclined to think it worked."

He smiled, enjoying her sense of humor.

"He's part Yorkie. Yorkshire Terrier."

He nodded, though he didn't know one dog from the next unless it was a German shepherd, golden retriever or a Labrador.

"I'll be back soon," she said to the animal. "Let's go."

He stooped to rub behind the dog's ears. "I've been thinking…"

Already on her way to the door, she stopped, turning slowly. "Thinking is good. Something specific?"

"Yes. I'm thinking that we should act as if we're friends since that's what I told your mother."

"Sure. You're right. We'll act like friends."

"What kind of friends? Close friends? Intimate friends? How well do we know each other?"

Her response was instant. "We know each other well enough to have dinner together."

"Which means?"

"Just that."

He concentrated on the dog's left ear. "Well, where I grew up, when you bring someone to meet the folks, it's more than a casual thing."

She stared at him. "Well, that's not the case in California. Here you bring a friend to dinner just because you're friends. Nothing more."

He could tell she was getting annoyed, when all he really wanted was to know why she'd gone along with his friendship ruse. He was pretty certain it wasn't because she liked him so much. "Okay, I get it. Just wanted to be clear so I don't screw things up."

"You'll be fine. I'm the one who'll likely screw up. I always do around my father."

Her tone was light, but he had the feeling there was truth in her words. A chink in her armor? A vulnerability. "Why do you say that?"

She shrugged off the comment, walked to the door, grabbing a small purse off a table on the way. "No reason. Forget I said anything."

He'd hit a hot button. He'd wondered what would rattle that cool facade, and now he knew—her father. Whatever the friction between Macy and her father, he'd bet it went back a long way. He'd had major conflicts with his own father and knew the routine well. "Okay. It's forgotten."

"We can use my car if you'd like," Macy said, when she saw a battered truck parked outside the gate.

"Why? You don't like my ride?" Rico laughed, then sauntered toward a black Jaguar.

Heat rushed to Macy's cheeks as Rico went over and opened the passenger door, then extended a hand to help her inside. "No…uh, it's very nice. I just thought—"

"That you were going to have to ride in that truck?" He climbed into the driver's seat.

Macy had to laugh. He was perceptive. A quality she liked, but she wasn't sure she liked it when applied to her. The heavy scent of leather inside the car indicated it was new. "I didn't know law enforcement paid well enough for a car like this."

He turned the key and the roadster growled to life. "Belongs to Jordan who, as you probably know, has other income besides his police salary. My car's in the shop getting new tires. Where to?"

"Beverly Hills. Bel Air to be exact." She rattled off the address. "We can take Wilshire to La Brea and go north…."

"I'm familiar with the Hills. I worked a beat for years."

She watched him in profile as he expertly wove his way to the Hollywood freeway going north. He seemed different tonight. He seemed…less intense. Relaxed almost. He made her feel more relaxed, too. "How long have you lived in L.A.?"

"Ten years."

"So, how did a guy from New Jersey end up working in law enforcement in California?"

He shrugged, keeping his eyes on the road. "Long story short, the move involved a girl who wanted to be an actress. That didn't last, but I liked it here and stayed." He exited the freeway onto Sunset Boulevard.

"Go to the end and turn left."

"Got it."

Anyone who moved across the country for someone had to be pretty serious about the relationship. A twinge of envy jabbed at her. She'd never had anyone feel that strongly about her. "And law enforcement?"

He shrugged again. "It's what I always wanted to do."

"Always?"

"Since I was eight and watched a policeman save my father's life."

She shifted to face him. "What happened?"

"My folks own a small family restaurant and one night when my dad was closing up, a gunman came into the store demanding money. My father, the original macho Italian, refused. Meanwhile, I was in the kitchen where the robber couldn't see me and called 911. After my dad refused to give the creep the money, the guy wigged out. Unfortunately, I didn't think of the consequences when I ran out to help my dad and within seconds we had a hostage situation and the place was alive with sirens and flashing lights."

"Oh, my goodness."

"I was sure the guy was going to kill us, but as you can see—" he winked at her "—it turned out okay. I thought the police were amazing the way they talked the guy into giving up. And, of course, my dad gave me hell for running out like I did. It was stupid, but what did I know?"

He looked at her and smiled. "And that's why I wanted to be a cop. Cops were superheroes in my book. They fought the bad guys and saved people and I wanted to do that, too."

"I can't imagine going through that, but I can see why you were impressed."

He took a moment to adjust a vent on the dash. "My parents didn't want me to be a cop. I suppose it's normal to want to protect your kid from danger."

They had something in common. She'd spent her whole life disappointing her parents.

"I guess it's a silly question to ask why you became an attorney."

She laughed. "Yes it is."

"So why aren't you working for your father?"

"I did for a while. But I should've known it wouldn't work. We have different philosophies. Bottom line, I wanted to choose the clients I represented." And she didn't want to be her father's puppet for the rest of her life.

After that, they fell silent, almost as if they'd both revealed too much. It was like that the rest of the way to her parents' estate, where Macy punched in the code for the gates. As soon as they pulled into the curved drive, the oversize double doors spread wide and Macy's mother stood in the opening looking small and fragile. As they pulled up closer, Macy saw uncertainty in her mother's eyes.

After the ritual greetings, Macy and Rico went into the family room, her mother clucking like a mother hen behind them.

"Make yourselves comfortable," Sarah said, "while I tell your father you're here." She started to leave, then whispered to her daughter, "Macy, dear. Can you please not upset your father today? He's had a very hard week."

Macy's nerves drew tight. Rico was far enough away that she didn't think he'd overheard, but she was embarrassed anyway.

"Something wrong?" Rico asked when Sarah left.

"Nothing that a stiff drink won't cure." Macy went to the bar in the corner and took out two glasses. "Scotch?"

"Sure."

She saw Rico taking in every detail of the room. "Nice place." He picked up a silver-framed photograph of Macy and her mother, studied it briefly and set it down again. "No pictures of all of you together?"

Macy poured a shot in each glass and handed one to Rico. "My father hates to have his photo taken unless it's going to be in the newspaper."

"What's up with your mother?"

"Nothing new. My mother is always worried that something isn't going to go right."

She sipped her drink. "Consider this visit your first session in Dysfunctional Family 101." She couldn't keep the sarcasm from her voice.

Rico didn't miss a beat. "I think I've already had that course."

"Well, this will be a refresher, then."

He laughed. "I could use one, especially since my family is coming to visit next week."

Macy felt her tension fade and she laughed along with Rico.

"Italian mothers are the worst," he said. "I bet your mother can't hold a candle to mine."

It was apparent from the love and admiration in his tone that regardless of what he said, he had a strong bond with his family.

"You'd better wait until after dinner before you make any wagers. Does your family live in New Jersey?"

He nodded. "Everyone but me."

"Do you have a large family?"

"My parents wanted lots of kids, a dozen or so, but decided somewhere along the way that seven was just the right number. I forget how many nieces and nephews I have."

"But apparently you're not in any hurry to start your own family."

"I would be if I found the right partner. But that's about as likely as me leaving law enforcement."

Interesting. "Did someone really hurt you somewhere along the line?" The actress, maybe.

He came closer, standing only inches from her, and she felt his warm breath against her mouth, smelled the scotch on his lips. Her heartbeat quickened.

"No," he said softly. "I've just never found anyone who's made me want to take the plunge."

"Oh, a drink before dinner, what a good idea." Macy's mother's voice trilled from the doorway as she and Macy's father came into the room.

Macy turned. "Hello, Father. I'd like you to meet my friend Rico Santini."

Wesley Capshaw nodded and held out a hand to Rico, all but ignoring Macy. "Nice to meet you, Rico." The pleasant words didn't match the stern look on her father's face. He was probably still miffed about their last dinner. Her father motioned for them all to sit on the two facing brocade couches.

A couple of stiff drinks seemed to help her father relax, and it wasn't long before he was teasing her mother about some computer glitch.

"I didn't mean to break your beloved computer," Sarah said. "I only wanted to learn how to use it like everyone else." She looked to Rico and Macy sitting together. Too close for Macy's comfort. "He wants to keep me in the dark ages."

Was that a note of dissatisfaction in her mother's usual appeasing tone?

Her father frowned. "If you want a computer, I'll get you one of your own."

"What's the problem with the computer?" Rico interjected.

"The whole thing went down. I'm sure I've lost everything. I'm going to have to call someone on Monday."

"Maybe I can help," Rico offered. "I know a bit about computers."

Her father's expression was skeptical.

"Have you tried to restore the programs?"

Wesley shook his head. "Not my forte."

"I can take a look at it if you want me to."

"Let him try it, Dad," Macy said.

It was obvious Wesley was taken aback. Then he grudgingly said, "It's in my office."

Both men started for the door.

"But Wes, what about dinner?" her mother blurted. "It's almost ready."

Macy's father was practically out of the room with Rico on his heels. "It'll wait," Wesley said. "This is more important."

"Well…" Sarah sputtered. "Isn't that just like a man."

Her mother seemed more than a little rebellious this evening. Not her usual appropriate self. Sarah rarely got angry at Macy's father, or if she did, she never showed it in front of anyone. Not even Macy. "Not all men, Mother."

Sarah forced a smile. "You're right. Maybe it's a good opportunity for the two of them to bond."

"Mother. Rico's just a friend. I told you that. They don't need to bond."

"*Good* friends." Sarah repeated Rico's words. "I think that's nice."

"Good or not, we're still just friends."

Sarah pursed her lips. "I saw how he looked at you. He likes you more than you think."

Macy was acutely aware that Rico wouldn't mind getting her into bed. *Liking her* had nothing to do with it.

"Well, what he likes and doesn't like isn't important if I don't feel the same. And I don't. We're friends. Period. End of discussion."

"Oh, sweetheart. Don't ever give up." Sarah gave Macy a concerned-mother look just as the two men returned.

"This guy's a computer genius," her father announced with one hand on Rico's shoulder. "Hardly a minute under his touch and everything is back to normal."

"It was an easy fix."

"Well, that's a relief," Sarah said. "Now let's have dinner."

With that, Macy's mother herded everyone into the dining room and indicated where each should sit. When they were all seated, Sarah gave Melanie, one of the staff, the nod to start bringing in the food. "So, I didn't break it after all." Sarah chortled with satisfaction.

"But we didn't know that," Wesley returned. "And since almost all of my personal records are on that computer, it could've been a disaster."

"But it wasn't. Now let's talk about something more interesting. Why don't you tell us a little bit about yourself, Rico?"

The rest of the dinner went along like that with Sarah asking questions and Rico responding with charm and patience. Listening with interest as Rico described his journey from MIT to the police academy in New Jersey and then to detective with the LAPD, it seemed the perfect segue to the questions she wanted answered. "As a matter of fact, Rico's working on a case right now that involves Haven's Gate."

Looking from Wesley to Rico, she said, "My father knows the physician at Haven's Gate. He could probably answer any questions you might have about the man."

Wesley glared at Macy, daggers in his eyes.

Finished with dessert, Rico touched his lips with a napkin and then said, "But like you, Macy, I don't talk about my cases outside of work."

A reprimand. Subtle, but enough to make her aware she'd crossed one of Rico's well-drawn lines.

"Good," Wesley said. "A man after my own heart. I never take my business home with me." That said, he and Rico launched into more talk about computers and a whole lot of tech talk she didn't give a rat about.

Rico had shut her out just as her father had always done.

Well, what had she expected? They were both cut from the same steel. Rigid. Unwilling to bend. And dammit, that upset her almost as much as being shut out. She'd started to like Rico. A lot. She'd even looked forward to spending the evening with him.

"Macy?"

Sarah was talking to her about something.

"What do you think?"

"I think…" Macy glanced at the time. "I think we should be going." She made sure her voice was loud enough for Rico to hear. "I'm expecting a call and need to be home for it." Macy stood. "Sorry to break up the conversation, you two."

After their goodbyes and a long silent ride home, Rico walked Macy to her door. Before she had a chance to go in, he stepped in front of her, his hands on her arms, making sure he had her full attention.

"What's wrong," Rico said.

She wiggled away, punched in her code and went inside. Rico caught the door and followed her to the elevator. "Can we talk about it?"

"There's nothing to talk about." She pushed the up button, the doors opened and she stepped in. Rico slipped in with her. He grabbed her hand to keep her from pressing the button.

"I think there is."

She faced him, anger and disappointment churning inside her. "Well, maybe you're right. We could start with how you cut me off at the knees. We could've had some answers, but instead you made me feel like—" She stopped. She'd learned early on never to act on emotion. It wasn't logical and it gave the opponent the advantage. Emotion now, regret later. That's exactly what would happen if she let herself go.

Only this was different. She wasn't in court and she didn't feel like being logical.

"I'm sorry about that," Rico said. "I only said what I did because it's true. I don't discuss cases in social situations. If I want to know something, I'll ask."

She was even more miffed. "Well, you didn't ask, so I thought I'd do it for you."

"I didn't ask because sometimes I learn more from listening."

Her anger abated a little, but adrenaline still pumped through her, heightening her senses. She was acutely aware of how close he was, that she could smell his aftershave, that she could lean forward and she'd be touching him. "Then why did you agree to come along?"

He moved even closer, radiating body heat. He brushed his fingertips along her jawline. "I thought that was obvious."

Desire pounded through her. Her breath came in short gasps, each shallower than the last. "Obvious to you maybe." Was that her voice? So low and husky.

His pupils dilated as he looked at her, and as if drawn by some invisible force she leaned into him. And then she was in his arms and he was kissing her, a slow drugging kiss. She kissed him back with unleashed passion, her hands all over him, his all over her. He pressed into her, her back against the elevator wall, and then her elbow hit the buttons and she felt the pull of upward motion and resistance as she explored his mouth, ran her tongue along his smooth teeth, savoring the taste of him. As the elevator climbed, she wrapped one leg around the back of his knee to secure herself, felt his hot hands skim down her backside and then up under her skirt between her bare legs. The sensuous touch of skin against skin made her want him even more.

It was dangerous. Exciting. And she was ready. Right here, right now.

Almost as she thought it, the elevator bumped to a

stop. She pushed away from Rico just in time to see her elderly neighbors standing outside the door. Quickly pulling down her skirt, she stepped out.

She motioned for Rico to come, too. But he didn't move.

"Can't," he said. "I'll be in touch."

Her neighbors avoided her gaze and hurried onto the elevator. The doors shut, and there she stood—alone in the hallway, clothes rumpled, lips swollen, chest heaving and unable to catch her breath.

She felt like a complete idiot.

CHAPTER SIX

IT WAS JUST A KISS. Okay, maybe it was more than that…
Macy opened her condo door, flipped on the light and
felt something smooth underfoot. A manila envelope.
Hercules was standing next to it, his tail whipping back
and forth because he was happy to see her.

She picked up both dog and envelope and went into
the kitchen for a glass of water. She always had the
bellman bring up legal papers if they came, but this
puzzled her. She wasn't expecting anything.

Placing the packet on the table, she nuzzled the dog.
"How are you doing, little guy?" Hercules stuffed his
nose into her armpit. After another snuggle, she set the
dog down and crossed to the watercooler, her thoughts
on Rico.

She should be mortified that he'd rebuffed her invi-
tation to come inside and finish what they started, but
she didn't feel that way at all. She felt supercharged. Excited. More excited than when she'd supposedly been
in love with Dylan once upon a time.

Maybe it was because she enjoyed Rico's company—without the emotional attachment. It was im-

possible to deny the sexual attraction. The man intrigued her.

She had no fantasies of anything more than that. It was better to be a realist where romance was concerned.

But then, he'd surprised her by revealing that he'd graduated from MIT. A cop with an engineering degree. A man who could carry on a conversation with her father. Who'd have thought it?

She headed to the bedroom to change her clothes and took the envelope with her. Sitting on the edge of the bed, she kicked off her shoes, then ripped the package open and pulled out a sheet of paper.

Her heart stalled. Ragged cutout letters were pasted on the paper with the message *Stay away or you'll regret it!*

"NOTHING EARTH-SHATTERING with the Board of Medical Examiners," Rico told Jordan. "A couple complaints, but none about quality of care." Macy's concern appeared unfounded.

"So how was the business dinner?"

"No big deal."

Except that his attraction to Macy Capshaw baffled him. Maybe abstinence was taking its toll? He'd pulled back from relationships after Angelica, a name that was as far away as Mars from the real woman.

"No insights on Wesley Capshaw?"

Rico laughed. "I wouldn't say that."

"How about your date? Any insights there?"

He shifted in his chair. "I wouldn't say that, either."

Jordan raised his eyebrows, got up and sauntered over to Luke, leaving Rico wondering what he should do about the woman crowding his thoughts at the most inopportune times. Hell, all the time. As much as he'd wanted to follow Macy into her condo last night, he'd waffled.

He didn't want to get into something he'd regret later. Or have her regret.

"Here's the stuff you asked for, Detective Santini." Rico looked up from his desk to see Mary Beth, the office assistant, holding out a ream of papers. "It's the birth and death records from Haven's Gate."

"M.B., you're the best."

"They were separated from the rest of the files, that's why you couldn't find them."

"I appreciate it."

"Uh… What're you looking for?" Mary Beth continued to stand at his desk. The woman wanted to be a cop so badly she tried to get in on everything. Apparently she'd taken the police exams, but couldn't pass the physical.

He shook his head. "I don't know. Anything that'll give me a fresh slant on this case."

"If you need any help—"

"I'll keep you in mind." He cut her off, anxious to find the entries for the two stillborns Macy had mentioned. Within 24 hours of each other.

"Oh," Mary Beth said before she went back to her desk, "if you don't find what you're looking for, you might want to check with the Department of Health's agency that licenses Haven's Gate. They have incident reports about everything that happens in licensed facilities."

"That's a good idea, M.B. If I don't find what I'm looking for here, maybe I'll do just that."

After three hours sorting through the records, he picked up the phone and called Macy again. He wasn't sure what kind of reception he'd get, but he hoped she'd understand.

Her secretary, Cheryl, answered and told him Macy wouldn't be back for several hours. "Does she have a cell phone where I can reach her? This is important. Important to her."

Cheryl paused. He remembered how young she'd seemed. Inexperienced. "I can try to get in touch and have her call you."

"I appreciate the effort." Macy was going to have to give him some kind of information on her client. If she didn't, he had nothing to go on. He could question all the parties at Haven's Gate again, but he didn't want to do that just yet. Macy was right. It might alert them that the facility and its staff were being scrutinized.

MACY WALKED with Karen Creighton back to their cars after leaving Billy with his new foster parents, an uneasy feeling getting the best of her.

"He'll be fine," Karen said. "This family is top-notch."

Maybe so, but Macy couldn't forget the forlorn look in Billy's eyes when she gave him a hug and said she'd be back soon. "Tomorrow?" he'd asked quickly. She felt another pang of guilt for leaving him with total strangers. He'd been discharged from the hospital and there hadn't been any time for him to get to know the foster parents first. She only hoped she'd made the right choice.

Both families she'd interviewed were experienced at foster care and she'd finally agreed that this placement seemed a positive one. Nancy and Joe Appleton were cheerful and responsible; they had two other foster children and one child of their own. So why did she feel so uneasy?

"He'll get friendly with the other kids and in no time he'll be right at home," Karen said. "I'll let you know how it goes."

She gave Karen a puzzled look. "You know I'll also be checking up on him. My job doesn't end with his placement."

An exasperated sigh was Karen's response. "Well, apparently you have a lot more time than I do."

Right then, Macy realized the difference between her and Karen. Macy didn't see Billy as a case she needed to *handle*. He was a lost little boy who needed love and affection—and someone who cared about his well-being. He needed more than custodial care, and she wasn't sure he was going to get it with the Appletons. She didn't know why, but her gut feelings were usually on target.

Macy's cell phone chirped, bringing her to attention. She fished the unit from her pocket. "Yes, Cheryl, what's up?"

Karen waved goodbye as Macy listened to her assistant and continued to her car.

"I'm sorry to disturb you, but Detective Santini called and he wants you to contact him right away. He said it's important."

Macy's stomach drew tight. Did he have some information on Haven's Gate or Dr. Dixon? Or was he calling about last night?

"Was I wrong to call you?"

"No, it's fine Cheryl. You did the right thing." The poor girl was barely out of high school and didn't know how to operate in a world that wasn't filled with drugs and violence. For a kid who'd been in jail for car theft six months ago and had no viable skills, she was picking up the job remarkably well.

Macy slid into the driver's seat, started the engine and headed downtown. She punched in Rico's number.

"Santini here."

"Hi, Rico. It's Macy. What's up?"

"Can you meet me somewhere? I need to talk to you."

"Personal or business?"

"Both."

Business was easy, personal stuff hard. "I'm in my car heading to my office."

"How about Pershing Square in an hour? That's close to your place and I have to go to the courthouse first."

When she didn't respond right away he added, "It's too nice to be inside."

Macy looked out the tinted car window. She'd hadn't even noticed that the sun was shining and wondered when she'd stopped paying attention to her surroundings. "You're right," she said as she pulled into the parking garage. "It is too nice to be inside. See you in an hour then."

Pershing Square. The oldest park in the city was smack in the middle of downtown L.A.—practically next door to her office and she couldn't remember ever going there. Certainly not on purpose.

Fifteen minutes later, she parked her car, rode the elevator to the seventh floor and headed for her office where she was bombarded with messages to return. Karen Creighton—when did she have time to call?—her mother, Marilyn Joffrey, her mother, Mark Weston, an attorney in her building who couldn't take no for an answer and her mother two more times.

She took off her suit jacket and opened the collar of her blouse one more button, then sat at her desk and prioritized. Her mother in file C; Mark, file C; Marilyn and Karen—both in the A file. She picked up the phone to call Karen first.

"Billy's locked himself in the bedroom and won't come out," Karen said without any greeting. "I thought you'd want to know."

"What happened?"

"Apparently nothing."

"Since we don't know Billy's history, we don't know what's bothering him. He might not remember who he is, but he does know he's been abandoned—that no one has claimed him. What kinds of issues might that create in a child? You need to get his therapy started as soon as possible."

"The foster parents will be taking care of all his needs, medical and otherwise. That's their job."

"Yes, but someone needs to monitor the situation. Isn't that your job?" It was Macy's job, too, but Karen had to take some responsibility.

A long silence ensued. Then Karen said, "It is. But there just isn't enough time in the day to give extra to any one child." Macy thought she heard sincere regret in the woman's voice.

"I know a couple of good child therapists. I can give Mrs. Appleton the names."

"As long as they're on the list of county-approved clinicians. I'll fax you the list so you can check."

"Fine. So what's the situation right now? What's being done about Billy?"

"Nancy said she's had this happen before. It's best to leave him alone. He'll come out when he's hungry."

Macy didn't think it was the best solution. She remembered how sad Billy looked when she'd left him. He may have felt abandoned again. Some children lashed out, others tried to do better, be better.

"I'll talk to you later," Macy said, then clicked off and punched in the Appleton's number. "Nancy, it's Macy Capshaw. I understand you're having a problem with Billy."

"No problem, except he won't come out of the bathroom."

The bathroom. Karen had said it was the bedroom. Her concern spiked. "Do you keep any medications in the bathroom?"

"Uh, just…some prescriptions."

"What kind of prescriptions?"

Nancy was silent for a beat. "I—I don't remember exactly."

Whatever medications Nancy was taking, she didn't want the foster care system to know about it. Great. Just great.

"Can you tell Billy I'm on the phone and I'd like to talk to him."

"You think he'll come out for that?"

"I'm hoping."

"I'll check."

Though it was only minutes, it felt as if an hour had passed before Nancy finally came back. "He wouldn't answer me, and—" Macy heard what sounded like a muffled curse. "Sorry about that," Nancy said. "He won't come out."

"What kind of lock is on the door?"

"It's on the doorknob and you push it in."

"Why don't you get a screwdriver and take the door-knob off?"

"Oh, I don't—wait. I hear something…. Okay, it's Billy and he's out."

"Please let me talk to him."

The other end of the line went silent and then, finally, a small voice said, "Hello."

"Billy. It's Macy Capshaw."

"Uh-huh."

"Why did you lock yourself in the bathroom?"

"I—I don't know."

"You had lots of people worried about you."

"Nuh-uh. Nobody wants me."

Oh, Billy. The child didn't think anyone cared about him…and why would he? He'd been abandoned and then abandoned again. "Well, *I* was worried. And I know Mrs. Appleton is very worried. We care very much about you, so please don't do that anymore. All right?"

Another silence.

"The Appletons are really nice people and they want you to stay with them."

"I—I want to go home." His voice quivered, his pain almost palpable.

"Where is that Billy?"

Now she heard a sniffle. "I—I don't know."

Oh, God. It wrenched her heart. "Look. I'm going to come over tomorrow and take you out for some ice cream. Would you like that?"

"O-kay," he said through another sniff.

Before Macy had a chance to say anything more, Nancy Appleton was on the phone again. "I think he'll be fine now. It's normal for him to feel some apprehension at being in a strange place. I'll do what I can to make him feel right at home."

"Good. And if he gets out of sorts again, remind him that I'll be there tomorrow to take him out for ice cream."

"What time?"

Macy quickly scanned her Day-Timer for appointments. "Three o'clock."

"That'll work."

Listening to the drone of the dial tone after Nancy hung up, Macy felt as sad as Billy had sounded. She'd had difficult cases before, but none that tugged at her heartstrings as much as this.

She tried to shuck off the thoughts. This was a case. Nothing more. An attorney, a court-appointed advocate couldn't afford to get emotionally involved. *She* couldn't afford to. It could color her ability to do her job. But with Billy, the task of remaining detached proved more difficult.

She took a breath and regrouped. Tomorrow she'd see Billy and also give Mrs. Appleton the names of the clinicians to make sure the woman would get the child's therapy in motion.

The intercom buzzed. "It's two forty-five."

"Thanks." Time for her to meet Rico. She was on schedule. Almost. She still had to call Marilyn Joffrey.

AVOIDING ANOTHER LOOK at his watch, Rico paced in front of the park bench and drummed his fingers against his thigh. Being late seemed to be a way of life with Macy. Or maybe she was only late when she had an appointment with him.

The thought irked him, but he felt more apprehensive about the meeting than annoyed at her. He rarely ever thought about how he approached someone on a case anymore. He'd been doing his job long enough that it came as second nature to him. But he'd started to think of Macy as a friend and he didn't want to hurt her.

He didn't know if Macy knew that her father had

worked for Haven's Gate, and he didn't know what she'd do with the information if he told her. She may have already screwed things up by mentioning that Rico was investigating Haven's Gate.

"There you are." Macy's voice came from behind. He turned. The sun reflected off her hair, a bright halo of light that made it look like spun gold.

He tapped his watch. "For a while now."

"I had some business to take care of."

"You also had an appointment with me."

She gave him a surprised look. "Is that a reprimand?"

Yeah. It was a reprimand. But he didn't want to start their conversation that way. "No, it's merely a reminder that my time is as valuable as yours." He motioned for her to sit on the bench.

A slight breeze ruffled her hair and she reached to brush a strand from her eyes. "I should've called. I'm sorry."

They sat together and he handed her one of two coffees. "It's probably cold by now."

Looking at the Starbucks label, she smiled. "Now I'm really sorry I was late." Her fingers brushed his as she took the cup. She brought it to her lips and sipped. "No, it's not cold. Thank you very much."

He polished his off to the soft strains of guitar music coming from another part of the park. The Square also served as a respite for a few homeless people catching naps on the grass and he wondered how Macy felt about that.

"I've never been here before. It's very nice."

He almost did a double take. "Your office is practically around the corner and you've never been here?"

"I work a lot. Remember? And speaking of which, I don't have a whole lot of time right now. What's up? You said it's both personal and business."

"I said that?"

She nodded. "Succinctly. Why don't we start with the business."

He leaned against the wooden bench slats. "I've been scouring the records from Haven's Gate we had on file from the Ray investigation."

"You have the Gate's records? I didn't see them in the file." She shifted, fidgeting with her cup.

"They were filed separately. The data is old and names are redacted, of course."

"What period do they cover?"

"A couple of years before and after the abduction."

She relaxed and leaned back against the seat with him.

After a moment, she asked, "Can you get the earlier records?"

"I'd have to have a good reason to get a search warrant. But I could get information from other sources that might be just as good if I had the specific date your client's baby died. And it would be even better if I had the name of your client." He leaned forward, elbows on his knees. "Frankly, without some kind of personal information, I'm stymied."

Macy took a long deep breath. Could she tell him the truth? If she did, would he keep it quiet?

He looked over at her. "Can you at least *ask* your client if she'd consent to give me that information?"

She tipped her head back and closed her eyes. Her

palms felt clammy and her heart rate doubled, as if she was about to go into a courtroom. She glanced at Rico. "Everything confidential?"

"Totally."

She focused on her hands in her lap. "It was me. My baby was stillborn. Twelve years ago. March 21, 1993." She brought her gaze back to his.

The surprise she saw in Rico's eyes lasted only a millisecond. Still looking at her, he said, "I'm sorry."

"It was a long time ago," she said. "But when I learned, just recently, that my friend's child had been stillborn the day before, I was dumbfounded. Twelve years ago I'd been told her baby had been fine, had been adopted. The physician and all the nurses told me that."

"Did you talk to her about it?"

"Not at the time, because she'd already gone home. I'd had a Cesarean birth and was under deep sedation. I wasn't really with it for a day or so."

"How did you find out her baby hadn't been adopted?"

"I talked to her last week. When I saw the name Haven's Gate on the back of the Ray baby's photo, I wondered if they'd taken a photo of my baby, as well, because…I'd never seen him. Then when I saw Dr. Dixon's name on the photo, I was shocked. I'd been told by my father that Dr. Dixon was only there for the birth of my child, and that I was lucky because he was one of the best."

"You think that has some significance?"

She moistened her lips. "Yes."

"Maybe Dixon simply decided to stay on at Haven's Gate after your child was born?"

"That's what my father said."

Rico blinked. "And you don't think that's the whole story?"

"No. Because they lied about my friend's baby. My father lied, too."

"Maybe they thought they were saving you from more bad news."

She'd thought of that. But her gut told her differently.

"You were very young," Rico said.

She nodded. "Barely seventeen." Looking down, she noticed her hands were trembling. Rico must've noticed, too, because he placed his hands over hers.

He let out a breath. "And you told me the other story because no one knows about the child you had twelve years ago."

She laughed weakly. "Great powers of deduction, Sherlock." That got a tiny smile from him, but he said nothing, apparently waiting for her to continue.

"My father thought it would harm his political aspirations. My grandparents don't even know."

His hand was warm and calming—and there was no judgment in his eyes, only compassion. He reached up and brushed her cheek. "That's a big secret to be carrying for so long."

After a deep breath, she said, "It was for the best."

His steady gaze said he didn't believe her. "Who's it best for, Macy?"

A knot twisted in her gut. She knew what he was getting at. She edged away from him, pulling her hand away. Too much revelation for her. She snatched up the coffee and took another long drink. Stone cold.

Rico didn't need all the details on how she'd gotten pregnant or by whom. "Well, you have the information you wanted," she said. "What are you going to do with it?"

He pulled back. "I'm not going to scoop it to the *National Enquirer* if that's what you're asking. I'll do what I said. More research."

Even though it wasn't warranted, she felt a sense of relief. Rico was a professional. He went by the book. It's why she'd felt she could tell him the truth. How ironic. His inflexibility, the part of him she disliked so much, also worked in his favor. "No, that's not what I was asking. I wanted to know the next step, that's all."

"I'll get more information, and if it fits, I'll try to get a search warrant for the records."

Finally.

"But a cold case won't be first on anyone's priority list."

"Well, it's a start." They both rested against the bench. "So," she said. "What personal stuff did you want to talk to me about?"

He cocked his head toward her. "I think we've talked about enough personal stuff. Don't you?"

Nodding, she agreed. There was no reason to talk about what happened in the elevator. The whole incident might be better forgotten. She reached into her purse for a breath mint and saw the manila envelope. "Oh, there is one other thing." She pulled out the envelope and the paper inside. "I found this inside my door last night."

As he read, she saw his body visibly tense.

"Do you have any idea who sent this?" Anger vibrated in his voice.

"Not a clue."

"I'd better get this down to the lab to check for fingerprints. If they find something, we can run it through AFIS."

"My prints will be on the letter. I wasn't being careful when I opened it."

"Mine, too," he said. "But neither of us will be in AFIS." He grinned. "At least mine aren't."

She gave up another smile.

"Are you sure you don't know anyone who'd send something like this?"

"No. The message is clear that I should stay away, but from what?"

"Are you working on a case that might be threatening to someone?"

She thought about the Joffrey case. A whole lot of people might be threatened. The health plan, the surgeon, the staff at the hospital. Maybe a few ex-husbands of women she'd represented in divorce proceedings. Some before the courts right now. "I'm always working on a case that might be threatening to someone. Right now, I have several pending and not everyone on both sides is happy, but I work attorney to attorney. I don't often have direct contact with opposing counsel's clients until we get to court."

"A jealous ex-girlfriend of someone you're dating?"

She shook her head.

"An ex-boyfriend?"

"I haven't dated anyone recently."

He grinned. "You invited me to dinner with your parents. That's a date."

Macy laughed. She couldn't help it. The guy never quit. "I didn't invite you and it wasn't a date."

Rico's hand went to his chest as if she'd just stabbed him. "No? What was it?"

"Dinner with a friend. Don't make it into anything more than that."

"Close friends, I'd say."

Now he *was* referring to the elevator. "Like I said, don't make it into something more than it was."

He held up both hands, that sexy grin still plastered on his face. "Okay. I'm cool. Friends it is."

How did he do that? He could lighten a serious moment in seconds. More than once he'd made her laugh, and she couldn't remember when she'd been so spontaneous. She couldn't remember when she'd felt such physical passion with someone, either, and remembering the elevator, desire, hot and quick, grew in her belly. "Are we done now, so I can get back to work?" She stood.

"Not really," he said, rising with her. "But we can come back to the rest later."

As she started to leave, he caught her by the shoulder.

"Be careful. Okay?" He held up the manila envelope. "People who do this kind of thing are usually a little off balance to start with."

CHAPTER SEVEN

IT'S FOR THE BEST. Why did Macy think hiding her past was best? Rico knew what secrets could do to a person. He rose from his desk and headed for the door.

But he only knew part of Macy's story. He didn't know what circumstances had brought her to Haven's Gate, pregnant at seventeen. But that wasn't any of his business, either. She'd only told him so he would help get some answers.

Problem was, he didn't know if he could.

Still thinking as he exited to go to the police garage, he nearly ran into Luke coming in.

"Yo," Rico said.

"Hey, New Jersey. What's hot?"

"Not much. Same old," he answered. "How about you? I hear you've got a political hot potato."

Luke gave a snort of a laugh. "Yeah. That and all the crap that comes with it."

"You're complaining? I'd give up my beer night to get a case like that. Money, power, politics, corruption, a sex scandal. What more could a guy want?"

Luke laughed harder. "It's becoming more of a pain

than anything. A homicide without a body...well, you know what that's like. Besides which, not too many congressmen like being investigated."

"Threats?"

"A couple."

"Seriously?"

Luke ran a hand through his sandy hair, which looked as if he'd combed it with a weed whacker. Rico remembered when Luke had been one of the best-dressed detectives around, giving up little ground to anyone except Jordan. Now on most days, Luke looked as though he'd just rolled out of bed.

"Nothing I can't handle."

Rico knew that was true. Luke was one of the best detectives on the force. He'd had a bad time of it after his divorce, but he was back now.

Moving to leave, Rico clapped Luke on the shoulder. "We're doin' a meet at the bar later. You coming?"

"Sure. If I can make it."

With that, they went separate directions, Rico to the parking garage and Luke into the bull pen. Reaching the department-issue sedan he'd picked up from the shop earlier that morning, Rico realized he only had a couple hours before state offices closed for the day and decided to call ahead, first the department of licensure and second, Vital stats. After telling the clerks what he needed and when he'd be there, he climbed into the vehicle and shoved the key into the ignition.

About to turn the key, he saw a package wrapped in brown paper on the floor on the passenger's side.

He gasped and in the same breath, bolted from the car and dived for cover—far enough away to be safe if it blew, but close enough to see if anyone else came by so he could warn them. His heart pounded. He punched dispatch. "Adam five, I've got a code 10 in the headquarters garage, second level."

The package hadn't been in the vehicle when he'd brought it back from meeting with Macy. Someone must've placed it during the past hour.

Less than three minutes passed before the bomb squad swarmed the place. He watched as they dismantled the thing in record time, after which the lead officer, Danny Chilton, came over. "Got yourself a pipe bomb. Not a lethal one, but meant to hurt someone."

Two threats, one directed at Macy and the other at him. Warnings of some kind? What was he getting too close to?

He went through the usual Q and A with Officer Chilton and gave him a list of recent arrests in which the suspects had threatened him. He rarely took those threats seriously because incarceration was usually in the suspect's future.

After the reports were filed, he went back inside to report in with Captain Carlyle.

"What aren't you telling me, Santini?"

An imposing black man who hovered at about six-five, the captain ruled his crew with an iron hand. Not much got by him.

"I wish I knew."

"Some husband after you?"

"I don't go with married women. Hell, I don't even date. Not since that schizo—not since Angelica."

"You think it was her?"

"No. She moved away after her arrest for stalking that other guy."

"She could've come back. She didn't like you testifying against her."

"I guess it's worth checking out."

"What else?"

"I don't know," Rico answered. The Ray case wasn't priority to anyone but him. "But if I'm ruffling feathers, that's good. It means I'm getting close to something."

A phone call interrupted them. "Make sure those guys get that stuff down to CSU," Carlyle said before answering. "And watch your back."

"It's done." Rico was relieved that the captain hadn't pressed him about what he was working on.

Before he was out the door, though, Carlyle stopped him again. With his hand over the phone he said, "If you get anything on the Ray case, let me know."

Rico grinned. Smart guy.

SOMETHING WAS WRONG. Macy heard it in Rico's voice when he'd called this morning before she headed for court and said he had to talk to her. She pulled into the public parking at the LAPD headquarters where the Detective Bureau was located. Twice she'd gone to see him now. Visiting Rico was becoming a habit.

Rico looked up when she walked into the room and called her over.

"This better be good," she said as she reached his desk. A couple officers sitting nearby were gawking at her. Maybe she should have hung a shroud over the red dress she'd worn to impress the jurors.

"Follow me," Rico said loudly, giving the other detectives the evil eye. "So we can have a little privacy."

She followed him into one of the interrogation rooms. He looked good today, his black shirt and jacket dressier than normal. "I know I didn't break the law, so this has to be about something else." The small room reeked of stale tobacco. It clogged in the back of her throat, making it hard to talk.

"Sit. Please."

She did as he requested.

"I went through the public birth and death records for the dates you mentioned."

"And you found—"

He held up a hand. "Let me finish."

Like her, he apparently didn't like being interrupted. She smiled. "Okay."

"Have you ever seen your son's death certificate?"

A strange question. "My parents took care of all that. My father."

He looked puzzled, shoved his hands in the pockets of his khaki pants, as if unsure what to say next.

"There was no death certificate on file for your son."

She blinked. Then blinked again. "What are you saying?"

"I'm not saying anything except that I didn't find a death certificate for the date you gave me. All deaths should be registered with vital stats. Maybe it was never entered into the computer, or someone failed to file the record properly...." Rico shrugged. "Bottom line, it's just not there."

Macy launched to her feet, then paced as far as she could in the tiny room that was bereft of anything except the gray metal table, the two chairs and a dirty ashtray.

"I found the death certificate for the stillborn baby of the day before. Haven's Gate was listed as the place of death and Dr. Dixon was the attending physician who signed the certificate."

"Carla's baby." She glanced at him quickly.

"It's probably a simple clerical error, but I thought you should know."

"And how will we find out if it was?"

"More research."

"What if it wasn't a clerical error, but something else?"

"Like?"

"Like maybe the shelter didn't file the death certificate because...they did something wrong." She stopped. Took a deep breath. The thought that negligence might have been responsible for her son's death was horrible. Anything else was even worse.

Rico nodded. "I've learned not to speculate. If your father took care of things, he should have a copy of the death certificate."

"Right." But she doubted he'd even talk to her.

"Are you going to look at the shelter's records to see if they filed the death report?"

"You know the answer to that. I'd have to get a warrant to look at their records from that time, and I'd have to have probable cause and rule out any administrative errors before that. Considering the amount of paperwork that department processes, the likelihood of a mistake is overwhelming."

He was right, of course. Probably clerical error. But that didn't make her feel any better. "You could say it's about the Ray case and get a warrant to look at their files."

He stood there for a moment, silent, his brows forming a deep V. "No, I can't. Because it isn't about the Ray case."

She nibbled on her bottom lip. That's what she thought. "Okay. So what's next?"

"Rule out error. That's all I can do right now."

Macy squared her shoulders. "Okay. But it's not all I can do."

Rico's frown deepened. "What do you mean?"

"Nothing." She went to the door and yanked it open. "Nothing that concerns you."

"If it involves the law, or breaking the law, it concerns me." He paused, shoved both hands in his pockets, then looked at her. "If it involves you, it concerns me."

Macy's heart skipped a beat. Concerned about her? Or did he mean he was concerned about what she'd do? Whatever, it was obvious that if she wanted an answer soon, she'd have to get it herself. "I—I'm sorry," she said, and rushed from the room.

Rico watched Macy leave. Dammit! He wanted to help her, but he couldn't—not the way she wanted him to. Apparently she was used to barreling ahead, all guns blazing, but that wasn't how things worked at the department. If he didn't follow procedure, any evidence he collected would be worth squat. Macy knew that as well as he did. She could screw up everything.

The more he looked into Haven's Gate, the more he believed there was a cover-up of some kind. Only the justice system didn't run on beliefs and he'd have to have a damned good reason to look at records from so long ago. A missing death certificate didn't cut it.

Five years ago, the clinic had threatened to sue him and the department for harassment because he'd been so dogged on the investigation. He'd almost been thrown off the case and demoted. If there was something to find, they'd go through the right channels to find it.

And the truth would come out.

CHAPTER EIGHT

MACY SWUNG HER CAR into the parking lot at Haven's
Gate, myriad memories playing like a B movie in her
head. If the death of her child was caused by negligence, she couldn't let it go. Not even twelve years
later. Not even if the information exposed her past.

Hundreds of children had been born at Haven's Gate.
How many of them had been at risk? How many had met
the same fate as her son?

The one-level building looked much the same as
when she'd stayed there. The exterior had been freshly
painted in adobe brown, a drab color for a sad place.
Most parents looked forward to the birth of a child, but
here it was different. With the exception of a few girls
who couldn't wait to have the ordeal over with, most
she'd met had mixed emotions about giving up their
child. The nurses doled out cheery platitudes and coun-
seled them on how their choice was the noble thing to
do. That because of their unselfishness, their child
would have a wonderful life with loving people finan-
cially able to care for them.

In theory, that was probably true, but when she

thought about it now, she remembered how persuasive those counseling sessions were—how some girls felt obligated to give up their babies since they'd received help from the center and believed they had no other choice. A knot twisted in her stomach. Well, so much for reminiscing. She exited the car, slung her briefcase over one shoulder and put on her court face.

Inside the building, the overwhelming sadness and feeling of loss returned with a vengeance.

She'd forgotten how tacky the place was. The pale green-gray walls devoid of decoration, the gray institutional tile floor and sterile hallways. A young woman, barely eighteen if she was a day, sat at the reception desk. Probably a former resident.

"May I help you?" she asked.

Macy handed the receptionist her card. "Yes, you can. I'm here on behalf of a client who was a resident at one time, and I'd like to speak with Dr. Dixon."

The receptionist looked from the card to Macy. "Oh, he's not here right now."

"Do you know when he'll be back or where I can get in touch with him?"

"No, I don't. But I can ask the director, Mrs. Brighton."

Macy remembered the name—and the woman. Twelve years ago Sally Brighton, referred to as Mrs. B by the girls, had been sitting right here at the desk answering the phones. She'd been over thirty then, which put her in her mid-forties now. Apparently Sally had climbed the administrative ladder as she said she would. "I'd appreciate it very much if you'd do that."

"I'm Danielle," the receptionist said with a smile, then pressed a button and spoke softly into the phone.

When finished, Danielle set the receiver back in the cradle. "She'll be out in a minute. You can sit over there to wait."

"Thanks, but I've been sitting all day." She wanted to ask the girl a couple of questions.

"Is someone in trouble?" Danielle suddenly said.

The wariness in her eyes put Macy on alert. "No, why do you ask?"

She shrugged, then looked down. "The only time anyone comes here is when somebody's in trouble."

"Who comes here?"

Just then a woman's sharp voice interrupted them. "What can I do for you, Ms.—"

"Capshaw." Macy held out her hand and continued talking, hoping the woman didn't recognize the name. "I'm representing a former resident at Haven's Gate, and I'm here to speak to Dr. Dixon."

"Dr. Dixon isn't available, but perhaps I can help. What is it you need?"

"Information on my client."

Mrs. Brighton frowned. "Client records are confidential."

"I'm aware of that. I'm also aware that a patient has a right to see her own records."

"Do you have a signed and notarized consent form from your client? If so, I can send her copies of the medical record, but the adoption records are off-limits. No matter what."

Macy knew that, but her blood pressure spiked anyway. She planned to request her own records if she didn't get the answers she wanted from Dr. Dixon today. "This isn't something you and I need to discuss. I came to see Dr. Dixon. Can you tell me when he might be available?"

"He's not available. You'll need to call for an appointment."

Macy stepped closer and, maintaining eye contact with Mrs. Brighton, she said, "Okay, make me an appointment."

"Sure," the girl at the desk spoke up. "I can do it."

Mrs. B pursed her lips. Her face flushed and she snatched the pen from the girl's hand. "That will take some time to research, Danielle. The doctor is booked for most of the month."

"That's okay. Make me an appointment anyway."

The older woman shook her head. "We'll have to check the schedule and discuss it with the doctor. But we'll get back to you."

Yeah, right.

Folding her arms across her chest and in a tone that brooked no argument, Mrs. B stated, "I think you'd better leave now."

Macy remembered Sally Brighton's little Hitler attitude. She'd liked power then and seemed to revel in it now.

"Okay. But please give Dr. Dixon a message for me." She pulled out another card and handed it to the woman. "Tell him Macy Capshaw wants to talk to him. Wesley Capshaw's daughter. And tell him it's very important."

Recognition flickered in the woman's eyes. She didn't take the card, so Macy laid it on the desk with the one she'd given the receptionist. "And tell him I have some grave concerns."

The glare Mrs. B gave Macy could've melted steel.

"Thank you for your time," Macy said, and strode out the door, her blood rushing. She hadn't intended to give her name. She hadn't intended to let them know she was looking into the shelter. Damn.

Later that evening, Macy settled on the couch and flipped on the television set. After her visit to Haven's Gate, she'd had another court appearance before visiting Billy. The boy had been sullen and wasn't about to enjoy himself, ice cream or no ice cream. She felt as if she'd failed him somehow.

Well, what did she think? That a trip to Baskin-Robbins was going to be a magical cure-all? The boy had problems that needed a therapist—not an ice-cream cone. She'd been happy to hear that his foster mother had made an appointment with one of the psychiatrists Macy had recommended and that after Billy had come out of the bathroom, the rest of his first day in foster care had been better. "Except for a fight with one of the other boys, he's getting along okay," Nancy Appleton had said. "I've done this before. Believe me, he'll come around."

Macy wasn't so sure. How could a boy who didn't remember anything about himself *come around?* And if he did remember, would that be worse? But she had to hope the woman was right—for Billy's sake. Still, when she'd taken him back to his new home, she knew he didn't want to stay. He didn't say anything, but his big, dark eyes pleaded with her.

She'd seen eyes filled with pain like his so many times in children of families she'd worked with, that when she'd first been assigned to work as a court-appointed child attorney, she'd vowed never to let down a child she represented.

But the problem with vows was that sometimes she didn't have a say. A child's disappointment wasn't always a result of something she did wrong, but more what she couldn't do. Sometimes she felt so helpless.

She patted her lap for Hercules to sit with her. He hopped up and snuggled into her lap just like a baby. She had to stop thinking about Billy. She was getting emotionally involved—and that wasn't good.

Just then the phone rang. She picked it up on the first ring, hoping it was Rico with new information for her. Or that Dr. Dixon had received her message and was returning the call.

"Hello?"

"Hello, is this Miss Capshaw?" A woman's voice. Young.

"Yes. Yes it is. Who's calling please?"

Silence ensued, except for muffled breathing.

"Who is this?"

"I—I can't say. But I have to tell you something. Something very important."

At the last words, Macy recognized the voice—the receptionist at Haven's Gate. "Okay. I'm listening."

RICO PLOWED THROUGH years of incident reports, looking for something that would trigger a new investigation or a search warrant in his niece's case. There was
nothing. After an hour and a half, he was ready to give
up. The Ray case went cold five years ago for a reason. Why couldn't he just accept it and get on with
his job?

Hell, he knew why. He didn't like failure. And he
didn't like knowing the answers were out there if he
could just find them. A child had been abducted, his
niece's child; there had to be clues.

Leaning back, his mind drifted to Macy again. He'd
never in a million years expected what she'd told him
yesterday. Why had she given up her child? It wasn't as
if her family couldn't afford to help. Did she not want
children? He didn't know any woman who didn't want
children, but he knew from experience that some people should never have them. Life wasn't always fair, but
when kids got hurt, it was life at its worst.

Absently, he flipped to another incident report.
Holly Magruder. The girl had come back to the center
after her child had been adopted and demanded him
back. He noted the date. Three months before Chelsey's
baby was abducted. He remembered talking to the girl's
parents. She'd been under psychiatric care before her
child was born. Afterward she was sent to the state
hospital.

During their earlier investigation, they'd made a point
to talk to all the girls who'd stayed at the facility when
Chelsey was there. They'd missed Holly because she'd

been hospitalized and any testimony she might have given would be tainted by her mental illness.

He flipped another page. LaVonne Smith had an unexplained cut on her wrist. He didn't remember talking to her, but knew the team would have. He flipped another page and another, finding a lot of little things, but nothing substantial. It was all stuff they'd already covered. Skimming the rest, he finally found another date—the night Macy's baby was born.

But again he found only a report of one child, not two. The Monroe baby. His instincts went on alert. All deaths in a licensed medical facility were required to be reported to the regulating agency.

Why wasn't Macy's stillborn baby recorded?

A LOUD RINGING jerked Rico from a dead sleep. He groped for the phone, dropped it once and finally wrestled the thing to his ear. "Yeah!"

"Rico, it's Macy."

He rubbed his eyes, then blinked, trying to focus on the red numbers of the digital clock. Instantly he came wide-awake. "What's wrong?" Had she received another threat?

"Nothing's wrong."

"Nothing? It's two o'clock in the morning," he mumbled, his mouth as dry as cotton. "And you called to chat?" Under normal circumstances he might be delighted, but he'd been out all night on a homicide and had only just gone to bed. As it was, he'd only get a couple hours of sleep before he had to be at the station early.

"I'm sorry. This is important."

He shoved himself to a sitting position, the clock throwing off enough light for him to see the half-finished can of soda on the chair next to the bed. "It must be if it can't wait another few hours." He grabbed the can and guzzled down the dregs. Warm and flat.

"I had a phone call…and I thought you should know about it."

"What kind of call?" His protectiveness shot up another notch. "A threat?"

"No, nothing like that."

"Well, what then?" He didn't mean to be irritable, but dammit. Between getting no sleep and thinking something had happened to her…

"I visited Haven's Gate today. And before you get all upset, I didn't do anything illegal. I simply asked to talk to Dr. Dixon."

"And did you?"

"No, he wasn't there. But I did talk to the director and asked to have the doctor call me."

"That's why you called at this hour?"

She cleared her throat. "No. The receptionist overheard everything and, because I'm an attorney, she thought I should know a couple of things about Haven's Gate."

He rolled out of bed and stretched. "I'm all ears."

"Well the receptionist, Danielle, said strange things happen at the shelter. She made me promise not to tell anyone she'd called, which I did. But I couldn't sleep thinking about it and finally I realized I had to tell you."

"Go on."

"She told me one of the residents had confided in her that she didn't want to give up her child. Danielle told the girl, who was only fifteen, if that's how she felt, she had to speak to the director."

Macy's voice sounded a little shaky.

"After that, Danielle said the girl became really sick. She had the baby and they disappeared that same night."

Rico waited a few seconds before he said, "That's it?"

"Yes."

"Maybe she had a change of heart again, signed the papers and went home."

"At night, after giving birth when she was so sick? Well, playing devil's advocate, that's what I said. And I asked why she, Danielle, thought it was anything more than that."

"And?"

"She said she couldn't say any more because she didn't want to lose her job. I thought you might want to follow up…find out what happened to her and the baby."

Rico sat on the edge of the bed, his feet on the cool tile floor. He rubbed his eyes. "Damn."

"You can't do it?"

"No. I can't question people on the basis of a disgruntled employee's rambling. I'd need something on file with the department, a missing person's report or a complaint of some kind. Is this Danielle willing to file a complaint?"

He heard Macy's disappointment in her deep sigh.

"I doubt it. I guess I hoped you might do what needs to be done."

The muscles in his neck tensed. "I always do what needs to be done. The right way."

"Fine. I'll handle it myself. I was going to do that anyway until I mistakenly thought you'd help."

"What do you intend to do?"

"I know someone who can get information I can't."

"I don't like the sound of that."

"You don't need to like it. If you can't help me, I'll get someone who can."

This was certainly not the time to tell her about his earlier finding. No incident report had been filed for the date of her child's birth and that, combined with the missing death certificate, gave cause for suspicion.

Hell, none of this would even be an issue if he wasn't so concerned about Macy. And, he realized, he was concerned about her because he cared about her. He wasn't supposed to care about her—not in the way he did. "Don't say anything more."

"Why? Are you going to arrest me for talking about an illegal act?"

The hair on the back of his neck prickled. "No, but I will if you commit one."

"Fine. I'm not going to do anything illegal."

Her tone wasn't convincing. "Look, I've had a long day. I also have something else I need to talk to you about, so maybe we can get together tomorrow to discuss all of this? Before you take matters in hand."

"I can do it now."

"I can't because I've had only an hour of sleep and I need to be at the station in a couple of hours. I'm cranky as hell and if I don't get some rest, I'll be worthless." And because he had a long list of criminals with explosive expertise to go through before he talked to her. There was a chance the warning wasn't just meant for him and the sooner he narrowed the suspects, the better.

Silence on the other end made him wonder if she was still there. Then she said, "I have some time around five o'clock tomorrow. Will that work?"

"Fine. I'll come to your office." After Rico hung up, he had second thoughts. If there was a possibility Haven's Gate was involved in a cover-up, and it was looking more and more like it was, he had to be careful what he told her.

If he told her and she went off on a tangent, she could ruin everything. He didn't want her destroying any chance he had of getting a warrant. He just hoped to hell she didn't do something before he talked to her.

CHAPTER NINE

MACY PLUMPED THE CUSHION with a good solid punch. Five in the morning and she was still awake.

She'd known a lot of cops and none of them had such rigid standards as Rico Santini. They improvised. They did what was necessary to get the job done.

Her father had to have a copy of the death certificate stuffed away somewhere. He was as thorough as any man could be, but getting him to even talk about her *indiscretion* was difficult. Still, she had to do it. And she had to do it before he left for Europe.

She waited a couple of hours until she thought he might be up. After five rings, the answering machine picked up, but just as Macy was about to leave a message, her mother answered.

"Mom, it's Macy. Is Dad there? I need to talk to him."

"He had to work late, dear, and he's not home yet."

"It's morning and he's still working?"

"Yes. That's what he said. Is anything wrong?"

"No, I just… When I had the baby twelve years ago, he took care of all the arrangements and I need to know if he has the death certificate filed away somewhere."

Sarah cleared her throat. "I don't know anything about that. And I don't think your father would like being reminded of it."

The words seemed pat. Something she'd been programmed to say. "Why do you need it?"

"I just need to see it, that's all. Can you please give Dad a message to call me when he comes home?"

"I may not be here when he gets home, but I'll leave him the message."

"What kind of business keeps him out all night?"

"I don't know, dear. I never get involved in his business. You know that."

Her mother's voice wavered. Something wasn't right.

"I know, Mom. But sometimes it's good to know what's going on. He is your husband."

Macy didn't understand how two people who'd been married for thirty years could know so little about each other. Their marriage seemed more of a business deal than anything.

No wonder marriage scared her. If she *ever* married, it would have to be a very different relationship than the one her parents had.

"I know you're right, Macy. And I've been thinking a lot about that lately."

"Thinking a lot about what, Mom?"

"About how your father is gone so much, and he and I don't communicate. Mary Lou, one of the new girls in the bridge club, says your father controls everything, including my life."

Macy nearly fell off the couch. This was not her

mother talking. Whenever Macy had suggested the same thing, her mother defended her father. He was perfect for her. They had a perfect life together.

"He loves you and you love him. Whatever works for both of you is just fine."

"That's the problem. I don't know if it's working. I don't know if it ever did."

"Oh, Mom. I'm so sorry." And she was. Not for her father's sake, but for her mother's. "I hate that you're feeling bad. Do you want to come over and talk?" she asked, even though they'd rarely communicated before. Macy had longed for it so many times. "Or I could come there?"

"No. It's okay. I'm going to take a pill. I'll feel better after that."

Macy didn't know what to say. Sarah might not be the independent person Macy sometimes wished she'd be, but she loved her nonetheless.

"I'm sorry, dear. I shouldn't have said anything."

"Don't be sorry. You can say anything to me."

"Thank you sweetheart. I may be just having one of my moments. Please don't mention this conversation to your father."

"Okay. You'll give him my message when he gets home?"

"I'll give him your message, but if he doesn't want to talk about it, please let it alone. I don't want anything to spoil our trip."

Macy had the feeling her mother thought the trip was going to fix everything. And maybe it would. "When are you leaving?"

"Tomorrow afternoon. We fly to New York and then Paris."

"It'll be wonderful. Please call me when you have a chance."

"I will. I promise."

"I love you, Mom." It was something she hadn't said in years, not since she'd had the baby and her parents had abandoned her. Oh, they'd provided for her physical needs, but emotionally, there was nothing. Maybe there never had been.

"I love you, too, dear."

It was a perfunctory statement and Macy felt more tense when she hung up than she had when she made the call. Why did she think things could ever be different? Why couldn't her father just tell her what she wanted to know?

It wasn't going to happen, she realized, not for the first time. Her father wanted to forget the whole thing and he was determined to make sure she did, too.

Good thing she still had the key to her parents' home.

"I'D LIKE TO SPEAK TO Dr. Dixon," Rico told the receptionist at Haven's Gate.

"Do you have an appointment?"

Rico flipped his shield. "No, I don't."

The receptionist's eyes almost bugged out. "Just a minute. I'll get him." She bolted from the desk and fled down a long hallway.

He paced the room. He doubted he'd get the answers he wanted, but he felt compelled to try. He'd like nothing better than to find Macy's son's death certificate and put her mind at ease. God knew what thoughts might've gone through her head.

Just then a corpulent man with graying hair entered the room.

"What can I do for you, Officer—"

"Detective Santini."

The man's brows came together in a frown. "Have we met before?"

Rico nodded. "Yes. Five years ago. The kidnapping of the Ray baby."

Surprise registered in the man's eyes. "Oh. Have you found new evidence?"

"Actually, I'm here to find out your procedure for filing birth and death certificates."

The man blinked. "I'm sorry, I can't help you with that. I sign the certificates, but our director takes care of the administrative procedures."

"Did you sign the death certificate for Macy Capshaw's child?"

Rico thought he saw a flash of awareness in the doctor's gaze, but then it was gone and his eyes looked like two gray stones.

"I'm sorry. I've signed hundreds of certificates and can't possibly remember each individual's name. Even if I could, our client records are confidential. Why do you want to know?"

"Because there's no death certificate on file for the child Macy Capshaw delivered twelve years ago."

The doctor stuffed his hands in his pockets. He

cleared his throat. "That would be an administrative error—if it were true."

"That's what I'm trying to determine. If someone on your staff sent the certificate to be recorded, then the problem is with vital statistics. All I need from you is to see your records that show it was filed. No names. Just the date when the report was sent."

Dr. Dixon's face flushed. "Our director is on vacation. But she keeps impeccable records and I'm sure she'll be able to locate exactly what you need when she comes back next week."

And that would give the good doctor plenty of time to make sure the records showed exactly what he wanted. But Rico had no other choice. He handed the man his card. "Have her give me a call when she returns."

Rico left the shelter, his nerves on edge. He was pretty good at reading people, and Dr. Dixon literally radiated negative vibes. It was obvious the guy was lying. If Wesley Capshaw had been on the shelter's board of directors, Dr. Dixon wouldn't forget Capshaw's daughter and the stillborn infant he delivered. Besides which, the young woman at the desk looked scared out of her wits. Something was going on at Haven's Gate, and he'd bet a pair of Super Bowl tickets that it wasn't within the law.

Back at his vehicle, he did a quick check to make sure there were no strange packages or any other paraphernalia, climbed inside, shoved the shift into gear and drove toward the freeway. Since the bomb scare, he'd been taking a different car every time he left headquarters.

When he walked into the office, Jordan immediately wanted details. "So, what's really going on at that place?"

"I have no proof of anything."

"Well, why don't you step outside the box and tell me what you *think* is going on. You don't need proof for that."

Rico had to laugh. In the time he and Jordan and Luke had been working together, they'd gone round and round about their different styles. Where Rico intellectualized, Jordan went with his conscience. Luke, on the other hand, needed immediate action. As close as the three of them were, they were as different as planets in the solar system and they'd had more than one conflict over it. But that didn't rule out mutual respect and good friendship outside the job.

"You remember the Erlicson case?" Rico said. "The one where everyone believed that dirt bag was guilty and set out to prove it? After ten years in prison, the DNA proved otherwise. I'm not accepting preconceived notions. They screw up a good investigation."

"Yeah, I remember. That guy needed to be put away anyway."

"Not for rape and murder, if he was innocent."

"Only a matter of time, my friend. Only a matter of time."

Unfortunately, Rico knew Jordan was right in many cases. But that didn't make doing the wrong thing correct.

Jordan sat at his desk and tapped his fingers, unwilling to let it go.

"Okay," Rico blurted, "I think there's something going on but I can't nail it down. Could be simple paperwork negligence, or it could be something more sinister. Like coercion to make vulnerable girls give away their children."

"Black-market babies?"

"It's a thought."

"What does Macy think?"

"We haven't talked about it."

"Why not?"

"Because she's a loose cannon. Tends to do things the way she thinks they need to be done. She's unpredictable."

"Ah. That's hard for some of us to handle."

It was true. He didn't like living on a precipice. Never had. "It's hard to handle because if she gets evidence without following procedure, it won't be admissible in court and that would screw everything up."

"And how does all this relate to the Ray case?"

Weary, Rico rested both elbows on his desk. "If the shelter is participating in one cover-up, there could be more."

Jordan nodded. "If you want help, I'm there. Proof or no proof. I'll help you get some."

His partner was loyal to the bone. But since the Ray case wasn't on the priority list, he couldn't let Jordan get involved. "Thanks. I've got it covered. I need to look at the medical records and to do that, I need a good reason for a search warrant. A missing death certificate and incident report don't cut it."

"What are you going to do?"

"I'm going to find a reason to get a warrant."

MACY FINISHED HER PHONE CALL to Nancy Appleton after learning that Billy was going to undergo DNA testing tomorrow morning. She made another call to make sure Rico's case was first on the list for cross comparison. Not that she could make it happen, but her requests were usually honored unless something else took priority. Two phone calls later, she realized it was time for Rico to arrive.

She took out the mirror from her desk drawer and checked her lipstick. Whatever he wanted couldn't be all that important or he would've said what it was last night.

Maybe he wanted to discuss their elevator encounter? Though now that time had passed, she didn't know if talking about it was even necessary. They'd had a moment. That was all.

Still, she wouldn't mind a few more moments like that with Rico.

A knock on the door startled her, since Cheryl had the afternoon off. "Come in."

Rico poked his head inside. "Is the coast clear?" He smiled—a big teasing smile. "No irate ex-husbands...or lovers on the prowl?"

"It's clear."

"Whew. I'm glad to hear that." Coming inside, he wiped a hand across his brow in an overly dramatic gesture, then dropped into the chair across from her.

His dark hair curled over his forehead in disarray and tiny beads of sweat dotted his brow just underneath. He looked as if he'd just run up the seven flights of stairs. He looked stomach-clenching sexy.

"So, what couldn't you tell me on the phone?"

He raked a hand through his hair and leaned forward, elbows on his knees. "Let me catch my breath."

She smiled. "Seven flights. I'm impressed."

He shrugged, breathing deeply, then sat back. "The other day after working on a case, I went to my car and noticed a small box on the floor."

"Not yours, I gather?"

"Right. So I called the bomb squad."

"Oh." She caught her breath. "Was it? A bomb, I mean."

He nodded. "Not a very potent one. Not meant to kill, but a bomb, nevertheless."

"Who? How? Why?"

"I don't know. But since it wasn't a killer, I'm taking it as a warning."

"About what?"

He stood and came around to stand at the window behind her and, hands clasped behind his back, he stared out at the city. "Like you, I can only surmise it might be someone I arrested and testified against. Or maybe someone who doesn't like what I'm digging up on one of my current cases."

She stood at the window beside him. "No ex-girlfriends as suspects? An angry husband?" If it was a possibility for her, it could be for him.

"No angry husbands I know of. I don't date married women. But I did have a stalker last year. A woman I'd gone out with once. That was all it took for her to decide we were meant to be."

"Really?" Macy couldn't hide her surprise. But she

shouldn't be surprised. She knew too much about stalkers—dealt with it all the time with the battered women she helped. "Is that what you meant when I showed you the letter and you said those kind of people usually had a screw loose?"

"Exactly."

"You don't think it's the same person, do you? Someone who saw you with me and…"

He shook his head. "I don't think so. The last I heard, she moved to the East Coast."

"So what happens now?"

"I found a number of leads, people with bomb-making expertise, narrowed it down and the CSU techs are on it to see if we get a match. We'll see. They didn't get anything on that letter of yours yet."

He placed his hands on her shoulders, sending an involuntary shiver through her. "I just wanted you to know about it so you could be extra watchful."

The concern she saw in his eyes almost undid her.

"Be careful. Okay?"

His voice was soft. He was looking at her mouth. She thought he moved closer. Whether he did or not, didn't matter. Her breathing deepened. "Okay," she said in a near whisper. "I'll be careful."

They stood like that for what seemed an eternity. What was it about Rico that made her want to jump off the defensive wall she'd built so long ago?

His mouth met hers. Or hers met his. She wasn't sure. It didn't matter. Her desire was suddenly overwhelming. His mouth was warm. His kiss demanding.

Her hands skimmed over the hardness of his chest. As he backed her into the desk, she felt his arousal. His kisses, his body pressing against hers, were like a drug, lulling her into euphoria. The backs of her thighs dug into the edge of the desktop. The effect was enough to make her aware of what was going to happen if she didn't stop.

She brought her hands between them against his chest and gently pushed.

Instantly, he pulled back, his eyes dark.

Regret? Anger? They were both breathing hard.

"I—I'm sor—"

He took a step away. "Don't be. I got the message."

IT HAD BEEN A LONG and delicious kiss. Even now, four hours later, her blood still pounded. "C'mon, Herc." She motioned for him to follow as she went down the hall to the bedroom.

She started to undress, an ache of need pulsed between her legs. She'd wanted to make love with Rico. Desperately. But she knew if she offered herself to him, she might want more.

She took a deep breath. Her life had been decided for her in one conversation with her gynecologist, and in that moment, all her girlish fantasies had disappeared.

Good God. She'd come to grips with that a long time ago. Why was she having such deep regrets now?

She stood there at the closet and ran her hands over her hips, her breasts. She wanted someone else's hands on her. Rico's. But when he'd asked her to be careful, she'd realized he really cared about her. Was worried. She'd never felt this vulnerable.

Everything was different with Rico. Dangerously different.

She grabbed a robe, put it on and flopped onto the bed. Rolling over, she reached for the phone. Her father had never returned her call. But then, had she really expected him to?

What time was it? Her parents should be on their flight to New York by now. She punched in the number.

"The Capshaw residence," a soft voice answered in a clipped English accent.

"Hillary, this is Macy. Is my mother…or father there?"

"Oh, dear. I'm sorry but your parents have already left on their trip."

Macy feigned disappointment. "Darn. Well, I'll catch up with them later. I hope you're taking a vacation, too."

"Yes, ma'am. I'm leaving in just a few minutes."

"Well, enjoy yourself, Hillary. You deserve it."

"Thank you."

Perfect. Macy hustled out of bed and put on her jeans, T-shirt and sneakers. Ready to set her plan in motion, she fished her parents' house key from her briefcase.

"Want to go for a ride, Herc?" The dog scampered at her feet, his tail wagging from side to side. She hated that she had to leave the little guy alone so much. Whenever she could, she took him with her.

She remembered her father's words. "Get rid of the animal. He'll just take up time that could be spent more productively." Her blood had boiled at the comment. Herc *was* her family.

"C'mon, fella." She picked up the dog, snatched her purse and was out the door.

Twenty minutes later, she slipped inside the big double doors at her parents' home and hit the alarm code.

Her father kept everything in his sacred library. If he had her son's death certificate, that's where she'd find it. But it was a big room with lots of files. She set Herc down and closed the office door to keep him inside. Retrieving the key to the file cabinets from the top drawer of her father's desk, she crossed the room to the files, hidden by two sliding mahogany doors that covered an entire wall. She went directly to the *H* file. Haven's Gate.

Everything was neat as a pin, files perfectly sorted. She would've expected nothing less. *Haven's Gate, Haven's Gate.* "Ouch," she sputtered at a paper cut on her index finger and stuck it in her mouth, the coppery taste of blood settling on her tongue. Hercules came over to comfort her. "It's okay, little guy." She ruffled the hair on his head.

Seconds later, she returned to the task, but found nothing. Where else would it be filed? *M* she decided. For Macy.

Nothing there either. Maybe *D* for Dr. Dixon.

Again, nothing.

After searching every possible file and coming up with zip, she sat in her father's chair to regroup. All she wanted was to see the stupid thing. Then everything would be fine. But her father was so paranoid on the subject, so worried someone might find out, that he'd wiped away any trace of the child she'd had. Her indiscretion as he'd called it.

She closed her eyes. It wasn't an indiscretion. The birth of her son had been a life-changing event. She had to know the truth. And her father *had* to have a copy of the death certificate. How would he have made funeral arrangements without it?

As she glanced at the clock on the desk, an idea formed. Haven's Gate would still be open. She picked up the phone.

The receptionist answered. Thank heaven. "Danielle, this is Macy Capshaw."

Danielle didn't respond.

"I wanted to thank you for calling me. It was the right thing to do."

She heard a muffled sound on the other end. "I—I wasn't sure…but if someone finds out—"

"No one will find out. But I need something else from Haven's Gate."

Danielle's breathing deepened.

"It isn't much. I need to get something from one of the files in the office and I don't want anyone to know about it."

"Oh, I couldn't—"

"It's okay. It's my own file."

"Your file?" she said incredulously.

"Yes, I was there a long time ago. But I don't want anyone to know I want to see it."

"I could get in trouble."

Macy felt guilty. She shouldn't have asked. She was grateful Danielle had even called about her suspicions.

"I'm sorry. You're right, of course. It's my problem, not yours."

"I get in trouble a lot," Danielle said. "Sometimes I forget to lock the side door when I leave and, since I'm the last one here, the one who locks up, they get mad at me when I don't do that."

Macy's interest was piqued. "Really? Well, you should be more careful then."

"I know. I'll probably forget again tonight when I go home. At six."

Macy couldn't believe what the woman was offering to do.

"If I forget again they told me I'll lose my job."

"You won't lose your job. I promise."

Finished, Macy leaned back in the chair and Hercules jumped into her lap. What would Rico say if he found out what she was about to do? Well, it wasn't illegal to enter an open door to a public building. That much she knew. Looking at the files, well, she wasn't going to think about that.

It was the only way if she wanted a real answer. Fact was, she didn't want to wait another hour, another minute. She felt an urgency about this. A gut-wrenching urgency.

IT WAS DARK when Macy pulled into the alley and parked where her car wouldn't be visible from the street. The side entrance to Haven's Gate led directly to the office, which was a separate area from where the residents stayed. Luckily, there was no light outside this door as there was in front.

After killing the engine, Macy left the car keys in the ignition, told Hercules she'd only be a minute, slipped out and quietly closed the car door. As she climbed the steps, her breathing became shallow and her hands felt clammy with sweat. She hoped to hell Danielle hadn't had second thoughts.

She checked around the door for any sign of an alarm system but found nothing. Key-holder flashlight in hand, she reached for the doorknob and turned. One click and it was open. Her heart leaped to her throat. *Thank you, Danielle.*

She inched open the door just enough to step inside and then closed it again, shining her flashlight along the floor to guide her. Within seconds, she found the record room. All she was looking for was something that showed her child had been stillborn and that his death had not been caused by negligence.

She pulled out a file drawer. Damn. The files only had numbers on them—no names. She quickly determined the numbers correlated with certain dates. The date the client came into the facility and the client's initials.

Knowing that, it shouldn't take too long to find her file. March 21, 1993. But these were current files, she realized. She needed old files and they didn't seem to be right here. She directed the flashlight beam from one corner of the room to the other, stopping at several stacked boxes on her left. Each had a label with a year on it. As she scanned them, her heartbeat quickened. *There. There it is! 1993.*

She couldn't move. All she had to do was find her file and see what had been recorded. Simple. She took a deep breath and pushed a chair over to the rack. As she did, she had the oddest feeling—a feeling that she wasn't alone—that someone was watching her.

Her gaze darted from one shadowy spot to another. Nothing. She was overreacting, that's all. Perfectly natural when one was doing something illegal.

It was a stupid thing to do. She knew that. But her need to know about her child far outweighed the consequences. She pulled down the box and took off the cover, fingering through the manila folders inside. *Yes.* There. Her blood rushed. And yet she felt a pall of dread.

Girding her resolve, she found the entry for the date of her baby's birth and flipped through three boxes before she found her file and pulled it out. She skimmed over all the entries for each day she'd stayed at the shelter until she reached March 21. But...what... What the—? The entry for that date had been blacked out. She flipped another page and another. The only entries after that pertained to her discharge.

Her hands shaking, she pulled the page and stuffed it into her waistband.

She went to the same date and found Carla's file. The entry verified that Carla's child had been stillborn. She was right about that. So, why had she been told otherwise?

Still trembling, she closed the box and hoisted it back in place and, as she did, she felt that same eerie awareness, as if someone was watching her. Turning, she saw nothing. No cameras even, that she could tell.

She had what she needed. After making sure the door would lock behind her, she left the building and drove home like a madwoman, her mind conjuring one scenario after another. Had her visit the other day prompted someone to delete specific information in her file? But why?

It was a question that needed an answer—and she was going to get it.

CHAPTER TEN

"RICO, IT'S MACY."

Something was wrong. And he could tell by the agitation in her voice that it wasn't a hangnail. He swiveled his chair to look the other way and keep the conversation private from Jordan. "What's up?"

"I need you."

"Well, I was wondering when you'd realize that."

"Please don't joke. I need your help."

"Okay. Shoot."

"I've heard there's a process to get information from a document even if it's been blacked out."

"Yes. CSU does it with forged checks, I think. What about it?"

She hesitated briefly. "I have a document. If I gave it to you, could you ask CSU to look at it?"

"I can if it pertains to a case. But I can't give them something personal."

"It might be pertinent."

"Where'd you get it?"

"You don't need to know that."

"Oh, man." He took a deep breath.

"If you can't take it to CSU, maybe you can find out what process they use, what chemicals and how they go about doing it. Maybe you could get some of their chemicals and—"

"What's in it?"

"I have a page from my medical file at Haven's Gate. And the information from the date I gave birth has been redacted."

"How did you get this?" He hoped she'd say she requested it through the proper procedure to obtain confidential records, but he had a bad feeling that wasn't the case.

"You don't want to know. Can you help me or not?"

"I want to help you Macy, but I don't think I can."

"You don't *think* you can—or you can't. Which is it?"

"Can't."

She was silent for the longest time, and then she said, "This is *really* important."

He heard the pain in her voice. Dammit. He felt helpless. Impotent. But he couldn't just barge into CSU and ask them to do something with illegally acquired information that didn't even relate to a current case. Or could he? What harm could come of it? His grip tightened on the phone.

"Have you tried the Internet? You can get almost any kind of information you want if you Google it."

"No."

"Look, Macy. I really want to help—"

"It's okay. I shouldn't have bothered you." Her voice

was distant, her words curt, and then the dial tone droned in his ear.

He slammed down the receiver. "Son of a bitch."

Jordan looked up. "That good, huh? Important call?"

"Yeah." Rico balled his hands into fists. "It could be significant."

"Well, then, do what you have to do."

When Rico didn't respond, Jordan added, "Not everything in the world is black-and-white. You of all people should know that."

Well, dammit. He liked things to be black-and-white. It's one of the reasons he was in law enforcement. There was order in what he did. He didn't want to be out there making his own decisions about what was within the law and what wasn't. Right was right and wrong was wrong.

"We have to make decisions all the time," Jordan said. "Right or wrong, we never really know until after the fact."

"This isn't in the gray area. There's no question of right or wrong." Rico stuffed his hands into his pockets and looked at Jordan.

Jordan smiled and nodded.

MACY PUNCHED IN another search on Google. Even if she found the information to get the ink off, she would have to find where to get the chemicals and it was probably too late for that. She slumped back in her chair and held the document up to the light one more time. If she could just see through the paper... No such luck.

She tossed it on the table. Damn. The sudden buzz of the doorbell made her jump. She shoved the paper under one of her law books and crossed to the door. No one she knew would stop by at this hour. No one she knew would drop by without calling first. And it had to be someone who had the security code. The only people who had that were her parents and her best friend, Amalia, both of whom were out of the country—and Rico.

She pressed the intercom. "Who's there?"

"It's Rico."

Barefoot and wearing a skimpy camisole top and boxer shorts, she wasn't exactly dressed for company. But after checking the peephole she opened the door.

"It's late. Has something happened?"

He shook his head. "I had an idea."

She stood still. "An idea."

He passed her and went into the living room. "Yeah. An idea. I have one once in a while."

She grinned. He seemed to be able to make her smile even when she felt horrible.

"You know how people do those rubbings and it transfers to the paper, I thought maybe that would work with the document you have if the writing was done with a heavy hand." He held up a brown paper bag and pulled out some tracing paper and dark pencils.

"Where's the document?"

"It's on my desk. But the writing is covered with black marker. I doubt it'll work."

In a few quick steps he was in her office. "Where?"

She pulled the document from under her books and handed it to him. His eyes bugged slightly when he saw the Haven's Gate imprint on the top of the page.

"I didn't break in or anything."

His skeptical gaze said he wasn't quite sure she told the truth. "Fine. But if someone didn't give this to you through proper procedures, don't say another word. I don't want to know."

Wasn't that just like him—determined to follow the damned rules, no matter what.

He shrugged off his jacket, laid the paper on her desk, right side down, placed a sheet of tracing paper over it and began to rub over it with one of the pencils. "Soft lead," he said. "I use it for drawing sometimes."

She liked watching him. Watching the muscles in his arms flex as he worked. He was dressed even more casually than normal in a white T-shirt and faded jeans. "You're an artist? I never would've suspected."

He kept rubbing. "No, I'm not. But I like to draw for my nieces and nephews. Cartoons and caricatures, mostly."

This was a side of Rico Santini she hadn't seen before, and she was even more intrigued. She knew he liked kids by his collection of keepsakes from his nieces and nephews. But she didn't know he had a creative side. Maybe he wasn't as inflexible as she thought. He was here, wasn't he?

"No big deal. Just something I learned to do out of boredom when I was at summer camp one year. My parents sent me because they thought it would get me away from the computer. I wasn't even allowed to take my electronic games along." He kept rubbing.

She moved closer to see how he was doing. "You poor thing. You were so deprived." She would've given anything to go to summer camp with friends. Most summers she went to Europe with her parents. Hating every minute.

He stopped what he was doing, shook out his fingers and turned to look at her. "I thought so at the time, but now I'm happy I had the experience. I learned that there was more to life than computers. And I made my parents happy."

"You're parents sound wonderful."

"They're all right. Hey, they'll be here this weekend if you want to meet them. My sisters and brothers, too.

She didn't know what to say.

"I'm having a barbecue. You can help me."

Help with a barbecue? "I'm afraid my barbecue experience is limited." Catered events for charity, usually. "You don't want me to help. Really. Take my word on it."

"Well, come anyway."

When she didn't respond immediately, he said, "I'd really like that. A friend thing. We are friends aren't we?" He smiled. "Your mother thinks so anyway."

Macy laughed. He had a way of getting her not to take herself so seriously. She'd been so focused on what she was doing, she'd forgotten how good it felt to simply let go—not think about the consequences.

"Tell me you'll come and I'll finish what I'm doing."

What could it hurt? "Okay. I'll come. As a friend."

Friend, shmend. At this moment she wanted to throw him on the desk and ravish his body.

"Great," he said and then went back to the paper.

"Does it look like it's working?"

"I think so…I hope so."

As she stood watching him, she felt the urge to touch him. His cologne teased her senses, a fresh ocean breeze.

"If this doesn't work, infrared light or laser photography might. One of the CSU techs told me that's how to separate the ink from the correctional fluid—or marker in this case."

Her heart swelled. He wouldn't do anything his ethics didn't allow, but he'd gone out of his way to find out what he *could* do to help her.

"There," he said and stood. "Let's see if it worked."

Oh, man. Her heart pounded. She hesitated. "I—I want to know what it says, but I'm afraid of what I'll find out."

"Do you want me to look at it first?"

She could feel her pulse pounding at the base of her throat. What a baby she was. She'd helped so many clients through crises and most of them had weathered the storm with dignity. "No, let's look at it together."

He took the tracing paper and walked to the couch. "The light's better here."

She followed him. "Let's do it."

He held the tracing paper to the lamp. The letters were smudged but she could make out a few words like breech baby and Cesarean. A bunch of numbers and then, *Healthy baby boy, 7 lb, 13 oz, 21 inches long. Vital signs normal.*

Oh, God! The room swirled and her legs started to buckle. She gripped his arm and at the same time felt him reach around, holding her up.

Her baby was born healthy. Did he die later?

Or not at all?

She dismissed the thought. That couldn't be. Her father had taken care of the funeral arrangements. They had a little vault where her child was buried. She'd been there.

Rico held her tight. What happened after Macy's baby was born healthy was anyone's guess.

He tried to get her to sit, but she pulled away, her eyes wild. "I—I don't understand. There's no notation to say what happened to him after that."

"Did you read the next pages in the file?"

"I read a couple lines and they were all about my discharge. I thought. Damn! I should've taken the whole file."

"Not a good idea."

She rounded on him, anger springing from every muscle. Hercules yipped and backed away. "This is my child we're talking about, Rico. Not one of your cold cases. And if you wanted a reason to get that search warrant, it won't get much better than this."

He clenched his teeth. Bit back a retort.

"They're my records, and I have a right to see them."

"Yes, but not to steal them. I'm as shocked as you are, Macy. But it won't help anything if we don't plan out what to do next."

She whirled around. "I know what *I'm* going to do

next. I'm going to find out what the hell happened to my baby. I'm going to find out why someone blacked out the information about him. I'm going to—" She flung her arms up in frustration. Her voice shook.

He gently took her hands, pulled her into an embrace and held her. "We'll figure it out," he said softly. "I'll help you."

He felt her tremble and his own anger flared. But for her sake, he kept it under control. "I promise you, we'll find out what happened." He drew back to look into her eyes. "But it probably won't be right this minute."

She went limp in his arms, as if all the fight had gone out of her. "Since we don't know what happened, and we can't do anything yet, how about I make you a cup of coffee?"

She gave a wobbly smile and let out a long breath. "Tea would be good." She sat on the couch and stared at the paper. "I feel so helpless."

He knew the feeling well. And he didn't want to leave her alone, not even to go to the kitchen. Not that he thought she'd do anything, but because he wanted to stay and hold her. Protect her. "I'll be right back."

"Freaking bastards," he said to himself on the way to the kitchen. Searching for what he needed, he picked up the stainless-steel teakettle, filled it with water and turned on the range, one of those flat-top jobs. He couldn't see where to set the damned kettle until he saw the red ring.

Yeah, he was frustrated, too—by his inability to get the answers Macy needed. And because she didn't even know the whole story and he couldn't tell her what he did know.

He had a couple ideas where to go from here. One, since Haven's Gate was a nonprofit organization, he didn't need a warrant to look at their financial records. He wasn't sure what that would show, but at least he'd know where the money came from to fund the place and where it went. Evidence could be buried anywhere. Two, if Macy's child had died, she could exhume the body and DNA would prove whether it was her child or not. All that was doable—and within the law.

He checked one of the cabinets to see where cups and tea might be.

"To your right."

Macy was standing in the doorway watching him.

"I'll get the tea," she said.

When the pot whistled, he poured the water over the tea bags she'd placed in the cups. "Maybe whiskey would be better," he said.

She actually laughed. "A lot of whiskey." But her mirth was fleeting. "I can't believe this is happening. Worse yet, I keep thinking that if I hadn't let my father handle everything, I'd know what happened. Maybe it's all nothing and I'm reading things into this."

Macy sat in a chair at the kitchen table, Rico next to her. "Maybe. We don't know *what* happened but we know something did. People lied to you. Reports are missing. Information blacked out. You're not reading anything into that. But let's not go beyond the facts. Not until we know more."

She tapped the rim of her cup with one fingernail. The sound almost echoed in the big ultramodern room. "Logically, I can rationalize missing reports and even why people lied if they were looking out for my well-being, which I don't really believe. But what I can't rationalize is not knowing what happened to my child after his birth."

"If your father handled everything, why don't you talk to him?"

She scoffed bitterly. "I tried to get him to tell me why he'd said Dr. Dixon was only there that one time and he wouldn't even talk about that. He hates that I had an illegitimate child. But I think mostly he hates that the baby's father wasn't acceptable to him and I became pregnant anyway."

"He's your father. I'm sure he was just protecting you."

She placed the tea bag on a teaspoon and wrapped the string around it to wring out the excess liquid. She leveled her gaze on Rico. "I'd like to think that was the case. But knowing my father…"

Bitterness laced her words. She obviously had a different kind of relationship with her father than he had with his. In his world, parents protected their children. Families stuck together, no matter what.

"Can you ask your mother?"

She scoffed again. "My mother is a Stepford wife. She's a robot who does everything my father wants her to do. She won't talk about it because he doesn't want her to talk about it."

"I'm sure if you tell them what you discovered tonight, they'll be honest with you." He waited a second, then added, "I'll go with you if you want."

She clasped her hands, weaving her fingers together, then looked at him with wide sad eyes. "They're on vacation. Probably in flight right now on their way to Paris."

"They left a contact number, didn't they?"

"They always stay at the same hotel. But it won't do any good to call them," she reiterated.

They sat in silence. He felt as if his hands were tied, and she felt…well, he didn't know what she was feeling. Hurt. Betrayal. Frustration. Uncertainty. He placed his hand over hers. "Why don't you get some sleep. Things might be clearer in the morning."

The resignation in her eyes made him want to punch whoever was responsible.

"I don't think so, but there's nothing else to do." She pushed her cup away. After a moment, her face lit up. "Yes, there is."

"Is what?"

"Something we can do. There's my father's computer. You heard him say he keeps everything on his computer."

"Like what?"

"Like everything."

"I'm sure whatever he has on file is password protected."

"But you're an expert. You could hack into it, couldn't you?"

He tensed. "I could, but that would be the same as breaking and entering."

"Not if you're with me. Not if I want you to do it."

If she had a key to her parents' home and took him inside, that wasn't a problem. But hacking into someone's computer…that was a violation of personal rights. "If your father is adamant about not revealing what happened twelve years ago, what makes you think he'd have anything at all on his computer?"

She nipped at her bottom lip. "He made the burial arrangements. He bought the vault. Even if he tried to clear the information, he has to have some record of that. I have to believe there's something there that will tell me what I need to know."

He shifted, more uncomfortable by the second. "It's really late. We're not going to get any answers tonight. I should go."

This time *she* reached out and took his hand. Her touch gave him an electric jolt.

"Stay with me."

Oh, yeah. And what would *that* do to the hormones raging inside him? Just talking with her, touching her hand, made him want so much more—when he should only be comforting and protecting her. If he stayed, who would protect her from him?

His feelings were out of place and removing himself from temptation was the solution.

"I have an extra bedroom."

The need he saw in her eyes made him feel like a jerk. She was going through hell and all he could think about was sex. *You're an ass, Rico. Plain and simple.* Ass or not, he had to leave.

"I'm sorry. There's something I have to do. But I'm only a phone call away." She would know he was lying. What did he have to do at midnight? "In the morning I'll talk with the people at Haven's Gate again."

"Again?" Her eyes widened.

"Uh-huh. I…went over after you told me about Danielle. I spoke with the physician and asked about their procedure for filing records."

"And?"

"And nothing. He said all he did was sign the papers. I told him your son's death certificate had never been filed and I wanted to see the log. He gave me some runaround—that I'd have to talk to the director and she was on vacation. So, I told him to have her contact me."

"Has she?"

"No. I don't expect her to, either."

"Why not?"

Because Rico didn't believe the papers had ever been filed. Because he didn't believe her child had been stillborn, and he couldn't tell her anything unless he had proof. "They don't seem too accommodating. It probably has something to do with my previous investigation. I put a lot of pressure on them." And nearly got thrown off the case.

Macy wasn't sure she understood, and two hours after Rico had gone, she was still trying to fall asleep. She finally got up and went to the bathroom. As she finished, she heard Hercules growling low in his throat.

She went to the bed and picked him up. "What's the matter with you, puppy dog?" she soothed him. Usually when she picked him up, he calmed down, but this time she felt the low growl vibrating like a motor in his chest.

She heard a rustling from somewhere down the hall. What on earth... She set Hercules down and he zipped past her, running toward the living room. She was about to call him back, but heard him bark ferociously, the way he did when he thought he was protecting her. And he kept on—barking and barking. Then she heard a yelp and suddenly it was quiet.

She started out the door. Another yip sent her heart to her throat. She froze. Someone was inside the condo.

How could that be? Her building had security codes and guards downstairs. What to do? Hide? Turn on all the lights? Her pulse pounded so hard she thought she'd stroke out.

She flew back into the bedroom, locked the door, picked up the phone and punched in 911. She gave her name and address first. "Someone's broken into my condo. Send the police!"

The dispatcher asked her to keep calm and not to hang up. "Did you see this person?"

"No."

"Can you hear him now?"

"No, it's quiet. But I didn't hear anyone leave."

"Do you know for sure someone's there?"

"I heard someone," she spat out. "I think he hurt my dog."

"The police are on their way, miss, just breathe deeply and...

She heard footsteps outside the bedroom. Panic seized in her chest. Oh, God! He's in the hallway. The doorknob's moving! *He's trying to open the door!* Where could she go? She dropped the phone and scrambled into the walk-in closet, feeling around in the dark for any kind of weapon. Her fingers touched the bat she'd bought for Billy.

A loud crash sounded against the bedroom door and then another. She left the sliding mirrored doors open just a hair so she could peer through the slit. It was too dark. She couldn't see anything. Another crash and the door banged open. Her fingers tightened, gripping the bat like a vise. She could see now—enough to know a man stood in the doorway, silhouetted by the nightlight in the hall. He had something covering his head. A mask.

And a gun in his hand.

Fear immobilized her. Was he there to rob her? Or hurt her? He had to have known the security code.

She watched him look around. He stepped farther into the room. Maybe he'd realize no one was there and he'd leave. Maybe...

Sirens pierced the air. The man froze, then making a horrible grunting sound, he stomped to the bed and ripped back the blankets. He turned, scanning the room. "Where are you, bitch!"

She flattened against the wall inside the closet next to the door, her heart pummeling her chest. Sweat beaded her skin. He was so close she could hear him panting.

Just then the closet door slid open and the man stepped forward. She swung out with all the power she could muster. There was an awful crunch. A horrible cry of pain. He stumbled backward then fell.

Fighting her panic, she darted around him. With the nightlight as her one source of light, she scrambled out of the room and down the hall—her only thought to get out of there before the man recovered.

Reaching the front door, she fumbled with the dead bolt, at the same time calling Hercules. "C'mon doggie," she whispered, her throat raspy. "Where are you?" God, she hoped he wasn't hurt. Something soft rubbed at her ankle. She reached down. "Oh, thank heaven you're all right." With Hercules in her arms, she ran out the door, afraid to look back because he, the burglar, the rapist, the murderer, whoever he was, might be right behind her.

In the hallway, she bypassed the elevator because who knew when it would reach her. But just as she reached the door to the stairwell, the elevator doors opened and three police officers barreled out. Guns drawn.

Thank God. "He's in the bedroom. I hit him," she said, panting, unable to catch her breath. "With a bat."

CHAPTER ELEVEN

RICO HEARD THE SCRATCHY dispatch and wheeled his car around, speeding back to Macy's. He wouldn't have even heard the call if he'd gone directly home instead of stopping for a hamburger.

All he'd heard was the code—burglary in progress. He recognized the address and the condo number immediately, and dammit, she was fine when he left her. Well, as fine as one could be, considering.

He banged his palm on the steering wheel. He should've stayed. God knew he'd wanted to.

How could someone break into her place? With all that security in her building, how the hell had that happened? His grip tightened on the steering wheel till his knuckles went white.

At her condo, he bolted from his car almost before he'd shut off the engine, and on his way inside, he flashed his badge to one of the blues at the door. Rico recognized the cop from the academy. "Hey, Melvin. What's going on? I heard the dispatch."

"Woman's apartment was burgled and she tagged the guy. Hard."

"Macy Capshaw?"

"Yeah, that's the one."

"Is she okay? She's a friend."

"Yep, but the guy isn't in very good shape."

Just then the EMTs pulled up, sirens blaring. "What's the MO?"

"Looks like a burglary," Melvin said. "The vic caught the guy and nailed him with a bat."

Rico waited impatiently for the elevator but when the doors opened, the emergency team shoved him aside and filled the space with their gurney outfitted with life support paraphernalia.

He hit the button again and waited for the second elevator. Man, it seemed to take forever. When he reached the top, the EMTs were getting back on the other elevator with a man on the rack. Rico tried to get a look, but the suspect's face was too bloody. The emergency technicians were slinging medical terminology and someone shoved Rico aside. Within seconds, they were gone and the sirens faded into the night.

When Rico reached Macy's, the door was still open and she was sitting on the couch with the dog in her lap. Two officers were questioning her.

His heart wrenched when she looked up at him, terror in her eyes. Her face was pale as chalk. He flashed his badge to the officers.

"He's a friend," Macy said.

Rico saw she was trembling so he sat beside her and put an arm around her shoulders.

"Are you okay?" A stupid question. "I mean are you hurt in any way?"

She shook her head. "But if the police hadn't come when they did…"

"Do you have any reason to believe it was anything other than a burglary?" one of the officers asked.

Macy looked at the man, her eyes dark. "He smashed down the bedroom door. I heard him say, 'Where are you, bitch!' and he was searching for me when I hit him." She took a shaky breath. "So, yes, I think he had something else in mind."

"Do you know anyone who'd want to hurt you?"

"Can't this wait?" Rico asked. "I mean you've got the guy and from what I understand, he's not going anywhere."

The officers eyed each other. One shrugged. The other said, "I guess so. I think we have enough information for now." He looked at Macy. "I'm sorry, miss. But we'll need to talk to you tomorrow, and we'll need a list of anyone you can think of who might want to harm you."

She nodded.

"You'd better get your locks replaced, too."

After they left, Macy went limp in Rico's arms, a small sob shaking her shoulders. He held her even closer.

"I should have stayed," he said, his anger rising. Anger at himself for leaving and anger at the creep who'd done this to her. "If I had…"

Sniffling, Macy pulled back. "It's okay. I think I handled things just fine."

She'd just had her life threatened and still, she had to assure him that she could handle herself. "I meant that if I had stayed, maybe the guy wouldn't have even come inside."

She stood, wiping the palms of her hands on her shirt. "They said he was critical. Th-that he might not make it."

"Well, don't expect me to feel sorry for the guy."

She rattled on as if she hadn't heard him, "What if he dies and all he wanted was money? I didn't need to hit him so hard, but I thought he wanted to hurt me, and I heard Herc yelp in pain and then he…the man broke down the bedroom door…I just…" She wavered on her feet.

Rico launched upward and caught her. "It's okay. You did the right thing." Helping her down on the couch again, he picked up a glass of water someone had put on the table and had her take a sip.

"You're going to be fine." He sat next to her, took her hand. "You did the right thing. You protected yourself. God knows what that guy wanted."

"I couldn't sleep and…"

"Shh. There's plenty of time to talk later. I think you better grab some things and stay somewhere else."

"Oh." She shook her head and motioned toward her office. "I can't do that. Everything I have is here. All my work."

"I don't think it's a good idea." With the guy in the hospital, it wasn't likely she had to worry, but he didn't see how she could sleep here.

"I'll call someone in the morning to fix the door and clean up the mess."

"And get new locks."

"That, too."

But for all that, her bravado wasn't convincing. Her eyes said she was scared to death. "Where's your booze?"

In her skimpy pajamas, with her ponytail hanging at half-mast and dark smudges under her eyes, she didn't look anything like the Macy Capshaw he'd met in her law office a few weeks ago. And every protective instinct he possessed filled him with a rage so raw, he wasn't sure what he'd do to the guy if he ever got hold of him.

She pointed toward a credenza of wood and glass and mirrors. "Over there."

He found a bottle of Jack Daniel's and poured them each a glass.

"I think I'm going to need a double," she said.

"That's cool. You can have as many as you want. No one's going to give you a DUI on your way to bed."

A wan smile tipped her lips. "But I'll need a designated walker to get me there."

It was obvious she was trying to lighten the conversation, probably for herself as much as him. But she didn't fool him one bit. "That's me. I'm staying here tonight and will gladly do the honors."

"Only I never get drunk."

Yeah. He could've figured on that. She wouldn't want to be out of control. Not for a second. "Well, there's a first time for everything. But I don't think this is it." He brought both drinks to the couch.

"Are you really going to stay?" she asked.

"Whether you like it or not."

"The man is in the hospital."

"Doesn't matter."

"Well, then, after this drink, I'm going to bed. I have some early appointments in the morning."

"I know it's not my place to tell you what to do, but I'd suggest you take the day off."

She gulped down the whiskey as if it was water. "Thanks for the suggestion."

But she wasn't going to take it.

She set her glass down and headed for the hallway, which he assumed led to the bedroom. After a few steps, she turned. "The spare bedrooms are this way." She pointed down the hall. "You can sleep in one and I'll take the other. I don't want to go into my own bedroom quite yet."

She started to go, but stopped again. "Thank you, Rico. I don't think I could sleep at all if you weren't here."

And he didn't think he could sleep with her in the next room.

MACY AWAKENED in a sweat, sheets damp and corded around her. Rolling over, she saw it was three in the morning. She'd barely slept at all. Then in a flash, it all came back to her. The man. The bashed-in door. His cryptic words. A body on the floor. *The blood.*

Oh, God! It wasn't a dream. Throwing off the covers, she waited a moment to get her bearings, then rose, went to the door and eased it open. Hercules was at her heels, so she picked him up. Across the hall her bedroom door hung crookedly off its hinges, smashed and splintered. But the man was in the hospital. Rico was in the next room. She was safe.

She took a few tentative steps and peered inside her bedroom. Everything but the door looked the same. She inched her way across the room toward the night table, then taking a deep breath, flipped on the light. Blood pooled on the floor by the closet. She gasped as she remembered the man had her security code. He knew how to get in. He had been there to hurt her.

And she didn't have a clue why.

She tore out of the room squeezing Hercules so tightly, he yelped. She stopped in the hall when she saw Rico's door was ajar and, pulse thrumming, peeked inside.

Rico catapulted upright, gun in hand and aimed directly at her. Her heart stopped. She reached for the door frame for support. "It's just me!"

"Oh, geez. I'm sorry." He laid the gun on the table next to the bed.

"I…I never thought about you having a gun."

"I should've mentioned it. I'm really sorry I scared you."

Finally able to breathe, she said, "My fault. Detectives are known to carry weapons. I'd just never thought about it, so it…surprised me." That was better than saying she was just plain terrified. That she didn't want to be alone. "I couldn't sleep."

"I can understand why. Come here." He patted the side of the bed.

It dawned on her then that she was wearing her

skimpy nightclothes, but she didn't care and walked over to the bed.

As if he understood her dilemma, Rico said, "Why don't we share the bed for what's left of the night. We'll think of an alternative tomorrow."

She put Hercules at the foot of the bed, but as she started to slide under the covers, Rico stopped her. "Uh, warning here. I'm naked."

She hesitated for less than a second. "I've slept with naked men before." Then she slipped under the covers and tucked the sheet between them. Although she wasn't touching him, and didn't plan to, it felt good to share a bed with someone.

No, not just someone. With Rico. "An alternative to what?" she asked.

Rico propped himself on an elbow to look at her. "An alternative to your staying here by yourself. That guy wasn't here for a little chat. I want to be sure you're safe."

His words were disturbing and yet at the same time, comforting. But did he want to make sure she was safe because he was a cop or because he was concerned about her? She wanted to think the latter.

"I'm sure it's okay now that he's in custody."

"Did you recognize him?"

"No. I told that to the police."

"Well, then, you don't know if he was out to hurt you or if he was sent by someone else."

The thought hadn't occurred to her. She lay there staring at the ceiling. "No," she whispered. "No, I don't."

A second later, she added, "But I don't know why

anyone would be that calculating. I'm not a witness in some high-profile case or anything."

"I'll find out more tomorrow. Hopefully the officers will have run the perp's prints through the system. In the meantime, I think you should find someplace else to stay."

He was right, of course. But her choices were limited. "I could go to a hotel."

"That would be less safe than staying right here. Here you have *some* security downstairs."

"But obviously not enough."

"What about friends? Your parents?"

Friends. Amalia, her best friend since grade school, was gone. The rest of her friends had married and had families. They'd either moved away or drifted away because they had nothing in common anymore. She didn't have a husband and children to talk about over long lunches, and besides, work took up most of her own time. "Nope. No friends close enough to stay with. My parents are out of town and I wouldn't go there anyway."

"Okay." He looked thoughtful. "Why don't you stay with me until we get this resolved?"

"With you?" She couldn't imagine.

"Yeah. I have room. And I'd be there most of the time."

"Oh. I don't think—"

"What?"

"I don't think that would look good."

"Anyone I care about would understand and I don't give a rat's ass about anyone else. They can think whatever they want."

She couldn't help a tiny smile. "Do the police offer to share their homes very often?"

"No, but you're a friend. Remember?"

Yes. It seemed they were friends. When had that happened? "I thought your family was coming."

"They are, but they don't stay with me. My place isn't big enough for the whole gang."

She looked at him, questioning.

"But it's big enough for one more."

What would it be like staying with Rico? She had to admit the idea appealed to her more than it should.

"I'd be there," he repeated. "Me and my gun."

That sounded good. Too good. "As inviting as that sounds, it just wouldn't work. I don't know what I'd do with Hercules."

"Bring him along. He'll get to run around outside for a change."

"You have a yard?"

"A small one. The house is small, too. One of those old California bungalows they built back in the twenties. But it works for me."

His eyes searched hers. Eyes that looked even darker in the soft glow of moonlight from the arched window. "So when is this barbecue then?"

"Sunday."

"But I have so much stuff. And my computer practically controls my life."

He arched his eyebrows. "I suspected as much."

"You know what I mean. When I'm not at the office, I work from home."

"No problem. Copy what you need onto a CD and

bring it along. I do have a computer. In fact, I have several."

She'd forgotten his geek side. "You should've been an attorney. You make a good argument."

He coughed. "Well, not everyone would take that as a compliment."

"Yeah, I know. But I happen to know a few attorneys who aren't so bad."

"So, you'll stay then? At least until we get a fix on this guy."

Relenting, she said, "Okay. But only if you promise not to make me obey orders." She was kidding but there was an element of truth in what she'd said. Rico was good at giving orders, and she wasn't good at taking them.

"Hmm. Jordan said I had a control problem. Maybe he was right."

Now she had to smile. "I've heard the same thing from various people about myself. But it's not true, of course." At that moment, Hercules jumped off the bed and ran from the room.

"Guess he didn't like the conversation," Rico said.

Macy rolled off the bed and started after the dog, a reflex reaction after what'd happened earlier. Embarrassed, she came back to bed and slipped underneath the sheet. Glancing at Rico, she saw his pupils dilate. Message received.

All her earlier apprehensions dissolved and she was suddenly acutely aware of his mouth. His perfect lips. Her desire. Her need—as palpable as the blood surging through her veins.

He trailed a fingertip gently down her cheek.

Her pulse accelerated. And in that one mind-spinning moment, she realized how desperately she wanted him. Right now, she wanted to make love with him more than she wanted anything.

She said softly, "I think it's time to get some sleep."

"You think?"

"No, not really."

His warm breath fanned her cheek. Anticipation pulsed through her with every beat of her heart. She turned so her lips were almost on his.

"Me neither."

As he breathed the words, his lips met hers. He kissed her hungrily, then gently and carefully, as if he'd suddenly decided she was a fragile China doll. She liked hungry better and kissed him back fiercely, opening his mouth with her tongue and letting him know she wasn't at all fragile.

She reveled in the raw physical need. She didn't want to think about this, she only wanted to feel. It had been too long since she'd lost herself in another human being.

Had she ever?

She felt transported. And all that mattered was this one moment. She pressed against him, instantly feeling his arousal on her thigh. He lifted her shirt and a gasp escaped her lips when he touched her breasts and teased her nipples, first with his fingers and then his tongue.

Somewhere between the kisses her shirt went over her head and then he slipped her shorts and panties below her hips. She helped remove them the rest of the way and then slid next to him.

His skin was hot. He was hot. And decidedly naked. "You always sleep au natural?"

"Uh-huh" was all the answer she got before he was kissing her again. Then he pulled back abruptly and muttered. "Damn. You have any condoms?"

"Don't worry," she said. "I've got it covered, and I have no diseases. How about you?"

"Nope. Cops get regular physicals." That conversation taken care of, he slipped a hand between her legs, rubbing gently, making her even more crazy with desire. She arched into him, letting out a deep moan, sounding like a wounded animal.

She needed him. *She loved him.* The thought was like a bright light, a beacon leading her from doubt to certainty. This was okay. They were okay. *For now.* He rubbed his fingers against her, harder and faster and yet his mouth never left hers, not even when he spread her legs and settled his body between them.

"It's been a while," he whispered. "And you're driving me crazy."

In the moonlight she could see his sleek, tanned body and was fascinated at how muscular he was. Much more so than he appeared in his clothes. She wanted to give him pleasure, too, but she couldn't think beyond his touch.

"We have all night, don't we?" she said. "I can't wait any longer, either."

He was ready and, in one swift move, he entered her.

CHAPTER TWELVE

RICO WOKE FIRST, smiling and feeling better than he had in a long time. Macy was spooned against him. He couldn't see her face, but he felt her slow breathing, felt her chest move up and down. Last night, she'd given herself to him with total abandon and he'd taken whatever she had to give.

Which begged the question, what did he have to give? Nothing. Absolutely nothing. He'd wanted to make love to her and had without a thought to the consequences. But she'd been right there with him. It was mutual.

He closed his eyes. He'd felt her deep need in every breath she took, in every moan and shudder. The truth was there and he was making excuses for it.

He'd taken advantage of a vulnerable woman.

Hell, she'd had her condo broken into, been accosted by someone, and he'd let his lust take over. Guilt lay like a rock in the pit of his stomach.

How could he have let this happen?

Macy Capshaw had managed to find a place in his heart, that's how. Was it love? He wasn't sure he knew what that was. Didn't love take a long time? First lust, then infatuation and then, eventually, the real thing. He wondered where he was on the list.

In the short time they'd known each other, they'd told each other things they'd never told anyone. That had to mean something more.

She stirred, then opened her eyes. She looked beautiful with her blond hair fanned across the pillow, her eyes sleepy and her lips full. He felt his groin tighten, and he wanted to make love with her all over again. "Hi."

"Hi." Her voice was low and heavy with sleep. She reached up to touch his chin. "I didn't think I'd sleep very well, but boy was I wrong."

He smiled. "Me, too. Slept like a baby."

Then they just looked at each other. Finally he said, "You okay?"

She nodded. "I'm perfect."

"I thought that I might've…that you might think I'd taken advan—"

Two fingers came up to quiet him midsentence. "I think you think too much."

Surprised, he said, "Maybe you're right. I've been told I need to just go with the flow."

She snuggled into him, her skin like fire against his. "Well, then. Let's go with the flow."

"WHAT TOOK YOU SO LONG?"

Macy shut her car door and glanced at Rico standing on the steps of the cutest little house she'd ever seen—and looking as anxious as she'd ever seen him. He stalked across the lawn to meet her in the driveway.

"I stopped at the hospital to see if there was any change."

"Yeah, I checked, too. No ID yet. Was he still unconscious?"

She nodded. "Then I followed your directions to get here. They weren't the clearest directions I've ever read. I had to read lots of signs."

"You should've followed me."

She shrugged. "Hey, I'm here."

"True." He opened the back door of her car and took out her two suitcases.

Her nerves hummed. This was probably the stupidest thing she could do. But wasn't she already emotionally involved? Even more reason why staying here was a bad idea.

Or maybe it was the best way for them to realize that good sex doesn't make a relationship. That an affair is all it could ever be.

"What do you have in here?" He dragged her suitcases toward the door.

She followed alongside. "One has clothes and the other some work I have to do."

"Lots of work, I'd say." He stopped at the steps. "Well, this is it."

"Your house is very pretty," she said. "Like one of those cottages in an English storybook."

He dropped her suitcases and reached for the knob, hesitating before he opened the door. "Just to warn you, the outside is not a good representation of what's on the inside. I'm not much of a decorator."

She figured that. Utilitarian would probably be his style. "Well, I'm not, either. I had someone else do my place. Saved me time and a lot of angst."

"Okay." He swung open the door. "Let's move you in and then we can both get some work done."

They walked right into the living room. No foyer. He was right. The place was small, and she could almost see the whole layout from right there at the door. Dining room on the right, and in the back through an archway, what looked like a family room that connected to the kitchen. She put Hercules down to sniff it out.

"He can go out back if he needs to do his thing," Rico said. "It's fenced. In fact, there's a doggy door that the previous owners put in. I'll just take out the nails and he'll be all set."

"The poor dog won't know what to do," she joked as Rico walked her down a center hall, to the bedrooms she assumed.

"Three bedrooms." He pointed them out. "Mine, my computer room and the guest room. One bath. And like I said, nothing fancy."

They'd have to share a bathroom? She'd never shared a bathroom with anyone, but she found it oddly appealing. "I hate to put you out like this."

He gave her a wicked look. "It was my idea. Remember?"

She did. And after last night, the idea was more exciting than it should be. "I remember."

"I'll let you get settled while I get the nails out of the doggy door."

"Great. I have to go to the office this morning and then I've an appointment to keep." She was going to see Billy. She'd told him they were testing his DNA and that she'd let him know when the results were available. But she really didn't expect it to be good news for Rico's case. "I'll take Herc with me because I don't think he'd like being alone in a strange place."

"Be cautious, okay."

"Definitely. But a person would be pretty stupid to try something with so many people around."

"There are a lot of stupid people out there, so don't take any unnecessary chances. I'll be at the station if you need to reach me. And I'm going to stop at the grocery store on the way home."

"Don't do any special shopping for me," she said, and the moment the words left her lips she realized how presumptuous that must've sounded.

"Maybe you want to come along? That way I won't get anything you don't like."

She felt her face flush. "I won't be back until five or so."

"Perfect. We'll do it then."

She was ready to do *it* right now. She felt as if he'd unleashed an insatiable lust inside of her. She'd never been as comfortable with someone as she was with Rico. He made her feel special, as if she mattered. And if she read the emotion she saw in his eyes correctly, he might be the one to get hurt if she let things go any further.

She couldn't let that happen.

Rico's first stop was the hospital to see if Macy's attacker had regained consciousness so he could question the guy—that's if the other officers didn't mind him horning in on their case. But the creep hadn't come to yet, and the docs weren't sure he would. "You get prints?" Rico asked the officer on guard. If their perp was in the system, they'd know right away.

"We're working on it."

But they didn't seem to be in any hurry. Next he went to the station and filled out the request to get Haven's Gate's financial records. He wouldn't hear anything over the weekend, but it was a start. Then he punched Dixon's name into the database and, waiting for the information to process, went back to Chelsey Ray's file. He was missing something. He felt it in his gut.

When they'd interviewed the staff and residents at the shelter five years ago, the questions hadn't been what he'd think to ask now. He had questions about the adoption process and record keeping. He wondered if the physical evidence collected at that time might be more useful now that they had better testing methods. Another avenue to check out.

He tipped back in his chair, hands laced behind his head to wait for the computer to spit out information. Jordan came in and sat across from him. He looked preoccupied and a little disheveled, a strange phenomenon for the always pressed and perfect Jordan.

"You look like shit," Rico teased. "What's up?"

Jordan rubbed his eyes. "Nothing. Didn't get much sleep, I guess."

"Woman trouble?"

His partner raised an eyebrow. "I wish."

Stupid question. Jordan never had woman trouble. The only trouble he had was too many.

"So, what then?"

"I approached my parents about finding my biological mother. They weren't too happy about it."

"Whoa. You've never mentioned that before."

"I had a checkup the other day and the doctor was asking about hereditary diseases. It got me thinking."

Rico sensed it was more than that. How could anyone not want to know something about the person who gave him life. He also knew how heartbreaking that search could be. "What if you found out something you didn't like?"

A frown creased Jordan's tanned brow. "I could handle it. What I couldn't handle is if it caused a lot of problems for my family, which apparently it would." He shrugged. "I'm not pursuing it."

"Okay." Rico knew how important Jordan's family was to him—even though they'd had their problems.

"You heard about last night?"

His partner's gaze narrowed. "No, what?"

Rico told him everything that had happened after he left Macy's. "Man," Jordan said, "I'm glad she wasn't hurt."

"So," Rico continued, "now I have a houseguest for a few days."

"Macy Capshaw's at your place? That's hard to imagine."

Rico feigned hurt. "Hey, don't dis my home. It's a palace."

"Maybe—if you'd been raised in a trailer park."

Jordan was joking, but it made Rico think. What was in his head? Getting involved with Macy Capshaw was a no-win situation. "She's safe. That's the important thing. It's nothing more than that."

Jordan coughed. "Methinks the man protests too much."

"Think what you want. Nothing is going to happen." A street kid from New Jersey, the grandson of Italian immigrants, and the daughter of a famous Beverly Hills attorney, a woman who never wanted for anything in her whole life—no way would they ever find common ground. No way but in bed. He smiled at the thought.

"That's the problem. You think nothing can happen and it's a self-fulfilling prophecy. You think too damned much."

He'd been accused of that so many times before he was starting to wonder if there was some truth in it. "Yeah, well, it helps to think because I have cases to solve."

Jordan raised his hands. "I'm cool."

Turning, Rico went back to the computer and pulled up the information he'd punched in earlier. It was a futile search. There was nothing on Dr. Dixon.

What next? He punched in a different name. Maybe that would get some results.

THE SUN WARMED Macy's face, the sunny afternoon a reflection of her feelings as she watched Billy playing with Hercules at the park not far from the Appletons' home. Despite her mixed emotions about staying at Rico's, the move had dispelled some of her worries about her own safety and she could concentrate on other things. Work.

Oddly though, she didn't feel the urgency about work she usually did. She was content to sit and watch Billy enjoying himself. More relaxed than she'd been in ages.

Maybe it was because she felt safe. Right now, with everything going on in her life she needed that sense of security. Even if it was temporary.

"Yay!" Billy shouted. "I got a point." Two boys had joined him and they were playing kick ball, with the dog running interference. Watching them, she felt that things just might be coming together. Billy seemed to be adjusting at the Appletons', and she was glad her earlier apprehensions had no foundation.

Just then, the ball bounced her way. She sprang to her feet and kicked it back and before she knew it, she was pulled into a game of kick ball.

By the time the other boys were called to leave, Macy was out of breath and crumpled in a heap on the grass. Hercules jumped into her lap and Billy tumbled down beside her, his brandy-colored hair tousled and hanging in his eyes. His cheeks were all pink from playing so hard, his clothes were dirty—and he was adorable. How could anyone leave a child like this to fend for himself? Any child.

"You're not like other grown-ups," Billy said.

She gazed at him. "What do you mean?"

He shrugged. "You're nice."

"Well, I think you're pretty nice, too. And so are the Appletons, don't you think?"

"Yeah, but they're not like you. They don't care about me."

Oh, my. She pulled him into a hug. "Of course they do, sweetie. You wouldn't be there if they didn't care."

He didn't answer, so she added, "You know what, I think they're going to have dinner ready any time now, so we should probably head home."

"Are you going to come back?"

She heard doubt in his voice. She couldn't blame him. He'd been abandoned by his own parents. But she saw a sparkle of hope in his eyes, as well, and there was no way she'd do anything to take it away. "Of course I'm going to come back. You're my best buddy." She ruffled his hair.

He gave a tiny self-conscious smile.

After she dropped Billy off and was driving back to Rico's, all the good feelings she'd had about Billy's stay at the foster home had dissolved. She'd been disheartened to read Nancy's daily journal, which detailed Billy's fights with the other kids, sulking in his room. Not talking. He'd started therapy and she'd hoped that would help him get comfortable in his new surroundings. But according to Nancy, it wasn't happening. If he didn't shape up soon, the woman said she'd have to talk to the social worker about finding him another placement.

Macy's grip tightened on the wheel. That was the problem with the system. Everything was temporary. If they didn't find Billy's parents or a close relative, he'd probably be shifted from one foster home to another until he was eighteen. Just thinking about it broke Macy's heart.

So, not only was she getting too involved with Rico, she was doing the same with Billy. What was that about? Billy wasn't the first child she'd worked with and he wouldn't be the last.

Pulling into Rico's driveway, she remembered they were going grocery shopping. She couldn't pinpoint when she'd last done that. She usually just grabbed a bite on her way home.

The front door opened as she stepped from her car, and Rico poked his head outside. "Why don't you pull into the garage. Your car won't be at risk that way."

She hadn't thought about that. "Is this a bad neighborhood?"

"No, but why take a chance? Teenagers are the same everywhere."

He hit a handheld remote and the door slid up. Ready to get back in her car, she stopped. "What about the groceries?"

"We'll take my car. It's bigger and we don't have to worry about getting it dirty." She set Hercules down in the grass and pulled the Mercedes inside. When she came out, Rico was holding the dog.

"I think he likes me."

"He likes everybody. Do I have time to change? My pants are dirty from playing kick ball."

"Kick ball? You?" He didn't disguise his astonishment.

"Yeah, me!"

"Well, I never would've guessed." He opened the door and went inside.

"Me neither." She didn't bother to explain and he didn't ask. Truth was, she'd been doing a lot of things since she met Rico that she never thought she'd do.

She changed into a pair of jeans and an hour and a half later, they were stalking the aisles at Albertson's Supermarket. Macy couldn't believe how much food Rico kept throwing in the cart, most of it for the barbecue tomorrow. Hot dogs, hamburgers and steak, so people would have a choice, he'd said. Beer, soda and wine. Beans and the makings for both potato salad and a pasta salad.

"So, who's going to cook all this stuff?" She hoped he wasn't going to depend on her for any of it. Not that she didn't want to help, she simply didn't have the experience.

"Me," he said, as if it was the most normal thing in the world.

"You cook?"

"Anything you want," he said proudly. "Grab a few bags of chips over there."

She did as he said and balanced them on top so they wouldn't get crushed. "Remember the restaurant I mentioned? Well, we all had to do our share and most of us learned to cook at home, too, in case my parents couldn't do it for some reason." He sauntered down the aisle, checking each side.

"Sounds like an ideal childhood."

"At the time I thought it sucked. We didn't have much money and we were forced to learn the meaning of hard work. I guess that was a good thing. Kept us out of trouble." He nodded toward a shelf. "Pasta."

She grabbed it and tossed it to him. "Growing up in a large family sounds wonderful."

"Most of the time it was. But we fought like hell, too. You get real territorial when you have someone snitching your stuff all the time."

"Is that why you haven't managed to get married? You don't want to share?"

"Yep. I'm selfish."

"Yeah, right. You're the most unselfish man I know."

"Well, no one in my family will believe that."

Rico navigated the overflowing cart to the checkout line and started chucking the food onto the conveyer belt. Macy reached to help him, wondering what it would be like to do this with someone on a regular basis. No, not just someone—with Rico.

Suddenly he tossed her a head of lettuce and she caught it on the fly. "Soccer, huh?"

She tossed the lettuce back, laughing. "Yes, soccer."

He shook his head.

"What? I don't look the type?"

"Excuse me, sir," the clerk interrupted. "That'll be $175.00."

"Sorry," Rico apologized and paid the girl.

On the way to the car, Rico said, "I think you'll like

my parents. They can be a little overbearing sometimes, but with them, what you see is what you get."

She smiled, but her stomach churned. She was actually nervous about meeting his parents. How bizarre. He'd said he'd told them she was under protection, so it shouldn't be any big deal that she was staying with him. And they did have separate bedrooms.

Right. If that's all it was to her, she wouldn't be having a problem. She liked Rico. She trusted him. He was honest, his integrity was beyond reproach and he was funny.

So there it was. She liked him and because she liked him, she was nervous about meeting his parents. It felt almost like being a teenager again.

"Okay, we're outta here," Rico said.

Back at the house, they carried in the groceries and set the bags on the blue ceramic countertop. The kitchen, small as it was, had a charm of its own. She could see that the original structure had been built in the 1920s because it had an Art Deco feel with rounded corners and arched alcoves.

She could tell someone had remodeled at some point, but not enough to change the ambience. The floor as well as the countertops were tiled in ceramic but in different colors. The old adobe tiles on the floor were perfect with the old-fashioned maple cabinets. The sink was white cast iron and the stove and refrigerator looked like something out of an old Bogart movie. Rico said he hadn't done anything to dress up the place. It was comfortable—bright and cheery and she felt bright and cheery standing there with Rico.

As they unpacked the food, the phone rang.

"Santini here."

She heard him rattle off a bunch of code numbers and the word homicide. When he hung up, he placed his hands on the counter.

"I gotta go. Sorry."

"It's okay. I can handle things here."

"You sure?"

"How hard is it to put groceries away?"

"Can you start the salads?"

"Start the salads?" She almost choked. "What do you mean?"

"Boil the eggs, potatoes and pasta."

"I've never made any of those things before."

"You can't boil eggs?" His expression switched from hopeful to incredulous.

"I didn't say I couldn't. I said I never have. Tell me what to do and I'll do it."

By the time Rico left, she had his cell phone number, had promised not to open the door for anyone, and had a list of cooking instructions as long as her arm. Lord, if she made it through the rest of the weekend, she'd be amazed.

Despite all that, she was glad to have something to do to take her mind off what had happened to her child.

RICO WORRIED ABOUT Macy the whole time he was away. He'd called twice and he could tell by her voice she thought he was overreacting. Now, pulling into his drive at 2 a.m., he noticed the lights were still on.

"Macy?" he said so she'd know it was him.

"I'm in here."

Her voice came from the kitchen. "Why are you still up?" The odor of burned food permeated the air. When he reached the kitchen, he stopped short. Dirty pots and pans filled the sink, but there were still two pots boiling on the stove. Macy was barefoot, wearing shorts and leaning on the counter, her hair half out of the ponytail and in her eyes. Her pink T-shirt was covered in something that didn't smell so hot, but he couldn't tell what. And the look she gave him warned that he'd better not say a word. She held up a hand to make sure.

"I've been following your directions," she said. "And again, they're not the best directions in the world."

He was speechless.

"Not for a beginner." She rubbed her cheek with one hand and shook the list in his face with the other. "For example. Here—" she pointed at the list "—here you say to place the potatoes in a pot and fill with water. Boil until done."

"Yeah. That's pretty clear, isn't it?"

She glared in exasperation. "You didn't say how big the pot should be, how many potatoes, if they were to be peeled or not, and you didn't say how long to cook them. And did you know that when they boil, the water goes all over the stove?"

"But what are you cooking now?"

Her mouth quirked sideways. "Potatoes. It took me a while to get it right." She flipped a hand toward the pots in the sink. "I burned the first batch. Then I had to go to the store for more."

He clenched his hands. "That wasn't a good idea. It's dangerous out there. A woman alone. At night."

"Oh? Well, if I hadn't gone to the store you wouldn't have any potatoes for the potato salad."

She looked so cute that, despite himself, he wanted to kiss her. "What about the eggs and the pasta?"

"Well…I had to get more eggs, too." She spun around, her expression serious. "I discovered that eggs will blow up if you let them go too long and the water boils away."

To keep from laughing, he went to the refrigerator for a beer. He pulled out a bottle of Bud and held it up to see if she wanted one, too.

"Sure, why not."

"And the pasta?" He was almost afraid to ask. "How did that go?"

"It's in the refrigerator cooling. There were good directions on the back of the package. And once I found a recipe for potato salad in one of your cookbooks, I figured out how to do the potatoes. Everything's okay."

He opened both bottles and handed her one. "Would you like a glass?"

She shook her head. "No, this is fine." Then she proceeded to guzzle about half the bottle. "Mmm. Wish I'd thought about this earlier."

She took another swig, then set the bottle on the counter. "So—how was *your* night?"

"Apparently a piece of cake compared to yours." He

couldn't help grinning, then went to check the potatoes on the stove. "Ten more minutes should do it. Why don't you go to bed and I'll take care of this."

"What comes next?"

"Next?"

"The food. When do you assemble the food?"

"Oh…uh, ideally, I would've made the salads tonight, but I'll do it in the morning."

"I can help, if you want."

He hoped his skepticism didn't show.

"It'll be easier since you'll be here to give me directions."

"Uh, sure. I'd love to have help. Now go to bed because we'll need to be up by six or there won't be enough time to get everything ready before the horde arrives."

She pursed her lips and swiped at a stray hair with the back of her hand. "Six? That's in four hours."

"Uh-huh."

Her expression said she thought he was crazy. But she didn't complain. "Okay. Good night then."

Watching her saunter down the hall made his breathing shallow and his blood start pumping. Just looking at those long, slender legs reminded him what they felt like wrapped around him. But he'd vowed to leave her alone while she stayed with him.

And if he didn't stop ogling her, he'd burn the second batch of potatoes.

CHAPTER THIRTEEN

WHERE ARE YOU, BITCH! Macy bolted upright in bed. Her nightshirt was slick with sweat and her heart raced as if she'd just run a marathon. *Just a dream. Only a dream.* She inhaled, filling her lungs with as much air as possible, then slowly let it out. No, a nightmare.

Only she was awake now and the man who'd attacked her was in the hospital under police guard. She blinked the sleep from her eyes and realized she wasn't in her own bed. She was at Rico's.

She was safe here. Safe with Rico. She lay back on the pillow and stretched her arms above her head.

The light filtering through the blinds told her it was morning. She heard a banging noise. Smelled coffee. Oh, no. Damn. She'd overslept. She got up, threw on a robe and checked to see if the bathroom was open. It was, so she grabbed her toiletry bag and hurried across the hall.

Rico's razor, shaving cream, toothpaste and toothbrush sat on a shelf to the right of the sink. A terry cloth robe hung on the back of the door. She brushed a hand against the fabric, then leaned closer, breathing in the clean masculine scent. Rico's.

Thoughtful, she went to the sink and set her toiletries on the empty shelf and stood back for a look. *This is what it's like to live with someone.* Sharing space. She liked the feeling. And yet…she was struck by intense loneliness. When she left here, she'd be alone again.

She needed a shower. *Stay in the moment, Macy.*

When finished, she pulled her wet hair into a ponytail and threw on white shorts, red T-shirt and her favorite flip-flops, and then headed to the kitchen, the rich scent of coffee teasing her nostrils. She stopped in the archway. Rico was standing next to the counter chopping something, and right then, her stomach growled. Loud.

Rico turned.

"Hey," she said. "Good morning."

"Good morning. I hope that sound I heard means you're hungry."

"Starved. But what I really need is coffee."

He poured her a cup. "Black. Right?"

"Good memory." She went over and took the cup from him, purposely brushing his fingers as she did. He smelled fresh from the shower himself, but his hair was dry, so he'd obviously awakened well before she did. "Sorry I overslept."

"No problem."

"What are you doing?"

"Chopping onions, peppers, cheese and ham. Can you eat an omelet?"

"I could eat a horse."

"Well, we don't serve that here. Eggs will have to

do." He poured some eggs from a bowl into a pan and hovered over it, spatula in hand.

"What about the food for the barbecue? What can I do?"

"It's all done. No help necessary."

The disappointment she felt surprised her. She'd wanted to help. But it was her own fault for getting up so late. "I'm sorry. I really wanted to…contribute."

He dumped the vegetables he'd been cutting on top of the egg mixture in the pan, and she watched as he flipped it over.

"There'll be plenty to do before the family arrives. Make hamburger patties, lemonade and Kool-Aid for the kids…."

"Okay. I feel better now."

He slipped the omelet onto a plate and set it on the table. Then he proceeded to make another. "Go ahead. Eat. Mine will take a couple extra minutes."

Sitting, she took a sip of coffee and waited for him anyway. "What time is your family coming?" Her stomach twinged at the thought. What was the big deal? These were people she would likely never see again. *Get a grip.*

"Sometime around noon. But with my family, you never know. Some come early, my parents usually, and the others dribble in. If we're ready before noon, we'll be fine."

Great. That gave her a few hours to get some things done at the office.

He slipped the other omelet onto a plate and sat beside her. "There's toast." He pointed to a plate already on the table. "And orange juice. Would you like some?"

She shook her head. "No thanks."

"Okay—then let's eat." He waited for her to take a bite. "It's good. I guarantee it."

She took a forkful, her taste buds salivating. "Mmm. You're right. It's wonderful."

Watching her, he seemed pleased that she liked it and then he dived into his own.

"I have to go to my office for a little while this morning, but I can be back in an hour or so to help."

"The office?"

"I need to get some things."

"Do you think that's a good idea? The place will be empty."

"I can't have you go everywhere with me, and I do have a job, I have appointments, court dates and clients need things."

"On a Sunday?"

"Well, no. But I'm behind."

"Can't you at least wait until we get a fix on the guy who attacked you? The detective on the case said he'd let me know as soon as the creep wakes up, and at the very least, we should know something tomorrow."

Again, he made a good argument. She wasn't all that comfortable about going to an empty building, either, but she couldn't just let everything slide. "It's possible that he just wanted to rob me and hearing me in the room, he decided to keep me quiet. Or maybe he just wanted to scare me. Like that note I received."

"Anything is possible. But until we know for sure, you're better off taking precautions."

She nodded. "You're right. If we haven't heard anything soon, I'll hire someone."

"Hire someone?"

"Yes. A bodyguard."

He thought for a moment, then nodded. "Yeah. I forgot you can afford to do things like that."

She didn't like the edge in his tone.

He finished his omelet, took his plate to the sink and stood there for a moment, as if reconciling something within himself. He turned. "Do what you need to do. But do it safely. That's my only concern."

A sharp ring of the doorbell interrupted them. "I'll bet that's my parents."

Macy's pulse quickened. "Already?"

"Finish your breakfast," he said and left to answer the door.

As if she could eat now. She heard their greetings and after a couple more bites, she took the dishes to the sink and was placing them in the dishwasher when Rico came up behind her. "Macy, I'd like you to meet my parents."

So much for going to the office. Macy wiped her hands on a towel and turned around.

"This is my mother, Josephine, and my dad, Mario." He smiled. "And this is Macy Capshaw."

The resemblance was there. Rico had his mother's sparkling eyes and Mario's big smile. Josephine, a well-endowed woman, immediately came over and hugged Macy, quickly followed by another hug from Mario. "We're so happy to meet you, dear," Josephine said.

Feeling awkward, Macy simply smiled and said,

"I'm pleased to meet you, too." Hercules hovered around Macy's ankles, so she picked him up. "And this is Hercules. Herc for short."

Josephine rubbed behind the dog's ears, commented about how cute he was, then turned to look at Rico. "What can I do? Or don't you need my help?"

"I always need your help," Rico said. "How about if Dad and I get things set up outside while you two finish here in the kitchen. Make the hamburger patties and lemonade, get out the chips and plates and all that stuff."

"That's it?"

"Mom, you're on vacation, remember?"

Mario gave her a look, too, the thick lines in his forehead deepening. "I keep telling her, but you know she won't sit down. She's always fussing over something."

"Go." Josephine shooed the two men out the back door, Hercules following as if he was one of the guys.

Macy was amazed at how quickly the pup had taken to Rico. Hercules hadn't warmed to her parents after four years.

"Well, there's not much for us to do, is there?" Josephine lamented. "But this place could use a little cleaning." As she was talking, Rico's mother went to the refrigerator and took out the hamburger.

Macy washed her hands, removed the chips from the bags, took out the lemonade, and searched for a pitcher to make the drinks. Josephine pointed to one of the cabinets.

"Do you visit Rico often?" Macy asked.

"Once a year. We like to take all the grandchildren to Disneyland and spend some time with them at the shore."

The shore. New Jersey-speak for the beach. "That's really nice." She couldn't imagine her parents doing the same if they'd had grandchildren.

"Maybe you and Rico will join us."

It wasn't exactly a question and before Macy could refuse, Josephine said, "But I know Rico will be too busy as usual. Too busy to come home to visit, too. It's that job." She enunciated the word *job* with distaste. "And I suppose he'll be too busy for Disneyland."

Oh, geez. Macy felt as if her own mother were talking. "I know how he feels. It's difficult to make time for both a career and a family."

Josephine rolled a lump of hamburger in her hand, pushing and shaping it into the perfect patty. "Working that much isn't good for anyone. Family is important. Very important." She smiled then. "Rico needs to settle down with a good woman. Have lots of kids like his brothers and sisters."

What could she say to that? I hope he finds someone?

"Macy," Rico called from outside. "Can you come here for a minute?"

"Excuse me," she said to Josephine and made a quick exit.

When she got close to Rico he whispered, "I thought you might need to be rescued."

Mario was cleaning the grill and they'd already set up extra chairs and small round tables near a very large redwood picnic table. Hercules leaped across the grassy yard like a gazelle, taking advantage of freedom from a leash. His personal nirvana. "Herc really likes the run of the yard, but I'll have to come out and pick up any messes before people arrive."

"I already did that."

"Really? That was nice of you."

He waggled his eyebrows. "I'm a nice guy. Glad you realized it."

How could she not.

"So, how's it going? My mom can be a little overwhelming sometimes."

"We were having an interesting conversation. I like her."

"No talk of me getting married? That's usually first on her list."

Macy laughed. "She did mention it."

"Well, just ignore all that and try to have a good time."

Just then another voice came from the house. "Rico, baby."

Macy looked up and saw a stunning woman with almost blue-black hair. Looking at her, Macy felt an odd sense of déjà vu. The woman seemed so familiar, but Macy couldn't think of where she might've seen her before. And since the family lived in New Jersey, it wasn't likely she had.

"Maria." Rico went over to give her a hug. "I'd appreciate it if you'd quit the baby thing. I'm not the youngest in the family."

She pinched his cheek. "But you're the cutest," the woman said, giving Macy a once-over as she moved rapidly toward her. "You didn't tell me you were bringing a date."

"This is my friend Macy Capshaw. Macy, this is my bossy older sister, Maria and—" Rico turned "—her husband, Tom."

Macy hadn't even noticed the man behind Maria.

"Have you told Macy you have a commitment phobia?" Maria said on her way to hug her father.

"Knock it off, Maria," Tom piped up. "Give the guy a break."

Macy's head practically spun listening to their banter.

"My big sister always knows what's best for everyone in the family. But that's just because she doesn't know what to do with herself now that she's celebrated her fortieth birthday and all the kids are in school or gone. Speaking of which, where are they?"

"They're coming with their *favorite* uncle," Maria needled.

Macy knew they were teasing each other, but she wasn't used to such kidding around and felt the odd man out. She couldn't think of a single thing to say and they'd probably all see her as some stuck-up prude. And after seeing Josephine's perfectly pressed skirt and blouse and Maria's fancy slacks outfit, she was pretty sure her short shorts and tank top weren't the right attire for this particular barbecue. Usually she was the one who overdressed.

"It's about time," Maria said glancing toward the back door. Macy saw three kids scoot down the steps, followed by another younger woman with dark hair and the face of an angel. With her, a blond man who towered over the rest of the group.

At Macy's side, Rico placed his hand at the small of her back. "This is Macy Capshaw, everyone." Then he looked at the smaller children. "And this is Anna, Tony and Michael." Rico touched each child's head as he said their name. "And the proud parents of this gang—" he made a wide sweep with his arm "—my middle sister, Angela, and her Viking husband, Eric."

"Pleased to meet you everyone," Macy said.

The dog bounded over and the little girl, Anna, squealed. Macy wasn't sure if the child was excited or frightened. "This is my dog, Hercules, and he really likes to play with children."

Michael frowned. "Hercules isn't a dog's name."

"Michael," Angela said firmly, "people can name their dogs whatever they want."

"Don't mind him," Eric said, shaking Macy's hand. Angela hugged her. By then, the children were chasing after Hercules and suddenly a half dozen other people burst through the door.

"Okay, everyone," Rico said holding up his hands, "I'm only going to do the intros once and then it's up to you. This is my friend Macy Capshaw, and the rest of this gang are—" he pointed to the new arrivals individually "—my sister Carly, the youngest and the only unmarried female in the group, my brothers Vinnie, Tony and Marco, and their wives, Nancy, Anne Marie and Delaney. The rest of these rug rats—" he pointed to four or five kids who'd already joined the others in the yard "—are my nieces and nephews, and you might get their names if they ever sit down."

Josephine came out the door. "Well, that's enough to confuse the poor girl for the rest of the day. Don't worry if you don't remember everyone's name, dear. I forget most of the time."

Macy smiled, realizing now where Rico picked up his protective nature.

"Macy has a mind like a steel trap," Rico complimented her.

"All right," the youngest brother, Marco, piped up. "Let's put her to the test."

Within seconds they'd all gathered around Macy. She felt trapped, but took a breath. "Okay, Marco—" she looked directly at him, then she turned and pointed to the person as she said each name.

"Amazing," Maria said when Macy finished. "The first woman Rico's dated who has a brain."

Rico glared at his sister. "And how would you know what kind of women I've dated?"

"I told her," another voice boomed from the back door and Jordan St. James sauntered over and gave Josephine a big hug. "Hey, Mama Jo. You look as beautiful as ever."

Josephine waved him off. Obviously he knew the family well. Macy knew Jordan and Rico worked together, but she didn't have any idea they were this close.

"You talking about me behind my back," Rico said to Jordan, not as a question but as a matter of fact, and then clapped him on the shoulder.

"Always." Jordan winked at Maria. The two men did the male bear hug thing, as if testing their strength against each other. She expected them to start butting chests any minute.

When they stopped, Jordan smiled. "Macy, nice to see you again."

"Where's the other Musketeer?" Rico's oldest brother, Vinnie, asked.

"Luke's on a call, but he'll stop by when he's done."

The rest of the afternoon and early evening went much the same way, everyone joking, eating and drinking. Everything was done as a group. Rico couldn't grill the steaks without Vinnie and his father telling him how to do it. Maria couldn't set the table quite the way Josephine wanted. And all the brothers and sisters chided Josephine and Mario about retiring and turning the business over to Vinnie, who'd apparently been working toward that goal for years.

Macy grinned. So much for Josephine's lecture on the evils of working too much.

Despite the fact that everyone in the family was as nice as they could be, Macy felt unable to participate. They seemed comfortable saying whatever they felt like to each other—the polar opposite of her family. With them, she'd had to weigh every word.

When Jordan went to one of the coolers and pulled out a beer, Macy edged next to him. "I'll have some of that wine while you're at it."

"How're you doing?" he asked. "This group can be murder on a newcomer."

"So I gather. I'm not sure what I should do. Try to blend in or just sit and drink a lot of wine."

Jordan laughed. "Hey, do what you always do. Schmooze."

Maybe he was right. While this wasn't the same event she was used to, she knew what to do in a roomful of strangers. She'd done it for years at home and then at all those charity functions she'd had to endure. While it went against her nature, she'd actually learned to be quite good at networking.

Watching Rico dazzle the children, she sat with Carla and chatted about the girl's major at Syracuse University. She admired Maria's outfit and Angela's hair. Rico bounced around much as she did, coming over to sit with her off and on, always asking how she was doing. When she gave a hand waggle of so-so, Maria, who'd been standing close said, "You mean you're not ready to give up everything for a life in the suburbs? Doing the same thing day in and day out? Be the chauffeur, cook, maid, baby-sitter and then switch to love goddess at night?"

Macy laughed. Apparently Maria had some issues being a stay-at-home mom.

Rico looked at Macy, as if curious to hear her answer.

"It's not even an option. I'm quite comfortable with my life."

Maria seemed a little tongue-tied by Macy's response, which was fine with Macy. When Rico left to go back to mingling, she did the same, finding Rico's brothers and his father, Mario, the hardest to get to know since all they talked about was sports.

When everyone finally left, somewhere around 9 p.m.,

Macy's jaw was sore from talking. She sat on the blue corduroy sectional in the family room and curled her legs underneath her, thankful that Rico's sisters had cleaned the kitchen already. "Your sister Maria looked so familiar," she said. "Something about her—I felt as if I'd seen her before somewhere."

Rico mumbled a response about everyone having those feelings now and then. He seemed agitated. Macy watched him go to the refrigerator for a soda, check outside to make sure the grill was off and there was nothing left to clean up. When he finally sank into the opposite end of the couch, he flipped on the television and clicked around from one channel to another.

It was almost as if he didn't want to talk to her—or be alone with her. "What's going on?"

He looked at her as if she had two heads. "What do you mean?"

"You're tighter than a vise, and you've barely said a word to me since your family left. Did I make some kind of major faux pas?"

His expression stilled and he clicked off the television. "You're right. I'm preoccupied. But not about anything you did. You were perfect as a matter of fact. And they all loved you."

"Well, what then?"

"I'm worried about tomorrow."

"Tomorrow? What happens tomorrow?"

"You tell me."

"Work. What else?"

He slid next to her, dead serious. "Since the man who attacked you is in the hospital, the police may not see a need to do anything. I contacted the investigating officer and requested a watch on your home. But you need to be cautious. At home and at work. The blues will make routine checks but they won't be around all the time."

She liked his concern. "I have to call someone to fix the door and replace the locks. I'll get a new security code, too."

He rested an elbow against the back of the couch, his dark eyes on hers.

"You don't have to go, you know. You can stay here as long as you want." His voice was soft, urging her to say yes.

She felt a ripple of excitement. But it was too tempting. Staying here was too comfortable. She wouldn't have a chance in hell of getting her life back to normal. Did she even want to?

"It would be safer."

"Thanks," she said quietly. "But I have to go home sometime." Home would be safer—emotionally.

He fingered a stray hair before tucking it behind her ear.

"It's a selfish offer. I'm enjoying the company."

His admission made her heart pinch. "I am, too," she said. "That's the problem."

He pulled back, obviously surprised. "That's a problem?"

She nodded. "Yes, it is. We're two people thrown together because of circumstances. We're attracted to each other, but…"

"Never the twain shall meet?" he finished for her and gave a wry smile.

"Something like that."

"Well, I like being with you, you like being with me, regardless of the circumstances, and yes, I'm attracted. Very much so."

Her pulse raced. "So what should we do about it?"

"We're adults. We can do anything we want."

He was right. Who said every relationship had to go somewhere?

"We can," she whispered. "We can do anything we want." Almost before the words came out, he kissed her. His hands were in her hair, and all the silent promises she'd just made to herself melted away like ice cubes in the desert.

Rico tasted the wine on her lips and felt as intoxicated as if he'd drank a whole bottle. But it wasn't the wine that made him feel that way. It was Macy. She was all the aphrodisiac he'd needed.

Right then he knew all those platitudes he'd just spouted were lies. He couldn't have a sexual relationship with her and not want more. He knew that as well as he knew how to collar a suspect.

Vaguely he heard the doggy door slap shut and was glad Hercules had gone out. He drew her onto his lap, his hands leaving her hair and working down to her waist. He wanted to touch her everywhere and everywhere he touched made him want more. His fingers felt on fire and he was suddenly acutely aware of everything about her, the softness of her hair, the sweet scent that was uniquely hers, the smoothness of her skin, the fullness of her lips.

He wanted her. Every part of her. He slipped his hands under her shirt, her smooth skin like balm on his. He unsnapped her bra and caressed her small but perfect breasts, only vaguely aware when she pulled off her top. As he deepened the kiss, she tightened her arms around him and gave him back even more. He wanted to be inside her. Make her his.

Excitement thundered through him, a rush like nothing he'd ever experienced.

Holding Macy in his arms, he stood and headed for the bedroom.

RICO WOKE FIRST. The early-morning sun shone through the blinds giving him a ladder of light to see by. He eased off the bed and looked at Macy, calm in sleep. She was beautiful, he thought, not for the first time. But it wasn't just a physical beauty. He liked how she fit right in with his family, how she didn't flinch at helping even though he knew she'd never done it before in her life. He'd made a 180 in his opinion about Macy Capshaw. She'd surprised him. Caught him off guard and found a place in his heart. And that was the biggest surprise of all.

He headed for the shower, quietly closed the door and turned on the water. As steam filled the room, he felt at odds with himself. He'd never been so drawn to someone. In the past, he'd always wanted to run the other direction when things turned serious. But this time, he wanted to keep her there with him. He wanted her to himself.

But she'd been up-front about what she wanted—or more to the point, what she didn't want—from the beginning. So what was his problem? Most guys would love the idea of a relationship without ties. Hell, that had been his MO most of his adult life.

So what was different now?

Two things he knew for sure. One was that Macy Capshaw would never give up all her comforts to live on a detective's salary—and he couldn't blame her. Two, he knew he'd never be a kept man. Both important points he couldn't forget just because he was in love with her.

In love with her. The realization made him feel as if he'd been hit with a knockout blow and was down for the count. He had no control over what was going to happen.

She was awake when he finished in the bathroom. "Good morning," she said as she stretched her arms, her body arching invitingly.

So much for the cold shower. "Good morning." He secured the towel around his waist and went to the closet for his clothes, pulling out a pair of jeans and a black Polo shirt. "I hope you slept well."

"For the first time in a week." She stretched again, then pushed to a sitting position, holding the sheet over her breasts.

"Well, stay in bed as long as you want." He grabbed his underwear from a drawer, dressed and took a sport jacket from the closet. "Just make sure you're careful. Don't go anywhere that isn't safe. Okay?"

"Aye, aye, sir." She gave a two-finger salute.

"Hey, I'm concerned about you."

"I know. I'm just giving you a hard time." He saw a teasing glint in her eyes.

He leaned over the bed and kissed her softly before he shrugged on his jacket. "Would you like some coffee?" he asked. It's made. There's stuff for breakfast, too, but I don't have time to fix it."

Surprise crossed her face. "I didn't expect you to. I rarely eat breakfast anyway."

"Now that's not good for—" He stopped midsentence. His sister Carly was right. He was *too* protective. "Never mind," he mumbled. "I have to go."

He started to walk away, but turned. "Here's a key, in case you decide to come back." Placing it on the table next to her, he added, "For whatever reason."

CHAPTER FOURTEEN

ALL THE WAY TO THE STATION Rico replayed the image of Macy sprawled in bed. It was true that she couldn't stay there forever and he couldn't protect her and still do his job. Pulling into the police garage, he saw Luke climbing from his Escalade. Luke always said he had nothing else to spend his money on, so he might as well enjoy his ride. He waited for Rico to park and they walked in together.

"Sorry I didn't make it yesterday. I got a good homicide."

Rico knew the feeling. While he'd teased Macy about never having fun, he was guilty of putting his job ahead of most everything else, too. "Anything on the cold cases?"

"All at different stages. Some are waiting CSU." Luke opened the door for Rico. "What's with you?"

"Nothing."

"You have a houseguest. That's something."

Rico looked up at Luke who only had an inch on him, if that, but his friend always seemed taller because he stood so straight. Military straight. "Temporary house-guest. She's going home today."

"Too bad."

"What do you mean?"

"All that money…" Luke gave a tsk-tsk sound and shot Rico a glance. "Hey, if you're not interested…"

Rico felt his blood pressure spike. Joking around had always been normal among Rico, Luke and Jordan, but Luke's humor seemed crude in reference to Macy. "She's not up for grabs," Rico stated. "So back off."

"Whoa. No offense meant, buddy." He followed Rico to his desk. "I mean it. I didn't know you were hooked."

He fell into his chair and drew a deep breath. "I know you didn't mean anything. Forget it. I'm just irritable. Not enough coffee."

"Not enough something," Luke muttered under his breath as he walked away.

Rico saw Jordan come in and bump shoulders with Luke on his way out. "Mary Beth gave me some information for you," Jordan said as he dumped a ream of papers on Rico's desk.

"The financial reports for Haven's Gate."

"What exactly were you looking for?"

"I don't know. Haven's Gate is a nonprofit agency, so the money has to come from somewhere and it has to go somewhere. I thought it might give me something else to go on."

"Maybe so. I took a look and—" Jordan flipped a couple pages "—and it seems the people who pay the medical care and other expenses are the adoptive parents."

"How much?"

"It's not defined. Just lump-sum deposits of several

million dollars per year. About a quarter of that is divided between Haven's Gate and another organization called Family Care Services, which could be the adoption agency."

"So the question is—where does the rest of it go?" Rico scanned the pages. Two numbered accounts showed a sizable amount of money funneled into both.

"For a nonprofit there's a lot of money that's not going back into the agency," Jordan said.

"Yeah. Let's get a trace on these two accounts. It's still within our purview. And I'll get the financial records for the other agency. They're probably nonprofit, too."

"Good. Anything on our guy in the hospital?"

Rico scanned the last sheet. "Not yet. AFIS was down for a while. And since I have to wait for the information to get here anyway, I'm going to interview some of the former residents."

Jordan scratched his head. "Yeah. But since the Ray case isn't on our priority list, we might want to pay attention to some of the cases that are."

Jordan was right. "Man, I'm sorry. I'll do this other stuff on my own time."

"Hey, I wasn't saying we shouldn't do it. I think you're close to finding something, and a case solved is a case solved, whether it's on the list or not."

"We? You keep saying *we* when you know I don't want you getting involved."

"I want to. I was on the old case, too. Remember?"

He could always count on Jordan to back him. Jordan and Rico were as close as Rico was with any of his brothers. Maybe even closer. Rico shook his head. "It could go nowhere. But if you want to help, maybe you can answer a question for me."

"Shoot." Jordan clasped his hands behind his head and leaned back in his chair.

"If you were going to find your biological mother, how would you start?"

Jordan looked surprised. "But I'm not."

"It's a hypothetical question."

His partner's eyes lit. "For Macy. Right?"

Rico didn't answer, but Jordan knew him too well.

"I'd register with every agency that lists parents and children who are searching for each other. I'd do an on-line search for anyone trying to find a child born on my birthday. If nothing showed there, I'd get the name of the adoption agency."

Jordan had obviously done some research on the subject.

"Then what? Adoption records are closed."

"Unless both parties involved agree to open them."

"You mean the biological mother and the adoptive parents."

Jordan nodded.

"And if the mother and adoptive parents don't agree?"

"You could hire an adoption investigator or find a way to let the biological parent know you're interested in making contact. And then the ball would be in the other court."

Rico knew the name of the adoption agency Haven's

Gate used. He wondered how difficult it would be to get information from them about how many babies they'd received for adoption from Haven's Gate on the date Macy's child was born. All he really wanted was the truth about what happened to Macy's baby.

"That's good information. Now let's get to work on the other stuff."

Jordan thought for a moment. "Yeah, well, I'm going to work on the Boling case. See if I can get some new results on the evidence collected at the time of the murder. I don't need any help for that."

"Thanks."

Rico spent the morning getting current addresses and phone numbers, then made calls and appointments to see three of the women he'd interviewed five years before.

On his way to Trudy Danko's place in Fullerton, he went over the facts in his head. The file showed that she'd left the facility the day before the kidnapping and one of the other girls had said she'd stood looking at the babies in the nursery for a long time. But her parents had picked her up right after that and took her home.

He located the address and went to the door. Though Trudy was willing to talk with him, after ten minutes with her, he was ready to climb the rafters. She'd had four more kids since her stay at Haven's Gate—all under five. She was fifteen then, which meant she couldn't be more than twenty now. But she didn't have anything new to add about Haven's Gate and what she did say was exactly what she'd said before. How did someone remember events in the exact details five years later?

LaVonne Smith and Terin Valetti were next. Holly Magruder was also on the list, but he hadn't gotten an answer at her place.

Three hours later, after his interviews with Smith and Valetti, he was sitting in his vehicle puzzling over the differences between the interviews today and the ones from five years ago. Every answer to every question was the same as five years before. He'd asked new questions about the doctor and the staff, and one woman's answer was almost the same as the next. As if they'd rehearsed. Had they talked to someone at Haven's Gate? Had they been coached? Paid off?

He looked at Holly Magruder's last address in Long Beach and decided to go even though he hadn't made an appointment. A surprise visit might get him a different response. He turned onto the freeway and headed down 210 to 405 toward the beach, glancing at his watch as he drove. It was getting late and he'd not heard anything from Macy. He punched in her direct office number.

"Macy," he said, relieved when she answered. "I've been trying to get in touch."

"Sorry about that. I had…a lot to do today. They fixed the door and the locks. I had a new security system installed, too."

Her voice sounded shaky, not firm and confident as he was used to hearing her.

"I didn't have time to get all my things out of your place yet. I'll come by to get the rest when I'm done here." She paused. "If that's okay."

"There's no hurry."

"Thanks. I appreciate your hospitality—"

"Why don't you stay another day or two?" he said. He could tell she was hesitant to stay at her place. Going there must've unnerved her. But would she admit it? Hell, no. "Just to get your bearings. It would be tough for anyone to go back to a place where—" He stopped. "Well, you know what I mean."

"I know what you mean."

"So you'll stay a little longer then?"

She didn't answer and he finally said, "I need to talk to you about some things anyway, so say you'll stay."

After another pause she said, "Okay. But I won't be finished here until about seven. And I have a lot to do that I didn't get done over the weekend."

He wasn't going to let her use that as an excuse. "Bring it along."

"I'll see you later, then."

"Good." He smiled, pleased with himself. He hadn't felt this good all day.

After talking with Macy, Rico was ready to go back to work and a half hour later, he pulled up to the building with the last address he had for Holly Magruder. He exited his vehicle and searched for the apartment number. The place was a wreck. Welfare housing was his guess. Finding number 228, he knocked and held his badge up to the peephole in the door so whoever answered would know he was there on business and wasn't a bill collector.

He heard a click, then another, and another. The door opened about three inches, held back by a chain lock.

An older woman, who looked as if she'd seen more than her share of bad days, peered out.

He held up his badge again. "Detective Santini. I'm here to talk to Holly Magruder."

The last lock slid off and the woman opened the door another few inches. "What did you say, Officer?"

"I'm Detective Santini. I'd like to speak with Holly Magruder. I talked with her parents five years ago about a case because Holly was in the hospital then."

The woman hesitated. "Oh, I remember. Her mother told me. Yes, Holly was in the hospital then."

"Right. I have this as her last address. Is she here now?"

She shook her head. "Holly's dead. Four years now."

"I'm sorry."

"Nanny, I want to go to the store now." A child's voice came from behind the woman.

"We will, sweetheart. In a little while."

Rico saw a child with dark hair pulling on the woman's housedress.

"My great-grandson," the woman said softly. "I take care of him."

The boy smiled and his eyes sparkled with mischief. He pulled back and hid behind his grandmother's legs.

"Holly's child?" Rico asked.

The woman shook her head. "No."

Well, that ended his afternoon of interviews, which hadn't netted him one shred of new information.

"Well, I'm sorry I bothered you," Rico said and went back to his car, which now had some tagger's artwork scrawled all over the side. Fortunately he still had tires.

He scanned the area for the perp but there was no one in sight. He wasn't surprised.

He swung the car around and headed back to the station. Most of the detectives on his shift were gone and the guys on the next watch were in the briefing room. He grabbed Chelsey Ray's file and headed back to his car, calling Macy while in transit. No answer. Odd. She said she'd be there by seven and it was now after eight.

He called Macy's office. No answer there, either. His adrenaline surged. He tried her cell phone. After five rings the recorder picked up. Damn. She should be there. Fear as he'd never felt before tightened like a vise around his chest.

"BILLY!" MACY CALLED OUT. "Where are you?" She rubbed her arms as darkness settled and the street lamps clicked on in the park, offering little light to find a missing child.

"Are you sure you checked everywhere in and around the house?" Macy asked Nancy Appleton.

"Joe and I looked inside and out. We've checked and double checked."

Macy's heart pounded. "Where would he go? Why?"

"He had a fight with Michael and I sent them both to their rooms. Later, when I called him for dinner, he was gone and the window was open."

"So if he left right away, he's been gone approximately how long?"

"Four hours or so."

Four hours. The boy could be miles away. "And when did you call the police?"

"Right after I talked to you. I didn't know he was gone until I went into his room." The woman wrung her hands. "After this, I just don't think I'm going to be able to keep him any longer. I'm going to talk to his social worker and see if she can find a different placement."

Macy stopped in her tracks, her anger flaring. "Billy is missing… He's five years old and he's out here somewhere all alone. We don't know if he left on his own or was kidnapped and all you can think of is yourself!"

Nancy looked away from Macy's accusing glare.

"If that's your attitude, then you damn well better not take him back or any other kids for that matter." Macy fought the urge to smack the woman. Finding Billy was more important.

Just then a squad car pulled up, lights rotating.

"Ma'am," one of the officers said. "We understand you have a missing child."

"He's a foster child," Nancy said.

"I'm the boy's court-appointed advocate. I came to the park because I took Billy here last weekend and he seemed to enjoy it."

"We live over there," Nancy said, pointing down the street.

Macy saw a couple of squad cars parked in front of the house.

"I know," the taller officer said. "We're getting information from your husband right now."

"What kind of information?" Nancy's eyes widened

and she had the guiltiest expression Macy had ever seen. "We didn't do anything wrong."

"I wasn't suggesting you did," the officer stated. "The information we need relates to what will help us in the search. Hair and eye color, how tall the boy is, what he was wearing. That kind of thing."

"Well, Joe is probably the last person to ask. He doesn't pay that much attention to the kids. Billy was wearing a red shirt, jeans and white tennis shoes."

"Then I'd suggest that you ladies go back home and give those officers that information, too. We'll put out an Amber Alert and hopefully we'll find him fast. It's better if you're at home in case he comes back."

"Okay," Nancy said and started walking toward her house.

Macy didn't move.

"Might be better if you go, too, until we determine what's going on."

"I'm not going anywhere," Macy stated. "Not until we find Billy."

She heard a faint ringing and remembered she'd put her cell phone in her purse. She pulled out the phone and recognized Rico's number. Lord, it was way past the time he had expected her. "Hi. Sorry I'm late."

"Late? That's an understatement. Where are you?" he demanded, anger vibrating in his voice.

"Billy ran away from his foster home and we're looking for him."

"Did you contact the police?"

"Of course. Several officers are here now. They'll

issue an Amber alert once they get the particulars. I'll be back when I can," Macy said.

"Let me talk to one of the officers, will you?"

Macy handed the phone to the closest cop. "It's a friend of mine, Detective Santini, LAPD."

While she waited, Macy scanned the area, noticing some tall shrubbery beyond the swings. Had she looked there yet? God knew she felt as if she covered the park shrub by shrub. But a little boy could be anywhere and if he was hiding, he could move around if he saw someone coming. She started toward the bushes.

"Wait a minute, Ms. Capshaw."

She stopped at the officer's voice.

"Here you are, ma'am."

She went back for her phone.

"Detective Santini asked me to tell you to stay put. He'll be here shortly."

"I'm just going to check over there." She continued to cross to the bushes beyond the swings. She was relieved that Rico was coming. They needed all the help they could get and she knew Rico well enough to know she could trust him not to interrogate Billy if they found him.

Reaching the bushes, she looked first for any sign that a child might've been there. Nothing. She searched underneath, around and behind the thorny branches. Nothing. Stumbling out from behind, she felt a strong hand steady her.

"Careful."

"Rico. I'm so glad you're here."

He held her briefly. "Where have you looked?"

"The house. The neighborhood within a mile and a half radius. Here at the park. Any place we thought he might go. Do you have any other ideas?"

He thought for a minute. "The bus depot?"

"But that's so far away and I don't think he'd even know how to get there. Why there?"

"Because that's where he was initially found. He's had several hours to figure out where it is and how to get there. If he was on the streets for very long when he was found before, he probably knows more about survival than you think he does."

Rico was right. "Let's go."

The next thing she knew, they were at the depot, checking the face of every child Billy's size, whether the child was with someone or not. After a quick sweep of the place, Rico went to the ticket counter and showed his badge.

"I'm looking for a boy. Five years old and he's alone."

"Dark brown hair," Macy added. "And he was wearing a red shirt, blue jeans and white tennis shoes."

The older man behind the ticket counter gave them a blank stare.

"Have you seen anyone who looks like that?"

"Nope. Kids aren't allowed to hang around without an adult."

Unable to conceal her disappointment, Macy's eyes welled with moisture. They'd simply wasted more time. She punched in the Appletons' phone number to see if Billy had come home.

"Yeah?" Joe answered.

"Joe, this is Macy Capshaw. Anything new?"

"Nope. And the cops say the longer he's gone, the worse the chances are."

Macy bit her lip. "Chances of what?"

She heard a deep cigarette cough on the other end. "The chances of finding him okay."

Words froze in Macy's throat. She knew the odds. She'd heard it more than once when other kids went missing. The first forty-eight hours are critical. "Thanks," she said. "We're going to continue looking and I'd suggest you do the same." She clicked off without saying goodbye, afraid her anger would grow into something unmanageable.

She glanced at Rico. "Nothing. They don't have a clue."

Rico suddenly grabbed Macy's arm. "What color did you say he was wearing?"

"Red."

Rico took off across the room, navigating the seats and the people sleeping on the floor, before disappearing into the men's room. Macy ran over, too, then waited. When he didn't come out right away, she decided men's room or not, she didn't care. But just as she reached for the door, it burst open and Rico came out with a child in tow.

"Oh, my God! Billy." Macy kneeled to hug him. "Oh thank God you're okay." She hugged him so hard she thought she might hurt him.

At the same time, she heard Rico making a phone call to the police.

Macy walked Billy to a bench and sat next to him. "What made you run away, Billy? We were so worried."

He looked down, chin practically resting on his chest. "I don't want to stay where I'm not wanted."

"Oh, Billy." She pulled him into another hug, but words cramped in her throat. What was she going to say. The Appletons care about you and want you to come home? "Why do you say that?"

"I just know it."

"Well, something must've happened. Something bad enough to make you run away."

"I was bad. They don't like me cuz I'm bad."

Her heart wrenched again. "Most kids do bad things once in a while, but that doesn't mean they're bad. And it's the parents' job to make sure they don't do it again. Discipline doesn't mean they don't like you. The Appletons were just doing their job, weren't they?"

He nodded, but she could tell he didn't believe it. He felt unwanted and if Nancy gave off the same vibes to Billy as she did earlier, she couldn't blame him. A child could tell when he was loved and when he wasn't.

"Why did you come to the bus depot?"

He kept his head down. "I thought maybe someone would look for me here."

"Someone?"

"My mommy or daddy."

Oh, Billy. Macy swallowed a huge lump in her throat and fighting back tears, she became aware that Rico was standing over her, staring at Billy. She remembered how desperately he'd wanted to see the boy.

"I think it's time to go home, don't you?" he said to them.

Billy's bottom lip protruded.

"Remember what we talked about, Billy?"

The boy nodded to Rico and then pulled himself up, squaring his tiny shoulders. "I remember and I can do it."

Macy trusted that whatever Rico said to the boy was the right thing. When they dropped Billy at the foster home, Nancy gushed over him, telling him she was so happy he was back. Macy didn't believe her act for a minute. It broke her heart to leave Billy there and first thing in the morning she was going to call his social worker to see if they couldn't work out a better placement.

"I see what you mean," Rico said when they were back at his house. "Billy couldn't be the Rays' child. He doesn't look anything like Chelsey Ray or the child's father."

She heard the disappointment in his voice. "They're still doing DNA and the results should be back soon. You never know."

"No. The minute I saw Billy, I knew in my gut he's not the Rays' child. You knew it, too. You said so."

"But I was only going on physical differences. Facial features. The eyes. The hair color. There's still a chance—"

"A chance he'll show up elsewhere, maybe. But Billy isn't the one. The case is as cold as it ever was."

"I'm sorry, Rico. I'm really sorry."

WHILE IT FELT GOOD to have Macy back at his place, Rico couldn't seem to shake his disappointment in finding out Billy wasn't Chelsey's child. For weeks, he'd pinned his hopes on Billy, which he knew now was a foolish thing to do. He'd lost perspective.

After a quick meal of Chinese takeout, Rico said he had work to do and went to his office. He needed time to think. Where did he go from here? As he sat there thinking, he felt a presence, turned and found Macy propped against the door to his office. "I'm going to do some work, too, but I wanted to tell you again how really sorry I am about tonight…about Billy and…everything. And to thank you for letting me stay here."

Everything. Damn. He'd been so preoccupied with his own disappointment, he'd almost forgotten all the other crap that was going on. He stood, crossed to the door and pulled her into his arms. "You had a tough night. A tough week. My disappointment is nothing compared to what you've been through."

Billy running away was only one of her problems. Probably the smallest one.

She pulled back. "What did you say to Billy today that made him want to go back to the Appletons?"

"Just a bunch of stuff about things not always turning out the way we want them to, but it's up to us how we deal with it. I said it's a big responsibility, especially for someone his age, and asked if he thought he could make the best of what he had to do right now."

She nodded. "That's good. I've said pretty much the same things, but he seemed to accept it better coming from you."

"Hey, us guys gotta stick together."

She smiled but just barely. "Okay, we both have work to do, so let's get cracking."

She was always on track, always proving herself. "Okay, but—" he glanced at the time "—only if you meet me in the kitchen at ten for a glass of wine."

She gave him a thumbs-up. "It's a deal."

Rico went back to his case file. Knowing that Billy wasn't Chelsey Ray's child instilled him with even more determination. Two hours later, he shoved the file to the back of his desk. Nothing. Nothing except the feeling the answer was right under his nose and he couldn't see it.

He went to the kitchen and was surprised to see Macy already there. The dog was curled up beside her on the couch. He opened the fridge, pulled out a beer and held it up.

"No thanks, I'd rather have a glass of wine if there's any left from the barbecue."

"Sure. There's more wine than beer. Chardonnay, Merlot and White Zin."

"Chardonnay is fine."

As he poured, she said, "I couldn't concentrate. What happened at my place affected me more than I was aware. I really am glad you convinced me to stay here." She worried her bottom lip. "I feel safer."

That she felt safe with him made him feel good. Better than good. He wanted her to feel safe—and protected. But did she feel anything else? "Is that the only reason?"

She took a sip of the wine he'd poured. "No. I came back because I don't think I can get through this alone."

He felt her need. She was the most stubborn, independent woman he knew. What had it taken for her to admit she couldn't do it alone? And where was her family? "You're not alone," he said. And he meant it.

If he hadn't gone to her office to find out about Billy, and then pressed the issue, she wouldn't have started probing into Haven's Gate in the first place. He couldn't discount the possibility that the threats and the break-in at her condo had something to do with the questions they'd been asking. Someone felt threatened, and it was up to Rico to protect Macy until he found out who it was.

"And there's the wine. That's another good reason for coming back."

He laughed. "And if the stock we have on hand is any indication, you'll be here for a while."

"And the sex. I came back for the sex."

He smiled at her bravado, trying to make light of a serious situation. As much as he wanted to make love with her tonight, he knew that wasn't what she really needed. She needed someone to hold her. Someone to make her feel safe and secure. And that's exactly what he was going to do.

CHAPTER FIFTEEN

IN THE MORNING, Macy stretched out and felt for Rico on the other side of the bed, but he was gone and Hercules was in his place. "Hello, sweet puppy dog." She ruffled his hair. "You kinda like it here, don't you, having the run of the place, going outside whenever you want." Hercules licked her nose and made her giggle. "I understand. I kinda like it, too."

Not good. Not good at all. She'd worked all her life to get to the place where she didn't need to depend on anyone emotionally. But being here with Rico made her realize that all she'd done was cut herself off. From loving. And despite her fight against it, she'd fallen in love with Rico.

Surprisingly, she didn't care.

Together right now was good enough.

Macy heard the phone ring and then Rico's low voice. She couldn't make out the conversation and decided it was time for work anyway. After a quick shower, she threw on her court ensemble, a black pinstriped suit and a deep lavender blouse, all the while ticking off in her head the things she had to do today.

Call Karen Creighton right away. Appear in court with Ginny Mathews who was certain her husband was going to violate the protective order. And knowing him, he might. She felt so sorry for that woman. For all she knew, Aaron Mathews had hired the man who'd broken into Macy's condo. He wanted his family back and had made no secret that he thought Macy was the one standing in the way, egging his wife on to get a divorce.

But those things were peripheral to getting the answer to the question plaguing her. What happened to her child? She'd tried calling her parents in Paris, yesterday and the day before, but couldn't make the connection.

She sat on the edge of the bed, picked up the phone for one more try. When she heard a click, her blood rushed. But it was only the answering machine. "Please call me," she said, then cut to the chase. "I need to see my child's death certificate. If you won't help me, I'm going to have his body exhumed. I'll be at the office today. Call me there."

When she finished, her heart was pounding like a jackhammer. Maybe she should go back to her parents and go through *all* her father records, her mother's, too, if she had any. Search everywhere. In fact, her resolve bolstered, she might go over there first, before doing anything else.

That settled in her mind, she picked up her small purse, stuffed it into her overflowing briefcase and went to the kitchen. Rico was standing at the counter and handed her a cup of coffee. "Sleep well?"

"I feel great. And I'm ready to get back into the fray."

He leaned against one of the bar stools, his expression serious. "I received a call from the hospital. The guy is still in a coma."

Macy slid onto the stool next to him. "Isn't there something else the police can do?"

"It's not my case, so I don't know all the details of what they've done except send the gun to CSU and the guy's prints to AFIS. We should know today if he's in the system."

"What if he's not in the system? What if he never comes out of the coma? We'll never know what he was doing in my condo or why. Maybe I'll call the officer in charge and find out what else they're doing. There has to be a way to identify him."

"You can call, but they might not be able to tell you everything. In an ongoing investigation there are always details that can't be released to the public."

"So, we just sit and wait?"

"And hope he wakes up soon and wants to confess."

"It's hell waiting for all this stuff to be processed. I'll remember to be more considerate when my clients get upset with waiting."

"Unfortunately, it's the way things actually work."

"Slowly," she added.

"Yep. And now I've got to take off."

"Me, too. Do you think it's okay for Herc to stay here today?"

"Mi casa, su casa," he said with a smile.

"WE HAVE A HIT on the adoption agency and the other two accounts," Jordan said to Rico, who was on his way to headquarters.

Rico switched his cell phone to the other ear. "Good stuff?"

"I'll let you be the judge."

"I'm on my way." Rico clicked off and gunned the engine onto the freeway. Finally, a lead. He knew it was good information by Jordan's voice. Jordan rarely got animated.

At the station, Rico saw a couple beat cops on watch. Since the bomb scare, the department had been taking precautions. He hoped Macy was doing the same. He'd asked for a house watch on both her place and his. He thought of calling her to be sure she made it to her office okay, but that would be acting like a mother hen again. He called anyway. She wasn't there yet, so he left a message.

On his way to his desk, Rico passed Jordan and clapped him on the shoulder. "Okay, buddy. Let's see your stuff."

A tower of papers sat on Rico's desk.

Rico set his thermal coffee mug down and leaned over the pile, one hand on each side, reading from a standing position. "Selena Burns, alias Betty Sells, alias…Sally Brighton? Sally Brighton is the director of the adoption agency *and* Haven's Gate?" He whistled in surprise, then tensed with the rush that always came when he was on to something.

"The woman has a long record of fraud and bilking senior citizens out of their money." Jordan came over to stand beside Rico. "She worked at a nursing home previously and was under suspicion for some missing jewelry and cash that belonged to the residents. She was also the beneficiary for two of the people who died there. But no convictions. And from what I can gather on the adoption agency, they farm out the adoptions to different attorneys."

"Anyone we know?"

"Don't know. It's coded so that all the money filters from the agency to Haven's Gate and back to the agency again. Probably to pay the attorney. Look here. Here the code is W.C., then it changes after that and later goes back to the code W.C."

"Yeah." He studied the sheet and saw the money going to the agency with the code W.C. spanned a five-year period, two years before Macy had her baby and three years afterward. The same time Wesley Capshaw was on the board of directors at Haven's Gate. Something else caught his eye. "Dr. Dixon is also on the board of the adoption agency."

"It gets even stickier. Get a load of the AFIS report underneath this one."

Rico picked up the papers and read the name. Herbert Burns.

"Look at the photo."

Rico flipped to it. Excitement coursed through him, the kind of excitement he always felt when he had his suspect dead-on and was about to make a collar. "Our guy in the hospital." He read some more. Military background. Explosives expert. Dishonorable discharge. He looked at Jordan. "That's it. We can nail him."

"Read."

Rico's skin prickled as he read on. Married three

times. Third wife, Sally Burns. Oh, man! "This is big. Big enough to have someone taken out if they got in the way." With all the evidence coming down on Haven's Gate, he regretted that he hadn't found a way to make a connection with the Ray case. "Has Brighton been to the hospital to see him?"

"No visitors."

Rico immediately called Judge Goldberg to get a search warrant for the Burns' house, and while he waited for it to come through, he had some other business to take care of. Business he couldn't get out of his mind.

On the road again, Rico replayed the conversation he'd had with Macy after they'd found Billy. Something she'd said put him on alert. He'd racked his brain all night for the answer—and came up with nothing. Nothing except the same gut feeling that the women he'd interviewed were hiding something.

The information about Burns and his wife was simply another piece of the Haven's Gate puzzle, of which there appeared to be many. He wasn't sure how they'd all fit together. Or if they even did. But how did any of this relate to Chelsey Ray's baby? He'd been hoping one thing would lead to another, but now he felt as if he was going backward instead of forward.

The thought sparked another idea. *Going backward...* He had to go back. But what if he was wrong?

MACY PULLED FARTHER into the drive at her parents' home so that her car wasn't visible from the gate or street. She hoped this wouldn't be another lesson in futility. What possible reason would her father have for being so secretive about her child? She'd gone along with keeping it a secret from others, but the thought that he wouldn't even give *her* any details was absurd. She was the child's mother, for God's sake. And that baby was the only child she was ever going to have. She deserved to know how he died.

An hour later, she knew she wasn't going to find a thing. Her father was too thorough. She felt weak and listless as if all the air had been sucked from her lungs.

She shoved the papers back into the files and tried to straighten the mess she'd made. There wasn't one file she hadn't gone through. She'd started in her mother's room and then gone back to the library. She sagged in the chair at her father's desk staring at the blinking message light on the phone. She'd noticed it when she came into the room.

Her father's business never quit, not even when he was away. Or maybe it was one of her earlier messages that he'd never answered. She pressed the button, ready to erase it if it was. Then an oddly familiar voice said, "Stop her, Capshaw. Do something, and do it now!"

Stop her? Do something? Who was the her in the message? A client? It seemed strange that someone was ordering her father to do something. She remembered how divorce cases among the wealthy were always bitter and messy. Still, Wesley Capshaw never took orders.

None of her earlier messages were on the machine,

which meant her father must've retrieved them—and chosen not to call her back. Why had she ever thought he would? Hoped he would.

She swallowed back the lump in her throat. She wasn't going to let this get to her.

Still curious about the odd call, she pressed caller ID. The voice had been familiar, but the number wasn't one she knew. She wrote it down anyway and stuffed it in her purse.

When she was finally back at her own office, she made all her other phone calls and was happy Karen Creighton willingly agreed to find another placement for Billy. He'd have to stay where he was for the time being, but as long as the change was in progress, Macy felt better.

Then she made one more call—to the number on the paper she'd copied in her father's office.

One ring. If the caller was one of her father's clients, the call was confidential and she shouldn't be doing this. Two rings. Okay, she'd hang up once she heard who it was. Or she'd just say she had the wrong number. Three. Just as she was about to hang up, she heard a click.

"Dr. Dixon."

Her heart thumped. *Dr. Dixon* was the one who'd threatened her father? Had the message been about her?

"Hello? Is someone there?"

Well, she'd wanted to talk with him before. Now was the perfect opportunity. "Uh, yes. Hello. This is Macy Capshaw, Dr. Dixon. Wesley Capshaw's daughter in case you don't remember."

It took a moment for him to respond. "What can I do for you?"

"I've been trying to get in touch with you about my stay at Haven's Gate. I'd like to know if your agency ever filed a death certificate on my child and what was the cause of death?" she blurted, getting it all out before he could refuse to talk to her. "And I'd like to know why you and your staff lied to me about Carla Monroe's baby." She wanted to ask about her record, why someone had blacked out the part about her child's birth, that the child had been born healthy and she wanted to know what happened. But then she'd have to reveal how she'd gotten the information. If she did that, she could not only get Danielle fired, but her own ethics might be on the line with the bar.

"I'm sorry, I don't know what you're talking about. I only sign the certificates. My director takes care of the rest. And I don't remember this Monroe person."

"She stayed in the same room with me. She had her baby the day before I had mine. She told me recently her child had been stillborn."

"I'm sorry, I don't recall. But rest assured, we take the very best care of every mother who comes through here. If there are problems it's usually due to poor prenatal care. Now I have an urgent call."

"Two stillborn babies within twenty-four hours isn't something anyone would forget. Especially not the physician who delivered them. And even if that were the case, you have records and I want—"

The phone clicked off on his end. Stunned, she sat

there holding the receiver. It wasn't one of her father's clients, but Dr. Dixon who'd called and left the cryptic message. The only thing she could conclude was that probing into her child's fate was a threat to him. The blanked out records were proof.

Listening to the droning of the dial tone, she suddenly felt as if her brain had been put on hold. She couldn't think of what to do next. But as she placed the phone in the cradle, she knew she had to tell Rico.

Only she had less than an hour to prepare for a court appearance, which made her even more irritated when the phone rang. She pressed the intercom and said abruptly, "I can't talk to anyone now, Cheryl." Macy pressed the no-call button.

But the intercom flashed again and wouldn't stop. "Yes, Cheryl, what is it?" she said too sharply.

"Ms. Capshaw, there's someone here to see you."

"I know we didn't schedule an appointment right now because I'm due in court."

She heard a muffled sound, then Cheryl said, "He says he doesn't need an appointment. He says he's your father."

Macy almost snorted a mouthful of coffee onto her desk. Her father? Here? He was in Paris with her mother. What on earth…had something happened to her mom? "Send him in and please call the court to say I'll be late."

God, she hoped nothing was wrong, but maybe that's why he hadn't returned any of her phone calls. He was on his way back because something had happened. Fear swept through her.

The door to her office jerked open and her father stood in the opening.

"What happened? Is it Mother?"

"No."

Something was wrong. He wouldn't come back from Paris just to visit her. She tried to appear casual, but it was tough when adrenaline was thundering through her veins like a freight train. "Well, then. To what do I owe this pleasure?"

That sounded rude. She shouldn't be rude, but when he hadn't bothered to come to her office since she'd opened for business almost two years ago, she didn't feel too many warm fuzzies about his coming now.

He shut the door behind him. "Don't start, Macy." He crossed the room to the window, his critical gaze making inspections on the way. "You wanted to talk to me, so I'm here."

"But…what about Paris? Where's Mom?"

"We came back early for a variety of reasons. You being one of them."

"Me?" Had he heard about the man who'd attacked her? Had he come back from his beloved Paris because he was concerned about her?

"Yes, you. You're getting into things you shouldn't be, and I'm warning you, it could be dangerous."

She bit her bottom lip so her disappointment wouldn't show. "Dangerous for whom?"

"I'm telling you to stop this incessant investigation into Haven's Gate. You can't change things now, so let well enough alone."

The message on his answering machine. *Stop her.* Dr. Dixon had ordered her father to stop her efforts to find out what happened to her child, and here her father was doing what Dixon asked. Warning her to back off.

Heat scalded her cheeks. She launched to her feet to face him. "What can't I change, Father? The fact that I don't know what happened to my baby twelve years ago? The fact that the records after his birth were blacked out to hide that he'd been healthy? There's no death record for my baby anywhere and you think I should just forget about it!" Her voice rose an octave with each word. "I want to know what happened to my child, dammit! All I need from you is the truth. If someone was negligent and caused his death after he was born, I'll deal with it."

He stared her down, just as he'd always done. But she wasn't going to be intimidated ever again.

Then, maybe with the realization that he wasn't going to stop her from finding out what she wanted to know, he let out a long breath. "I did what I thought best at the time. What's done is done."

Moving forward, she stood toe-to-toe with him. "That's the problem. I'm the child's mother. I need to know what happened."

"I did what's best for you."

Her body started to shake. "You know, with every fiber of my being, I don't believe you. Maybe I'd feel differently if I thought you cared one iota about me. You do what's best for you."

Just then the door opened and her mother charged in.

Macy closed her eyes, her emotions as raw as a piece of meat. "All I want is the truth. Tell me the truth and let me deal with it."

Sarah glared at Wesley, her arms crossed and her feet planted firmly. "Tell her, Wesley! You owe it to her."

Surprised at the vehemence in Sarah's words, Macy's head started to pound. Her mother shouting at her father. Disagreeing. That just didn't happen.

"Tell her now or I'm leaving you." Sarah turned to face Macy. "I'm sorry for all this, sweetheart. I know apologies don't fix anything, but I didn't know until it was too late. And then it seemed—"

"W-what? Too late for what?" Macy felt powerless as if her world was spinning out of control.

"Too late…to get the baby back," Sarah said.

Macy's mouth fell open. "Back? From where?"

"Tell her, Wesley, you spineless bastard," Sarah spat out. "I'm not going to let you destroy Macy as you did me."

Her father looked as if he was preparing to give a sharp retort. But he just stood there, his face getting redder by the second. He stormed from the office, Sarah right after him. Macy hurried to catch them, then stopped. She reached out, hands flat on the wood of the door to hold herself steady.

Get the baby back?

She stumbled back to her desk, her hands trembling and her heart beating erratically.

After a few minutes of staring into space, tears blurred her vision and then huge gulping sobs came from so deep inside she thought she might die from them. She buried her face in her hands and rocked back and forth, crying until she couldn't cry anymore.

"I REALLY NEED TO GET IN TOUCH with her," Rico pleaded with Cheryl. He'd left three messages and still no return call. "It's important. Urgent."

"I'm sorry, I don't know where she is. Her father and mother were here, and a while after they left, Macy went out without a word. She was supposed to be in court—"

"I thought her parents were in Europe?"

"They came back."

Okay. That meant Macy was safe. And he was glad to hear Macy's father had returned. He had to talk with Wesley Capshaw about his role in the adoptions at Haven's Gate. If the shelter was part of an adoption ring and Capshaw had been one of the attorneys who arranged the adoptions, how much did he know about what they were doing? Was he part of it? At the very least, he might be able to shed some light on what was going on.

Hanging up, he saw the captain staring at him. He went back to completing his reports from the day before.

"Everything okay?" Jordan asked.

"Yeah. Fine." Rico couldn't get into the details with his partner yet. Before he even talked to Capshaw, he had to settle something with the mothers who were at Haven's Gate during Chelsey's stay.

Knowing people were sometimes more willing to testify when they knew they weren't alone, he'd decided to get all his witnesses together. By noon, he'd contacted five of the women and they'd agreed to come in the next day. As he hung up from the last call, he looked up to see another woman standing in the doorway. Macy.

He raised his chin, indicating she should come over, but she shook her head. He rose from his chair and crossed the room toward her. As he came closer, he saw her eyes were red and puffy and the pain etched on her face sent all his protective instincts into overdrive. "What's wrong? You didn't get more threats, did you?"

"No. Can we go somewhere to talk? Outside maybe?"

"Sure. There's a little balcony garden a couple of floors up."

"As long as it's private."

He led her to the elevator, his hand at the small of her back. He wanted her to know that whatever it was, he was there for her. They rode to the fourth floor in silence, and walked out onto the balcony. "This okay?"

Macy nodded, but didn't say anything. It was almost as if she couldn't speak or didn't know where to start. He took her hands, led her to one of the chairs and then sat next to her, still holding her hands.

After a deep breath, she stated in monotone, "There's no reason to continue trying to find out what happened to my child."

He pulled back, surprised.

"I know what happened. My mother told me." She pushed to her feet. "I had a visit this afternoon from my parents."

"They're back early." He stood, wanting to touch her, but she edged away.

"Yeah." She gave a wry laugh. "You know, today was the first time my father has been to my office and he came because he wanted to tell me to quit probing into Haven's Gate. He said it was dangerous."

"He came back from Paris for that?"

"Ironic, isn't it. Well, at that point, I lost it and said some things about the missing birth certificate and the medical records, and then my mother came in. She was acting in a way I've never seen before, shouting at my father to tell me. And then it came out that my child hadn't…wasn't…stillborn."

Rico took a deep breath, stepped closer and rested his hands on her shoulders. "Are you okay?"

She nodded. "As okay as I can be after hearing something like that." She waited a moment and then said, "You don't seem surprised."

He wasn't, but he couldn't tell her that. "Did your mother say what happened to the baby?" He'd suspected all along the child had been adopted.

A tear fell on Macy's cheek and he raised a hand to brush it away.

"No. They were angry and stormed out of my office. I tried calling them at home and on their cells but didn't get any answer. I can only assume the baby was adopted."

"Did you sign adoption papers?"

She shook her head.

"Well, if that's the case, someone else had to." And

he had a pretty good idea who it was. Wesley Capshaw. If he was working as the adoption attorney for the shelter at the time, Capshaw would know exactly what happened to Macy's baby—and many others. Rico's gut churned at the thought that Macy's father, any father, could do this to his own child and then lie about it.

What some people did to the people they supposedly loved was unbelievable. Unfortunately, he saw it all the time in his job.

She paced the small balcony like a caged animal. "I imagine my father signed the papers. I was underage and I'd agreed to do it when I first went in. Then I changed my mind. Papers relinquishing all rights to a child must be signed after the mother leaves the hospital. I thought my child was dead—never relinquished anything."

She took a deep breath. "So, I have to get the name of the adoption agency used by Haven's Gate."

He could only imagine the hurt she'd feel if she knew her father was more than likely involved in the actual adoption. And for Macy's sake, Rico hoped to hell Wesley Capshaw had no knowledge on anything else that was going on at the facility.

"I need to find my child. He has to know I didn't just give him away like a sack of old clothes."

"He may not even know he's adopted."

"I *have* to find him, Rico. And I think you have probable cause to get a warrant to search the adoption records at Haven's Gate."

Even if there was probable cause, which he doubted, it had to be the worst idea she'd had. "Adoption records are sealed and it would take an act of God to get them." And doing that could screw up everything he'd put together on the case. Not only that, he'd seen the heartbreak of a child finding a parent who didn't want anything to do with him. If the child didn't know he was adopted, it might work in reverse for Macy and she'd be hurt even more.

"I don't think it's wise, Macy. This is between you and your parents."

Her eyes filled with disbelief, her voice soft. "You won't help me?"

She nearly broke his heart. "I can't help you. And I don't think you should pursue finding the child. This is your desire, not his."

She jerked away from him. "You don't know that."

"You're right. I don't. But I do have experience with adopted children finding their parents and I know how it can disrupt lives and lead to heartache. I know because—"

"Don't, Rico. Don't say anything more. You want to play God with other people's lives just the same as my father. Your experience doesn't mean a thing to me."

Her breath hitched and the look in her eyes said if he couldn't support her in this, he'd betrayed her every bit as much as her father had.

"I don't think we have anything more to talk about." She banged open the door and ran to the elevator.

Before he could reach her, the doors shut in his face. And for the first time in his life, he despised the part of him that always had to do the right thing.

CHAPTER SIXTEEN

RICO WAS ON A MISSION. After stopping for a coffee refill, he found LaVonne Smith's place and banged on the door four times before a husky bald guy answered.

Showing his shield, Rico said, "I'm here to speak to LaVonne."

"LaVoooonne," the guy yelled. "Some cop is here to see you."

The big guy left Rico waiting at the door. LaVonne was the only one of the girls he'd called who couldn't make the group meeting later today. When she appeared several minutes later, hair mussed and wearing a pink robe, he knew she'd just rolled out of the sack.

"Can I come in? I'd like to clear something up regarding our previous conversation."

The woman backed up, wary, yet she motioned him inside. "It's a little messy."

"No problem," he said, doing his best to put her at ease. He sat on the couch.

"Did I say something wrong before?"

"No, not at all. I just wanted to make sure what I heard is what you meant. I have a couple other questions, as well."

"Okay."

"You have a pretty good memory for something that happened five years ago."

The girl hesitated. "Uh, I guess I just remembered it like it was yesterday."

He took out his notes from their previous interview. "Here's what you said the other day." He went on to read her answers to each question, then asked. "Did you see anyone near the Ray baby before he was kidnapped?"

LaVonne looked at him blankly.

"Your answer the other day was, 'I didn't see anyone, except Chelsey.'"

"That's right."

"Originally, you said you didn't see anyone but Chelsey talking to Sally Brighton."

"Uh, I guess that's what I meant."

"What were you doing by the nursery when you saw Chelsey?"

The girl looked confused. "Chelsey and I were talking. Then she talked to Sally."

"What were you talking about?"

"She didn't want to get rid of her baby."

"I understand. How did you feel about having your baby adopted?"

LaVonne's eyes opened as wide as frisbees. "I didn't want to but I couldn't do anything else."

"Were you given any other choices?"

She shook her head. "No. I didn't have any money. They paid for everything and they said if I couldn't pay them back, I had to do it."

He nodded. "Did you willingly give up your child?"

She frowned, shifted in her chair nervously. "That's why I was there."

Okay. Wrong question. "Who referred you to Haven's Gate?"

"The doctor I saw at the free clinic."

"Dr. Dixon?"

"Uh-huh. He said Haven's Gate could help me through the pregnancy because I had no money."

"Were you planning to give your child up for adoption?"

"Not at first, but the counselors said it was a good thing for my baby."

"Did you feel coerced?"

"What do you mean?"

"Did they convince you not to keep your child?"

Her gaze went to her lap where she was twisting the ties on her robe into knots. "It was better for the baby. I know that now."

Rico took a long breath. "Thank you, LaVonne. I appreciate your help. I only have one more question. Why didn't you mention any of this in the other interviews?"

"No one asked."

No one asked. *He* hadn't asked. He'd thought he'd done everything by the book. They'd been so focused on the baby being taken by the father that they'd glossed over anything else. An agency that coerced mothers to give up their children might do anything to cover up other things. A kidnapping. An illegal adoption.

"The other young women who stayed with you at the

time said they were paid by someone to tell the same story they did the first time. Is that what happened to you?" It was a lie, but he had to know her story before he talked to the others.

LaVonne's panic reflected in her dark eyes.

"It's okay, LaVonne," he said softly. "The others are willing to testify that they were coerced to give up their babies. Can you do the same thing?"

Tears brimmed in her eyes.

"Nothing bad will happen to you. We'll make sure of it."

"But I took money… and they said I'd be in trouble if I breathed a word to anyone."

"Who gave you the money?"

"The lady who runs the place."

When Rico finished with LaVonne, his spirits soared. He had probable cause for a warrant to search records at Haven's Gate…and the adoption agency. Maybe. He'd have even more if the other women corroborated LaVonne's story. Yeah, he'd lied to LaVonne, but he'd gotten his answer and, more importantly, he had a case.

With an hour before the interviews, he decided to see Holly Magruder's grandmother again. Five years ago, he'd talked with the girl's parents. But since Holly had later lived with her grandmother, maybe the woman knew things the parents didn't. He knocked several times and was about to leave when the door opened a couple inches.

"Yes," the old woman said, squinting through the small opening.

"Mrs. Magruder, Detective Santini. I was here the other day."

"Oh, yes."

"Can I come in for a minute?" He pushed the door a little, not wanting to take no for an answer.

She opened it the rest of the way. "Might as well."

The place was small, one room that was a combination kitchen and living room. Dingy curtains hung at half-mast over the only two windows in the place. The woman didn't look well.

"I remember you," she said directing him to sit at the kitchen table. "I remember you because I thought you were nice. And I thought maybe you wouldn't put a sick old lady in jail."

"Now why would I do that?" He tried to smile but it didn't come off.

"Because I helped Holly."

"You mean before she died?"

"When she came home with the baby. She'd been in the hospital you know, that crazy people hospital, and when she brought him home she couldn't take care of him. So I did."

His records showed Holly had given up her child.

"When Holly got sick, she told me the boy she brought home wasn't her son. She said it was her friend's baby and she'd taken him to help."

It took a moment for Rico to realize what the woman had actually said. He fought to control his reaction. "Are you saying she had someone else's child?"

"She said she was helping a friend. She didn't want

me to tell her parents because they'd make her give the baby away. I loved her and I didn't know what to do. She was really sick all the time." The woman touched her head. "Up here. It wasn't her fault."

Rico's hands shook. "When did she do this?"

"I don't remember. It was after she came home from that place that took her baby away, but before she was put into the crazy hospital. I had to take care of Adam while she was in the hospital."

"You didn't tell anyone?"

She shook her head. The lines in her face seemed deeper than when he came in. "If anyone knew, they'd keep her at that hospital and I couldn't care for such a little baby any longer."

"How long was she hospitalized?"

"I don't know. A couple of days maybe."

Rico's head swam. This was surreal. Holly wouldn't say she'd taken someone's child for no reason at all. Even if she was mentally ill. Or would she? What about the grandmother? Maybe she was lying. But why?

"When she came back she took real good care of Adam. She loved that boy. When she died I just kept on. I thought about finding his mother, but I didn't know who she was and the boy doesn't know anything else. He only knows me as his Nanny. He'd be scared with someone else."

His emotions vacillating between excitement and disbelief, Rico asked, "Where is he now?"

"Preschool. Head Start it's called."

"When does he get home?"

"My neighbor will be dropping him off in a few minutes. I don't drive," the woman said absently. "It's hard for me to do things for him now, and I'm worried about what will happen to him if I... You're not going to arrest me, are you?"

Rico took a calming breath. This boy could be Chelsey's child. But he couldn't get his hopes up again. Just because Holly had taken someone's baby didn't mean he was any closer to solving the case. For all he knew, the woman was making the whole thing up to get someone to care for the boy.

A knock at the door caused Rico's lungs to constrict.

"That's him," the woman said. Trying to get up off the couch, she didn't make it before the door opened slowly and a young woman poked her head inside. "Granny, are you there?"

Rico lurched to the door. "Yes, she's here." And as he stood there, a little boy bounded past him to hug his grandmother. Rico's heart stalled.

"Adam, this nice man is here to talk to us." The boy turned.

A boy with a mop of dark brown hair—and sea-green eyes.

RICO'S HEAD FELT as if it was going to burst. Finding out that the Magruder boy might be Chelsey's baby and then doing back-to-back interviews with the other young mothers from Haven's Gate had him so preoccupied, he'd made a wrong turn. He didn't want to get too excited, but he couldn't help it. He turned off at the next exit and circled back to 405 heading north to Hollywood.

He focused again on his conversation with Evelyn Magruder. While he felt ninety-nine percent certain he'd finally found Chelsey's child, he couldn't be sure until tests were taken. A quick trip to social services had given him some sense of relief. Everyone was willing to work together because they understood that if the tests showed a positive match they'd have to transition Adam to his real parents with care. Ripping the boy from the only home he'd ever known would be traumatic.

Macy had said the same thing about Billy, and he'd been too bullheaded to understand.

He'd been shocked at the grandmother's tale…he was still shocked, and he wasn't about to say anything to anyone until he had proof. He could only imagine Chelsey's disappointment if it turned out to be a false lead.

If it was true that Adam was her son, he'd finally be able to close the case. Five years too late, but they'd have closure—not only for Chelsey, but for him.

It didn't let Haven's Gate off the hook. The situation surrounding Macy's baby and his other suspicions about illegal adoptions had to be put to rest. He was going to start with a visit to Wesley Capshaw.

Twenty minutes later, he pulled into the circular drive of the Capshaw estate, surprised that the main gate was open. Climbing the steps in front, he was met at the door by Macy's mother. She seemed flustered and not too happy to have an unexpected visitor. "Rico. What a surprise."

He'd wanted the element of surprise when he talked to Capshaw, so the attorney didn't have a chance to come up with some story to cover his ass. "Hello, Sarah."

"Is Wesley expecting you? He didn't say anything to me." She looked away. "But then he's not talking to me much lately."

"No, he's not expecting me."

"Is this about Macy?"

"In a way." Rico took a step inside. "Can you tell him I'm here?"

"Yes, of course. I'm just leaving anyway."

Rico saw some suitcases stacked by the door. "Another trip?"

"You might say so."

Before Rico had a chance to ask, she disappeared and he could hear her telling her husband he had a visitor. Wesley Capshaw emerged from a room off the foyer as Sarah hurried up the curved staircase. "It was nice seeing you, Rico."

Capshaw stood in the doorway to the room, an imposing figure. "Rico. To what do I owe the pleasure?"

"It's business, I'm sorry to say. Can we talk privately?"

"Of course. Come in." The older man motioned Rico into the library and closed the door. "Have a seat."

His nerves were as taut as a tightrope and the last thing he felt like doing was sitting. But he did anyway, getting right to the point. "I need to ask you about Haven's Gate."

Capshaw scowled. "Have you been talking to Macy?"

"I have, but that's not why I'm here. I want to know about your involvement with adoptions during a five-year period when you worked with the Family Services Adoption Agency used by Haven's Gate."

The briefest hint of surprise flashed in the man's eyes. He sat in the chair beside Rico. "You know, that was a long time ago."

"Seven years to be exact. Do you want me to tell you the specific time period?"

Capshaw shrugged. "I handled private adoptions for the agency for a period of time. Lots of attorneys do private adoptions."

"I'm aware of that. Dr. Dixon is a friend of yours, isn't he?"

"A former friend. We've had limited contact since I did the work for the shelter."

"Did you know he referred girls from the free clinic to Haven's Gate and they in turn worked with the adoption agency?"

"No, I wasn't aware of that. It makes sense, though. What's your point?"

"The point is that I have several women willing to testify that they were coerced into giving up their babies. Did you know anything about that?"

"Never heard a thing. I was only involved after the decision for adoption had been made. Sometimes the agency found viable parents for the unwanted children and sometimes I did."

"Viable?"

"People who wanted the children and who could afford to take care of them. Believe me, the children who were adopted through Haven's Gate have much better lives than they would have had staying with their biological mothers."

Rico tensed at the condescending tone, the superior attitude. "Does that include Macy's child?"

Capshaw's expression didn't change. "Yes, that includes her child." His voice was cold, matter-of-fact.

"It's too bad Macy doesn't feel the same way." Damn. He hadn't intended to get into this.

"Macy doesn't know what's good for her. Never did. She's too emotional and can't see the real picture."

"But as the mother of the child, adoption's a decision she should make. Not you."

"I did what was best for my daughter and I don't see how this is any of your business."

Undaunted, Rico went on. "It's my business because many of the adoptions you signed off on were illegal. Macy's included."

Capshaw scoffed. "You'll have to prove it."

"I have witnesses."

"If you're counting on the statements of a few street sluts, I could blow holes in their testimony in seconds. I'm afraid your evidence wouldn't hold up in any court."

"I didn't say anything about who the witnesses are."

"I said *if,* Detective. My answer was hypothetical."

The guy was good, and Rico had no doubt an attorney of his caliber *could* blow holes in the character of some of his witnesses. But he wasn't going to let him get away with what he'd done to Macy. "Does Macy know you're the one who arranged the adoption of her child?"

"Of course not. And she never will."

"She will if I tell her."

Capshaw leaned back in his chair, a slow smile forming. "Okay. I get it. How much do you want?"

Rico clenched his fists. Anger suddenly burned like fire in the back of his throat. "Odd as it may seem to you, Capshaw, I'm here to see justice for all those mothers who had their babies illegally adopted. I'm here because I care about Macy. She needs to know the truth."

"Nice altruistic sentiments, Detective. How much do you want?"

"Twenty-four hours. That's what I'm going to give *you* to tell Macy the truth. If you don't, I'll tell her." It went against everything he'd just told Macy about seeking out her child. If he did what he was threatening, he'd be giving her the exact information she'd need. Man. His stomach churned. It didn't matter what he did, each action had bad consequences.

Ultimately the choice wasn't his. Macy had to know about her father's involvement. That would give her access to the name of the adoption agency. What she did with the information was up to her, not him. He could only hope she'd do the right thing.

Wesley Capshaw was on his feet. "She was seventeen. She didn't have any idea what taking care of a child would be like. She only wanted to keep the baby to spite me, to remind me of the worthless kid who'd fathered the child. She still doesn't know what it's like to be tied down with a responsibility you never wanted in the first place."

Bitterness edged Capshaw's words, and Rico knew the man was talking about himself. Was that why she felt she never measured up? Had her father let his own bitterness affect his relationship with his daughter? The thought sickened him.

"Twenty-four hours."

"You can't blackmail me," Capshaw sputtered.

"Twenty-four hours or I'm telling Macy about your involvement at Haven's Gate and the adoption of her child." He paused, then added, "And if the same information gets leaked to the media, don't be surprised."

MACY PICKED UP HERCULES well before Rico was due home and headed back to her condo. Rico couldn't know the emptiness she'd felt for twelve years believing that her child had died. The knowledge that she'd never have another made it even worse. Now, finding out her son was alive—and out there somewhere— changed everything. There was no way she could simply ignore it.

If she'd willingly given her baby up for adoption, it would be different. But she hadn't. Other people had taken the decision from her. She'd never forgive her father for that.

She stood in the hallway of her condo, still hesitant about going back. Opening the door, her pulse quickened. A vision of the attack flashed in her head and she couldn't move. She could hear her heartbeat in her ears. But the new alarm system was installed, the door had been replaced and the cleaning people had taken care of the rest. Still clinging to Hercules, she forced herself to take first one step and then another. Reaching the living room, she glanced around furtively. Everything *was* the same. She let out a breath of relief. Everything was fine. *She* was going to be fine.

She stopped by the door to the guest bedroom where she'd spent the night with Rico. Despite the circumstances that had brought them together, her short time with him had been the most wonderful experience of her life. He'd opened her eyes to how normal families lived. Made her realize how narrow her world had become.

An all-too-familiar ache of loneliness enveloped her. How could something so perfect end so badly?

It wasn't really a question because she knew the answer. The fact that she couldn't have children wasn't negotiable. It wasn't something she could even tell Rico, because although she'd only known him a short time, she knew him well enough to know he'd probably say it didn't matter. Only it wouldn't be his choice. She knew how important choices were—and she knew how much he wanted children.

If he gave up his dream for her, he'd eventually come to resent her. She knew that as well as she knew family law—she'd lived with that kind of resentment all her life.

The door buzzer sounded, sending her heart to her throat. Who knew she was home? Who had the security code to get upstairs?

On the fourth ring, she went to the door and peered out the security hole. *Rico.* She hit the intercom. "Yes?"

"Macy, it's Rico. I need to talk."

She just stood there.

"I need to talk to you in person."

Her hands shook as she let him in.

"Are you okay?"

"I'm fine, thanks." Keeping her distance, she motioned for him to sit. She took the chair across from him.

If she remained distant, she wouldn't get caught up in other dynamics. "I went over to your place and brought my things home."

"I gathered that when I found no one there. But I can't say I didn't have a few moments of concern."

"I left a note."

"I know. I found it."

"I'm sorry if I worried you. I received a call from Officer Malloy. He said they'd had a positive ID on the guy who attacked me and he felt it was safe for me to come home. Did he tell you that?"

The soft, attentive way he was looking at her cut to the bone.

When he didn't answer immediately, she realized his visit wasn't just to check on her.

"Yes. We have an ID."

"Officer Malloy didn't say who the man was or why he was here. Do you know?"

"They're still looking into it, but they have a pretty good idea."

She wrung her hands together. "What is it?"

Now he was looking everywhere in the room but at her. If he had something to say, he was having a hard time doing it. That was so unlike him.

When he finally looked at her, he said, "If there was a leak, it could ruin our investigation."

"A leak? How would that happen?" It was a stupid question, she realized. She'd shown him more than once that she had no compunction about doing what she thought needed to be done. She lifted a hand. "Don't answer. I'm sorry my methods don't meet your expectations."

His eyes shot to hers. "That's not it at all. This has nothing to do with my personal expectations. And as far as those go, all I expect is respect and honesty." He stood, turned away and raked a hand through his hair. "The ID on your burglar shows that he's married to a woman named Selena Burns. That just happens to be one of Sally Brighton's aliases."

Macy's mouth fell open. "Sally Brighton has an alias? She's married to the man who broke in here? No." She shook her head. "That can't be right. If the man who attacked me is Sally's husband—" Macy abruptly stood. "Do you think Sally was behind the attack because I was getting too close to finding out what happened to my child?"

He nodded. "Yes, but that's not all. We have reason to believe Dr. Dixon and Sally Brighton have been running an illegal adoption ring. For a long time now."

"Oh, my god." Macy took a step in one direction, then another. Finally she managed, "Do you have proof? Do you think that's what happened to my child?"

Rico was torn. If he told Macy the whole story, told her about her father's involvement, that he'd been the adopting attorney, she'd be deeply hurt. It would also give her carte blanche to find her son. She might do something to screw up the rest of the investigation.

But she'd find out anyway once they arrested Dixon and Brighton, wouldn't she? "Have you heard from your father within the past two days?"

She barked out a laugh. "No, and I doubt I will. Why?"

Rico took a deep breath.

"There's more, isn't there?"

"Yes. The department is going to reinvestigate the Ray case. It turns out that many of the young women who went through Haven's Gate believe they were co-erced into giving up their babies. I believe we have enough evidence to make an arrest."

Her face lit up. "Does this mean you have the name of the adoption agency?"

"I do, but...I can't give that to you."

A muscle twitched in her jaw. He saw her hands clench into fists. "Then why are you telling me all this?"

Dammit. Because he couldn't keep something so important from her. "Because I know who can give you that information."

Her gaze narrowed. "Who?"

"Your father. He worked for Haven's Gate as their adoption attorney during your stay there."

The shock on her face made him want to snatch back the words. *She didn't know.* He thought she might've suspected her father was involved since she knew he had to have signed the adoption papers. Wrong. Rico reached out to her, but she pulled away.

Shock switched to incredulity, incredulity to anger and then rage. She rounded on him. "You've known this all along, haven't you? You've been investigating Haven's Gate based on the information I gave you and you couldn't trust me with what you discovered—even knowing my son had been illegally taken from me!" She shook with anger, her eyes wide with disbelief. "I can't believe this is happening." She sagged into the chair and covered her face with her hands.

He knelt in front of her. "I didn't keep anything from you that could be shared. Hell, I shouldn't be telling you this now because we haven't made any arrests yet. But if I'd told you before we had all the information to nail these people, and it got out, I never would have had a lead on the Ray case."

Macy's hands dropped to her lap. "You didn't trust me."

"I couldn't take the chance. I gave you more information than I've ever given any civilian."

She looked thoughtful, as if just realizing something. "Did you say you have a lead on the Ray case?"

He nodded. "I think so. We're waiting for the test results. I haven't told the child's parents yet, because I know how disappointing it would be if this kid turns out not to be their son." He leaned back, sitting cross-legged on the floor.

"How did you find him? Did Haven's Gate have something to do with it?" Her voice was an even monotone, as if her anger had faded—or all the fight had gone out of her. She slipped from the chair to the floor and sat next to him.

"No, but information on the old case is what led us to him. *If* it's really true."

"I hope it's true. I can only imagine the mother's joy if it is." She looked down.

He realized that as happy as Macy was that he might've found Chelsey's child, she wished it was her own son who'd been found. Her hands were trembling, and he wanted to engulf her in his arms, to comfort her. He wanted to tell her everything. But he couldn't. Her father had to tell her the rest.

"I'm sorry about your father, Macy. Sorry I had to be the one to tell you."

She stiffened. "So why did you?"

He looked into her eyes. "I thought you needed to know." And because he loved her and couldn't bear to see her unhappiness.

Leaning forward, elbows on her knees, she seemed to struggle for words. "I appreciate your telling me about my father—even though you think it's wrong for me to want to find my son."

He took her hands. "I don't think it's wrong for you to want to find him. That's natural. But I don't want to see you get hurt."

Rico rubbed a hand against his chin. He'd never told anyone, except Jordan. "My sister Maria had a child when she was sixteen. She gave the baby up for adoption. It was a girl. Eighteen years later, the child decided to find her biological mother. She said she was pregnant and needed her family's medical history. The girl found Maria, but my sister had a new life. Her husband and children didn't know anything about the child she'd had."

"And?" Macy asked expectantly.

"My sister rejected her. Maria didn't want anything to do with the girl. She especially didn't want her husband and children to know. Heartbroken, Maria's daughter found me, hoping to make some kind of family connection."

"Was she pregnant?"

He nodded, his words choking in his throat as they came out. "I referred her to Haven's Gate. Chelsey Ray is Maria's daughter. My niece."

"Oh, Lord." She slumped forward, forehead against her raised knees. After a moment, she sat up and flipped her hair back. "That's why Maria looked so familiar. I saw the photos of Chelsey in the case file. Maria and Chelsey have the same unusual eye color."

"Yes, and it was your feeling of déjà vu that had me thinking in different directions. When I interviewed the grandmother of one of the girls who'd been at Haven's Gate, the woman was taking care of a little boy, and I noticed something familiar about him, but I couldn't put my finger on it. I realized later, it was the eyes. He had the same green eyes."

Macy slid next to him and took his hand. "You referred your niece to Haven's Gate. That's why you felt responsible for the baby's abduction."

"Logically I knew I wasn't responsible, but I carried it with me every day. In addition, I broke the rules. I shouldn't have worked the case, but no one knew she was my niece. I was too close and I screwed it up."

"Knowing you, I doubt you screwed it up. But now I know why you were so adamant about seeing Billy."

He nodded. "For all the good it did me."

"I'm sorry. If I'd known—"

"Nothing would've changed. You had a job to do."

"Like you."

He felt as if something significant had just passed between them. Understanding. Forgiveness.

"So, what happened with Chelsey and Maria?"

"Nothing. It's sad. Maria didn't want a relationship with Chelsey—she didn't want her family to know. Chelsey was heartbroken, but after a while, she accepted it. I see her once in a while, but not often. She's happy with her own family, and now, if this works out, she'll be even happier."

"It'll work out. I know it will." Macy was quiet. "So it won't bother you then that there was no DNA match for Billy?"

He gave a wry smile. "I knew when I saw him there wouldn't be."

She leaned back, her weight on her hands behind her. "I had a message from the social worker that a woman called today to say she thinks she's Billy's aunt. I hope it's true. He's such a precious boy, he doesn't deserve what he's been through. No child does."

"Yeah," he agreed, emotionally spent. Hercules

jumped into his lap. "Hey little guy." He rubbed behind the dog's ears. If Macy disappeared from his life, he'd never see Hercules again. What an odd thought. But that's when he knew he couldn't let that happen.

"So, where do we go from here?" Macy said on a long breath.

She was talking about the case, but he took the opportunity to change the subject. "You could come back to my place."

She frowned. "Am I still in danger?"

"No, you could come back because you want to. Because I want you to."

Macy pushed to her feet. She rubbed her forehead as if she might have a headache. "Please don't do this, Rico. I can't. Not now."

He stood, too, and gripped her shoulders so she had to look at him. "I love you, Macy. We'd have lots of things to work out, but I think we could do it."

Macy's breath hitched. She couldn't let this go on. God knew, she wanted more than anything to spend the rest of her life with Rico. "There are things that can't be worked out, Rico."

"Anything can be worked out if we love each other. If you love me we can do it. If you don't, then it doesn't matter."

What could she say? He didn't know all the facts, and if he did, he'd probably say things he'd regret later.

"Do you love me?" he asked.

Tears blurred her vision. She loved him so much she hurt. She should tell him she didn't love him and be done with it. But she couldn't bear to hurt him that way. Finally she said, "Yes. I love you."

He started to smile.

"But love isn't enough."

His hands fell to his sides. When he spoke his words were chill. "Not enough for what? Is it the money? You can't imagine a future with someone beneath you?"

"Oh, God." She turned away. "That's so far from the truth it's laughable. I live in my grandfather's condo and the office I use also belongs to him. The money I receive from my trust supports me, and the money from my cases goes right back into the business to help people who can't help themselves. And I'd give up every penny I have if it made one iota of difference to us. But it doesn't."

He ran a hand through his hair, his frustration obvious. "If it isn't the money, what is it?"

She had to tell him or he'd always wonder what he'd done wrong. "A few years ago, I had an ovarian infection that left me sterile."

He stared at her, blank.

"I can't have children, Rico."

"That's it? That's why you don't want to spend the rest of you life with me?"

She nodded.

A big smile preceded his response. "This is too funny."

"Excuse me?"

He led her to sit on the couch. Placing his hands on her arms, he said, "Why do you think I haven't gotten married?"

"Your mother says it's your job."

He shook his head. "No, what do *you* think?"

"You told me you haven't found the right woman."

"That's right. And the right woman is you. I don't care about having children. I care about you."

"You said…that you wanted a houseful of children."

"I always say that. In my family, that's the expectation. Everyone believes I'll follow the Santini tradition, and it's always been easier to go along with it. Yes, I've used my job and all kinds of excuses for not getting married, but I can't do that anymore."

His eyes locked with hers. "I can't do that anymore because I met you. I love you and I want us to have a future together. Kids or no kids. Don't get me wrong, I love kids, but I don't need them."

Despite Rico's words, Macy shook her head. "It's so complicated. When a person gives up something and it's not his choice, resentment is bound to creep in."

He blinked. "I don't have an answer for that. I can't predict the future." He frowned suddenly as if he'd just realized something. "That's why it's so important for you to find your son. Isn't it?"

Macy took a wobbly breath. "He's the only child I'll ever have and he's out there somewhere. I need to know if he's happy. Let him know I didn't give him away."

"There are ways to do that without disrupting his life. You can register with an agency that reunites biological parents with children who wish to be reunited. Someday he may contact you and then you could tell him."

"Or he may not be interested."

"That's a possibility. You could also write a letter to him and ask your father to give it to the adoptive parents. They could decide whether to give it to him or not when he's older."

"Like that would ever happen."

"Just a thought."

"I see you've done some research on this."

"A little."

"I could also get the name of the adoptive parents from my father and go see him myself."

"You could."

But he didn't think she should. "Why are you telling me all this when you think it's so wrong?"

"Because I love you," he said without hesitation.

"And that's worth going against your principles?"

"You were right. What you do is not my decision to make. And I also believe you'll do the right thing."

CHAPTER SEVENTEEN

MACY SAT IN HER CAR and stared at her parents' home. The mausoleum where she'd spent half her life. She wasn't as confident in her own judgment as Rico seemed to be.

Even though he'd said he loved her and would be happy without children, she couldn't let him make that sacrifice. It would mean living under the specter of resentment for the rest of her life. She'd done that for too long already. She didn't see any way to resolve the issue.

She had to see her son. And her father had the information to enable her to do that. Boosting her courage with the mental image of what her boy might look like now, she stepped from the car, walked up the steps to the front door and rang the bell.

Did her son have Jesse's dark hair and eyes? Or was he blond and fair like her? It was hard to imagine.

"Macy, I'm so glad you're here." Hillary, the housekeeper, practically pulled her inside. "Your mother packed her things and left. She said she was going to a hotel and would call you later."

"She left? By herself?" Macy didn't know what

planet she'd just landed on, but it wasn't one she recognized. "Why?"

"She said she could no longer live with your father and she was going to make a new life for herself."

Macy didn't know whether to laugh or cry. Her mother was the most helpless person she knew. She sure could understand her mother's feelings, but why now? She'd lived the same way for thirty years.

"I know it's not my place to say, but frankly I'm worried about her."

"It'll be okay, Hillary. I'll check on her." Macy tried to calm the woman who'd worked for her mother since before Macy's parents were married. "Is my father here?"

The housekeeper motioned toward the library.

"Thanks. I'll call you later after I hear from my mother." Then she marched into her father's study without knocking.

Wesley was sitting at his desk. He jerked his head up when she entered, obviously surprised to see her. She was surprised by him, too. He was unshaven, his clothes looked as if he'd slept in them, his hair was unkempt and the room reeked of alcohol.

She'd never seen him like this, not even on weekends when she was growing up. But whatever was happening between her father and mother wasn't as important to her as getting the truth about her child.

"I came to get the name of the couple who adopted my son."

Wesley leaned back in his chair, raising one hand in a weak dismissal. "Your mother's gone. She's left me."

"I know. And if that's what she wants, I say good for her. I want the name of the people who adopted my child."

"I can't give you that."

"Why not? Would it be unethical?" She couldn't keep the sarcasm from her voice. "I'm sorry but I think you crossed that line twelve years ago."

Wesley pushed to his feet, went to the bar and poured himself another drink.

"I'm going to get it one way or another, even if I have to get the media involved."

He downed his drink in one swallow, swaying a little as he did. "Don't threaten me, Macy. It didn't work with your detective friend and it won't work for you."

Detective friend? Had Rico talked to her father? "What do you mean? What won't work?"

"Blackmail. Your detective said he'd do the same thing if I didn't tell you the truth. But like everyone else, he was blowing smoke. Keep this up and you'll be sorry."

"I'll be sorry! Why? What are you going to do to me? You gave away the only child I'll ever have, so anything else pales in comparison."

After refreshing his drink, Wesley grunted, resigned. "I can't do it because it would ruin everything I've worked for. It would destroy me—beyond what your mother is trying to do."

She walked over and placed her hands on the desk in front of him and leaned forward. Keeping her voice even, she said, "I don't give a damn about you."

"You'd better leave or I'll call the police."

Macy felt cold. Very cold.

"As far as I'm concerned, you're no longer my daughter.'

She straightened, shoulders back. "Was I ever? When did you ever make me feel I was important to you? When did you ever tell me you loved me?"

"I did everything for you and this is what I get for it. Well I'm done. You won't see a penny of my money."

She crossed the room to leave, then stopped and looked back. "You know, that's really funny. Because you never did anything for me except tell me how I wasn't good enough. Nothing I ever did was good enough for you." Her veins pulsed with wasted anger and hurt and bitterness.

"I never cared about the money! Ever. And it's all you cared about. You didn't care about Mother or me. I hope Mother takes all the Delacourt money and leaves you penniless."

"Get out!"

"Gladly. You're pitiful and I'm ashamed to say you're my father." Macy walked out of the room, her heartache burning like fire in her gut. All her life she'd hoped that someday her father would tell her he loved her.

At the front door, Hillary stopped her.

"Take this," the housekeeper said and handed her an envelope. Macy's name was on the outside in her mother's scrawly handwriting. "She told me to give this to you."

Macy sat in the car and took a paper from the envelope. Blinking back tears, she read her mother's apology for keeping such an important thing from her and that she hoped someday Macy could forgive her. *I know this won't make up for anything, but I finally found this in-*

formation. Reading on, Macy's heart literally stopped at the next sentence. Oh my God!

Her mother had written the names of the people who'd adopted her child. And Macy knew why her father would be ruined. Her mother also listed the school her child went to, the church they attended—and her son's name. *David.* Her son's name was David.

Her throat closed. Tears streamed unchecked down her cheeks. She crumpled the paper to her chest. *Thank you, Mother. Thank you, God.*

MACY DIDN'T KNOW what to do first, but after a few hours of indecision, she found herself on the road to Santa Barbara, her pulse racing.

Arriving at the middle-school playground, she parked and sat in her car watching several boys playing kick ball, searching their faces for something familiar. Would she recognize him? Would he look like her? Or Jesse? Her hands were clammy and her stomach churned. If she saw him, what would she say? What would she do?

And then—there he was—and all her questions were answered. He looked like Jesse, only he had her blond hair and fair complexion. He was tall for twelve, like both her and his father. Lord, he was the most beautiful boy she'd ever seen.

This was her son. The boy who'd been given away without her knowledge. She wanted to shout, to tell him she loved him and make up for all the lost time.

My son. My son. Love swelled inside her. A mother's love.

As she sat there, the ball sailed out of bounds and bounced against her fender. Without thinking, she got out of the car, picked up the ball and held it until the boy came over.

Her son. Her beautiful son.

"Thank you, ma'am," he said politely. "I'm sorry, I hope the ball didn't damage your car. We'll pay for it if it did."

Macy felt as if she was frozen. She couldn't stop staring at his face. "Uh, no." A cool gust of wind flicked a long strand of hair into her face. She reached up and pushed it back. "Don't worry about it. It's fine."

He looked at her strangely. "Do I know you?"

Her hope blossomed.

"Are you one of the new teachers?"

One of the teachers. As if she couldn't be anything else. "No—no I'm not. I…uh, was looking for an address and stopped to look at my map."

"Well, thanks again," the boy said. And then he was gone—back to the playground—and she stood by the car door, knowing she couldn't continue watching him or someone would think she was a stalker. Yet she couldn't tear her gaze away.

He was so beautiful. He was her son.

Finally, she got back behind the wheel. He seemed happy. Really happy. Quickly, before he left, she took out her digital camera, zoomed in and snapped four shots.

Just then a car pulled up in front of her and a man climbed out. She recognized him immediately. Senator Hadly. The boy ran over and gave his father a handshake-type hug, the kind guys give so they don't look like sissies. As they talked and laughed, she could see the camaraderie—and the love between them. Then the boy tossed the ball to his dad and they climbed into the big black sedan and drove away.

Macy watched until the car disappeared, then closed her eyes against the gut-wrenching sense of loss. He was her son. But he wasn't. He had her genes and Jesse's genes. That was all.

She drove home like a zombie, barely noticing the lights or signs. Inside her condo, she paced, unable to work, unable to think about anything except what had happened today. Rico. Her father. Her mother. *Her son.*

And in the end, one significant thing remained. Rico had said he loved her. And she loved him.

She didn't know what she could do about it, but with everything else gone, she couldn't let that go, too.

RICO CALLED FOR BACKUP as Jordan climbed from their unmarked car in front of Haven's Gate, a surprise visit to Dr. Dixon and Sally Brighton on their agenda. They went in together.

The receptionist's eyes almost bugged out of her head. "We're here to see Dr. Dixon and Sally Brighton."

"I—I don't know if—"

"Call them," Rico ordered.

The girl picked up the phone. "There's some officers here to see you, Dr. Dixon. And they want to see Mrs. Brighton, too."

Within seconds, Dr. Dixon appeared with Sally Brighton at his side. "Gentlemen, what can I do for you?"

"You can turn around and put your hands behind your back. You're under arrest for tax evasion."

Jordan cuffed the two while Rico gave them their Miranda Rights. Tax evasion was the only thing they could legally charge them with at the moment and make it stick, but that was only temporary. They had a whole list of charges they were working on. Including kidnapping and running an illegal adoption business under the guise of a nonprofit association.

"People from social services will be here before long," Rico said to the receptionist. "They'll help the residents find other accommodations."

After booking Dixon and Brighton, Rico and Jordan headed for the bar. But after two beers, Rico said, "It's time for me to split."

Jordan looked surprised. "Stick around for a little while. Luke and Tex are coming by."

Rico tried to smile. "I see them every day."

"Well, do you have something better waiting at home?"

Jordan had him there. No, he didn't. He had nothing to go home to—no one. "I've got a date with my couch and the TV. I like it that way, and it's better than listening to you rowdies all night." Yeah. Who the hell was he kidding?

So he stayed. But even after four beers, he couldn't stop thinking about Macy. He was surrounded by his best friends—and still, he'd never felt so alone. "I'm out of here."

"You're not going to drive are you?"

"No." He handed his keys to Luke, who wasn't drinking because he was on call.

In the car, he cranked up the music so he wouldn't have to talk or think anymore. But when they pulled into the driveway at his house, all bets were off.

"HI," MACY SAID when Rico walked in. Her nerves hummed under her skin, her apprehension impossible to contain.

He stood at the door, glanced first at her and then at the suitcases sitting in the hallway. Without a word, he walked over, picked up her luggage and carried it down the hall, apparently to the bedroom. She hoped.

She was sitting on a bar stool in the kitchen when he came back.

He stood next to her. "I'll get us something to drink."

Hercules wiggled and she let the dog down. Her emotions were still on high frequency and she couldn't keep what had happened today to herself. "I saw him, Rico. I saw my son." She hoped she'd see understanding in his eyes. When she didn't, she said, "His name is David. He's a beautiful boy. He's tall and blond."

He handed her a glass of white wine and she took it gladly, her fingers trembling.

That's when she noticed how tired Rico looked. Drawn. And she felt partially to blame for pulling him into such a mess. Still, she had to tell him.

She took a sip of wine, moistening her lips with its sweetness. "But…" She cleared the lump in her throat.

"Only he isn't my son. I know that now." Tears suddenly choked off her words, yet she kept talking because if she didn't, she'd fall apart. She might anyway. "I know the people who adopted him. Isn't that ironic? They're good people. Important people. No wonder my father said it would ruin him if anyone found out." A fact that meant nothing to her. She didn't give a damn whether her father was ruined or not—but she did care about her son's happiness.

"When I saw him, how happy he was, I knew biology didn't mean anything compared to twelve years of love and caring." Her voice faltered. "I'm not his mother, Rico, no matter how much I want to be."

He looked at her, sympathy in his gaze, but he didn't move to comfort her. "Are you okay with that?"

She closed her eyes and felt a warm burn behind her lids. Getting control, she said, "I—I don't know. But seeing him, how happy he is, there's no way I could disrupt his life."

He continued to look at her, as if trying to figure something out. He seemed distant. Preoccupied.

"What *do* you want?"

Could she say it? Would he reject her, too? If she didn't take that chance, she would never know. "I want you, Rico. I want us."

He looked surprised, then frowned. He glanced around, gesturing with one hand. "Take a good look, Macy. What you see is what you get. This is me. This is how I live."

"I know," she said. "What I see is what I want. For as long as you want me."

Disbelief flickered in his eyes. Then he pulled her roughly into his arms. "Are you sure? Because I want you forever, Macy. I want it all."

His intensity was overwhelming. "I've never been more sure of anything in my life."

As if she'd said the magic words, he relaxed his embrace, but he didn't let her go. "I love you, you know."

She smiled. "I know."

"And I want to marry you—if you think you can live with a cop who's got a crazy schedule and who doesn't make a whole lot of money."

"I can live with that." Her breathing deepened. She wanted him so much. In every way. She pulled back a fraction of an inch. "And what you see here is what you get, too. Can you live with a mongrel dog and an attorney who can't cook?"

He nodded. "I can manage. But then there's my family."

"And mine. I think they cancel each other out."

They laughed together and for the first time, Macy knew what it felt like to be loved. Rico had gone against his beliefs, told her how to find her child—even though it was wrong. He'd told her because he believed in her. And that meant more than money could ever buy.

Her heart filled with a happiness she hadn't thought possible.

"I love you, Rico. More than anything."

And when his mouth met hers, she knew her life had just begun.

Turn the page for an excerpt from
AND JUSTICE FOR ALL,
book two in the COLD CASES: L.A. *trilogy*
by Linda Style.
AND JUSTICE FOR ALL
(Harlequin Superromance)
coming in early 2006.

CHAPTER ONE

EDDIE WAS LYING ON HIS SIDE, his back to her and facing the cushion. An acrid scent assaulted her nostrils. She smacked him on the leg, anger and a deep disappointment flaring within her. How could he.

"Damn you, Eddie." Laura nudged him in the small of his back with her knee, this time a little harder.

Again, he didn't move. Odd. Even when he'd been at his worst she could get a grunt out of him. But…he was too still.

Abnormally still.

A terrifying realization swept over her.

Her pulse pounded in her veins as she stepped closer, and then leaned over to see his face. His eyes were open. A dark stain soaked the pillow under his face. She lurched back. *Oh, God!* Bile crawled up her throat.

Caitlin. Covering her mouth with one hand, Laura swallowed back nausea and glanced toward the bedroom to make sure her daughter hadn't come out. *Think. Do something.*

Her hand shaking uncontrollably, she reached out to

find a pulse in his neck. Nothing. *Oh, God!* He couldn't be... She reached out again, touched two fingers on the pulse point in his wrist. The air left her lungs. He was cold. His body rigid.

Nine-one-one. She had to call for help, but she couldn't seem to move. He was dead. Oh, God. He was dead.

Her heart raced triple time, her thoughts reeled just as fast. Was Eddie so depressed about going away that he'd killed himself? No. He wouldn't do that. He'd been upbeat when she talked to him last night. He was hopeful about making changes in his life. Most importantly, he'd never do such a thing with Caitlin there. *Caitlin.*

Caitlin said she'd seen someone there earlier. Fear stabbed in her chest.

What if he'd seen her? No...that didn't make sense. If the person had known Caitlin was there...saw her... she'd be—Laura's breath caught, the thought so awful she couldn't even finish it.

Oh, Lord. She bolted for the bedroom. Her little girl thought her father was sleeping. She had no idea he was dead.

"I gots everything," Caitlin said proudly when Laura appeared in the doorway.

Laura hid her trembling hands behind her back and pasted on a smile. "That's great. You said you saw a man here earlier. Did he see you?"

"Nu-uh. I was peeking through the bedroom door cuz

I heard loud voices. Then I went back to bed because it's not nice to interrupt people."

Relieved, Laura asked, "Did you recognize the man?"

Caitlin frowned, then shook her head. She stretched her arms in the air and yawned. "I'm still tired, Mommy. I want to go home to my own bed." She flopped back on the bed like a limp noodle.

"We will, sweet pea. In a few minutes. You stay right here while I check for anything you might've left in the other rooms." Halfway out the door, Laura turned. "Stay where you are. Don't move. Okay?"

"Okay."

In the hallway, she filled her lungs with air. If she called nine-one-one, then Eddie's death would be on the news and everyone would know Caitlin had been here during the murder.

Eddie's killer would know.

She had to get Caitlin out of there before anyone saw her. Then she'd make an anonymous call from a pay phone. Propelled by fear for her little girl, Laura tore through the small house, snatching up everything that belonged to Caitlin. A red tennis shoe from the bathroom floor, socks and Caitlin's toothbrush…anything that would indicate a child had been there. Seeing nothing else, she went back to the bedroom. Caitlin was curled up on the bed and rubbing her sleepy eyes.

"Okay. We're ready."

"I wanna say bye to Daddy, too."

Laura's mouth went dry. "Uh…you know…it's not even six o'clock yet, and Daddy's really sick. I think we should just let him sleep. Okay?"

Without waiting for a response, Laura reached down, scooped Caitlin into her arms and ran like hell.

BLACKBERRY HILL MEMORIAL

Almost A Family
by **Roxanne Rustand**
Harlequin Superromance #1284

From Roxanne Rustand,
author of *Operation: Second Chance*
and *Christmas at Shadow Creek*,
a new heartwarming miniseries,
set in a small-town hospital,
where people come first.

As long as the infamous Dr. Connor Reynolds stays
out of her way, Erin has more pressing issues to
worry about. Like how to make her adopted children
feel safe and loved after her husband walked out on
them, and why patients keep dying for no apparent
reason. If only she didn't need Connor's help. And if
only he wasn't so good to her and the kids.

Available July 2005 wherever Harlequin books are sold.

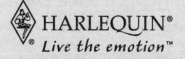

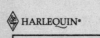

If you enjoyed what you just read,
then we've got an offer you can't resist!

Take 2 bestselling
love stories FREE!
Plus get a FREE surprise gift!

Clip this page and mail it to Harlequin Reader Service®

IN U.S.A.
3010 Walden Ave.
P.O. Box 1867
Buffalo, N.Y. 14240-1867

IN CANADA
P.O. Box 609
Fort Erie, Ontario
L2A 5X3

YES! Please send me 2 free Harlequin Superromance® novels and my free surprise gift. After receiving them, if I don't wish to receive anymore, I can return the shipping statement marked cancel. If I don't cancel, I will receive 6 brand-new novels every month, before they're available in stores. In the U.S.A., bill me at the bargain price of $4.69 plus 25¢ shipping and handling per book and applicable sales tax, if any*. In Canada, bill me at the bargain price of $5.24 plus 25¢ shipping and handling per book and applicable taxes**. That's the complete price, and a savings of at least 10% off the cover prices—what a great deal! I understand that accepting the 2 free books and gift places me under no obligation ever to buy any books. I can always return a shipment and cancel at any time. Even if I never buy another book from Harlequin, the 2 free books and gift are mine to keep forever.

135 HDN DZ7W
336 HDN DZ7X

Name	(PLEASE PRINT)
Address	Apt.#
City	State/Prov.	Zip/Postal Code

Not valid to current Harlequin Superromance® subscribers.

Want to try two free books from another series?
Call 1-800-873-8635 or visit www.morefreebooks.com.

* Terms and prices subject to change without notice. Sales tax applicable in N.Y.
** Canadian residents will be charged applicable provincial taxes and GST.
   All orders subject to approval. Offer limited to one per household.
   ® are registered trademarks owned and used by the trademark owner and its licensee.

SUP04R   ©2004 Harlequin Enterprises Limited

Montana Standoff

by **Nadia Nichols**

Harlequin Superromance #1287

Steven Young Bear is ready to fight
the good fight against the mining
company whose plans threaten to
destroy a mountain. Molly Ferguson
is fresh out of law school and
representing the other side. Steven
and Molly are in a standoff!
Will love bring them together?

Available July 2005
wherever Harlequin books are sold.

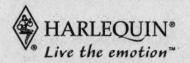

HARLEQUIN®
Live the emotion™

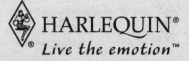

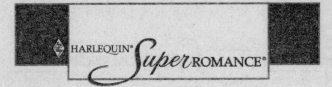

COMING NEXT MONTH